Murder in the Morning Calm

By

Bob Warner

Copyright © 2001 by Bob Warner
All rights reserved.
No part of this book may be reproduced, stored in a retrieval system, or transmitted by any means, electronic, mechanical, photocopying, recording, or otherwise, without written permission from the author.

ISBN: 0-75963-260-X

This book is printed on acid free paper.

1stBooks - rev. 04/30/01

Dedication

I dedicate this book, in part, to Barbara Murphy, wherever she may be now. I also dedicate it to my wife, Kilsun, who put up with a lot while I was writing it (and even when I wasn't), and to Bill Speicher, who stayed by my side when I was being wrongfully accused of selling goods on the blackmarket.

Chapter One

Sweat was dripping down my back. I always hated the humid summers. This house was no help either. It'd been closed up since the body was found. It seemed to be about fifty degrees hotter inside than out, even with the windows open. The suit didn't help either. The shoulder holster seemed to stick to my skin even through the light shirt and T-shirt. The sweat was pouring off my face. I mopped my forehead and the handkerchief came away soaked, but that didn't seem to help. Almost as soon as I finished wiping my forehead it looked and felt like I hadn't even attempted.

The Military Police Investigators, MPI for short, had this case until yesterday. A new twist developed that took it out of their hands and dropped it squarely in ours.

I'm Jim Stewart, special agent with the U.S. Army Criminal Investigation Detachment (CID) in Taegu, Korea. My partner, Louis Linke, and I were handed the case this morning when we arrived at work. It was more than just a murder. MPI agents Ernie Compo and Keith Reese had found a locked cash box in a collapsible closet in the victim's house. When that box was opened, the need for CID became readily apparent. The box contained three hundred ration control plates. That was about two hundred ninety-nine more than the victim would ever have needed alive, legally, and three hundred more than he'd need now.

I guess I should explain what role ration control plates play in life, as well as this story.

When members of the military are assigned overseas, the host countries often have different customs laws. As a result, they don't like having American goods flooding their economy without the benefit of customs tariffs being paid.

On the other hand, military bases have stores operated by the Army and Air Force Exchange Service, called post or base exchanges — PX or BX for short. The military also operates commissaries, which are similar in many ways to American food markets. American goods are sold to GIs and their legal families for their consumption only, free of local tariffs and taxes. Though these stores are in the host country, soldiers and their families can get food and dry goods at Stateside prices or less, while local Koreans would pay an arm and a leg for the quality items we take for granted. If Koreans could get their hands on these items at even 200 percent of the cost, they'd be happy. Lucrative dollar signs pop up in the minds of even the most staid Americans when they think of this. But only those few who are willing to take the risk of getting caught black marketing actually see those dollar signs materialize into money in the hand — for a while. That's when we step in. Put simply, black marketing is smuggling.

To help control the flow of duty-free goods, a ration system was established, with ration cards issued only to those authorized to buy in the exchanges and commissaries. This way, the system could also track family expenditures on a monthly basis, control the amount of cigarettes and alcohol bought and consumed, and limit the number of higher-priced items sold, such as stereos, refrigerators, cameras and the like.

Branch ration control offices are set up in each of the five-area support groups, all answering to headquarters in Seoul. Each group appoints their own ration control clerk to issue cards to eligible people. The appointees are supposed to be the honorable sort who have no criminal intentions, whatsoever. Sometimes one slips by, however, as in the case of our victim. I guess I can name him now. The family's been notified and the body's been claimed.

Army Staff Sergeant Timothy E. Rostock was a thirteen-year veteran with an excellent record. Having served in 'Nam, he was a proud recipient of the Bronze Star for heroic action and two Purple Hearts, one of which came as a result of the same action that also brought him the Bronze Star. While there, he rescued his company commander from a foxhole caught in a VC crossfire. As he was pulling the wounded C.O. across fifty feet of open territory, two VC rounds caught him. One took him in the side, a flesh wound. The other hit his leg and shattered a bone. He was MEDEVACed to the U.S. and patched up at Fort Sam Houston, Texas. Unable to return to combat, he was assigned to several headquarters companies worldwide. He continued to serve honorably, even helping to modify some missions to make them more efficient, thus earning the respect of commanders wherever he served.

He arrived in Korea about two years ago and immediately requested an extension to remain one extra year. Another nearly approved extension was working its way up to Seoul for final approval at the time of his death. He wouldn't need that anymore. Someone ended that extension prematurely.

When he arrived in Taegu the commander noted his impressive record without hesitation, and appointed him the primary ration control clerk. Rostock seemingly filled the bill for the job like no other. Sometime during that two years, however, something went wrong enough for him to be found dead with three hundred ration cards in his possession.

Louis and I were sent there to try and find out what happened and why. That included finding the killer and bringing him or her to justice, which never proved to be an easy task. It never is, no matter how it sounds in books and on TV. It always involves a lot of hard work and many tedious hours of checking, double-checking and rechecking everything.

Being with the Army in Korea didn't help either. There are some forty million Koreans in an area about the size of Indiana. Of these, there is a small faction of dissident students, some of whom are radical. Taegu had its share of these radicals lately. They'd been voicing their extreme desire for us Yankees to go home. Along with their sincere wishes, some had even threatened to kidnap Americans found alone or in small groups in an effort to emphasize their demands. There was no telling what would happen if they actually kidnapped someone and that victim were to put up a fight. While the radicals proved to be, for the most part, non-violent on a one-to-one basis, a situation such as this could turn fatal.

Why does this hinder things a bit? Because the Korean National Police, or KNPs, while maybe sympathetic, don't really seem to care if we Americans knock each other off. Therefore, we'll get little help if a Korean is suspected.

Two things are "helping" us out here, though. One is the fact that Rostock met his fate with a .45-caliber slug. There aren't too many Koreans who have this type of weapon. If they do, they would have stolen it from an American. Rostock had to have died at the hands of another American, narrowing the field of potential suspects down from some forty million to about forty thousand — the rough figure of the number of American service people assigned to Korea.

The other "helper" is the three hundred ration cards in Rostock's house. This sparked enough of an interest with the Korean authorities to call in the Korean Customs Agency. This is mainly because if someone is caught black marketing, hefty fines are levied by the Korean government for the goods that find their way illegally into the local economy. We'd receive their undying support in this case, even if it involved one of their own.

During the initial three weeks since the body was found, the only time the KNPs were there was after the initial report of a death in Bongduk Dong in southern Taegu. Their presence seemed to vanish after that. The customs people appeared, however, when Louis and I took over the case once the black marketing angle came out. In fact, they arrived at the house before us and were waiting impatiently to be admitted. Once inside, they scurried about, taking interest in every little thing and talking up a storm. They appeared to be into this with a fervor.

They sorely wanted to take possession of the ration cards, but knew they'd never get that to happen in a million years. Even the legal cards are the strict property of the United States Government. More so the illegal ones. All of them are heavily

Murder in the Morning Calm

controlled items, allowed only in the hands of the rightful recipients after issue. Before issue they are only authorized to be handled by ration control clerks. Even installation commanders can't legally get their hands on "extras." There was no way the Korean authorities were going to get their hands on these or any other ration cards. But I could swear these customs agents were drooling just the same over these cards.

The taller one, Mr. Park, who was apparently the boss, finally stood up from his crouch with the other, a Mr. Song, introduced himself and his partner. "Forgive my manners," he said without sincerity. "We waited so long for your arrival and we were anxious to see the evidence." His English wasn't too bad, but his accent was typical to millions of other Koreans, with the Rs and Ls that sounded alike and the THs that sounded like Ds. "Please to introduce yourself," he said and I mentally noted his first error in otherwise concise English.

At this, Song tore himself away from the box of plastic ration cards long enough to shake hands during the introductions, then rambled off through the house, noting various aspects of the crime scene. Park spoke again.

"Mr. Song is good man. He is excellent investigator. Mr. Song does not speak English very well, though, and will need me for translation. Please to talk to me if you need something say to Mr. Song." We all agreed for the time being and returned to work.

Under the watchful eyes of both Korean agents, we inventoried each of the ration cards and, with gloved hands, put them into separate evidence bags, taking care not to smudge any possible prints. The print boys would need the cleanest cards we could give them. The sheer numbers were making it a very tedious task at best, especially in this stifling house. Was it my imagination or did the temperature rise another ten degrees since we arrived? I was about to take off my suit jacket when Louis tapped me on the shoulder.

That small activity caught the eyes of the two alert agents. They were bending over our shoulders to see, listening to Louis even though he whispered. "Here's one with your name on it, Jim." How right he was and this didn't escape the attention of our two Korean chaperones. They started talking in a frenzy, all the while pointing at me. I could see Song wanted to pick me up on the spot and take me away to a Korean jail cell. Park held him off, though, and I radioed in to the duty agent.

"Charlie Delta One, this is Sierra Alpha One. Come in."

The radio crackled for a split second, then the duty agent answered. "Go Sierra Alpha One. What do you need, Jim?"

"We've got something interesting here. Could you ask the commander to come over right away?"

"Roger that, Sierra Alpha One. Out." The radio fell silent. I returned the radio to its belt holster and turned to Mr. Park.

"Ajushi," I addressed him politely in Korean. "I have called for my commander, Colonel Walsh, to come here and see what we have found."

"I am aware of this," he replied, adding that he also told his partner about the call. "This will mean you are, as you Americans would say, off the case?" he inquired.

"Yes. And I will be investigated before I can return to duty," I answered.

Song jabbered and Park translated. "Mr. Song says that you will return to work only if you are found innocent. We plan to be there when they investigate you." Boy, they must have wanted to sink their teeth into someone real fast on this. I guess, in their minds, it would be real icing on the cake to bag an American CID agent in the process.

It took Colonel Walsh nearly half an hour to get there, even though the house was only five minutes' walking distance from the gate of the base. Korean traffic, at the best of times, was horrendous, with all drivers showing a "me first" attitude when it came to intersections. This attitude showed up especially where stop signs supposedly controlled the flow of traffic. They were largely ignored by all. And at 6 p.m. the "rush hour" crowd was all over the place, making traffic slower than during the normal daytime crawl outside the gates of the installations. Even nighttime was no better. With the roads unjammed, taxis and buses zoomed along at top speed to get where they were going, endangering all in their paths.

We heard the sharp, loud Skreeee! of the outside gate first, and then the colonel's gruff but friendly voice. "Jim! Louis! Whatcha got for me, guys?" As he came in the door, he spotted the two customs agents assigned to the case. "Ahn nyong hashim nikka?" he said in polite Korean, wishing them good day as he extended his meaty hand. "Have they been keeping you busy, Mr. Park? The last time I saw you was at the police officer's convention in Seoul."

"Yes suh, Kuhnul Walsh. They have been keeping us very busy, Mr. Song and I."

Walsh then excused himself from the two customs agents and turned to me. "What is it, Jim?" he asked. It wasn't unusual for him to call me by my first name. MPI and CID are such small units that the commanders usually know us on a first name basis. But, while we might know his first name, we still addressed him as colonel or sir. I handed him the bag containing the card with my name on it. It was the last thing Louis and I had been able to do before the Koreans virtually halted all progress.

He looked at the front of the card, turned it over, then studied the front again. "What's your social?" he asked, meaning my social security account number, that was part of the batch of numbers at the top of the card. He didn't even look up as I rattled off the nine-digit number that controls so much of everyone's life. He just looked to see if the numbers matched those on the card. When I finished, he looked at Mr. Park and informed him the number on the card did not match mine, which it honestly didn't. The Koreans talked heatedly for a moment before Mr. Park turned back to the colonel.

"But kuhnul. The numbers wouldn't match if this were a second card issued for illegal purposes," he protested.

"I understand that. It doesn't change the fact that Special Agent Stewart will be suspended pending an investigation, but I wanted you to know that they did not match." Mr. Park said that he and Mr. Song understood.

The commander asked if Mr. Park and Mr. Song knew of another James Stewart, a famous American movie actor.

"Is he related to Jimmy Stewart?" asked Park. Most Korean people don't realize that Jim or Jimmy is to James and Bob is to Robert like "ajushi" is to mister: that is, they're interchangeable. They think Jimmy Stewart and James Stewart are two different people. In this case it was true, to an extent, since I had been named after the actor my mother would have married had he ever asked her. But the fact remained that, formally, we were both "James," even if that was only his stage name.

The colonel tried to explain this to the agents to no avail, and he chuckled knowingly when they failed to comprehend. After explaining that he wasn't laughing at them, Walsh told them that I was suspended and would be investigated thoroughly. They were only happy when Walsh agreed they could follow the investigation personally, if that was approved by their headquarters.

The colonel turned to me and, more for the benefit of the Koreans who watch American police shows on TV than for official protocol, asked for my badge and gun, giving me a sly wink as he did so. I added the radio to the collection and he handed them all to my partner, Louis, telling him, "Go over later and see how he's doing." Louis nodded and Walsh turned back to me. "You are hereby restricted to your quarters until further notice," again for show in front of the two customs agents. He'd stop by later to lift the restriction. With that he turned and left and, after saying good-by to Louis, so did I. It would have been an insult to the Koreans if an alleged criminal addressed them, so I left without so much as a nod in their direction, but saw out of the corner of my eye that they both wore wide grins.

Louis was going to have to turn in the government sedan by himself tonight. I walked to the main road and looked for a Korean taxi. I had no reason to return to the office, so I would go straight home. As I waited for a taxi to stop I had time to think about what would happen next. They'd call Seoul and get the records for all legal and illegal purchases made with both ration cards bearing my name. They'd check the signatures on the many receipts sure to be on file. Then they'd bring both lists to my house and compare them with major items in the house.

If I were a regular GI, the local MPI would handle the "show and tell," as it's called. Since I'm CID, they'll call in a team from Seoul, Japan or maybe even Hawaii, to get an unbiased report on the investigation. No matter where the team came from, though, they'd know I was in law enforcement simply because they'd been called in, rather than the local office handling it. It wouldn't go easy. Quite on the contrary, they'd be much harder on me than they would on a regular GI.

It doesn't matter whether you're a military or a civilian cop. To a cop, one of the worst things is another cop gone bad. Yeah. It was going to be rough. There was no doubt in my military mind. No one liked show and tell for the implications, let alone the hassle of just having to do it. It implied that you were being accused or suspected of smuggling.

That's a hard hit to a good cop. I've been in the Army nearly ten years, all of it in the CID. Four years of that time was spent right here in Korea. I'd never done anything illegal, except maybe drive a little above the speed limit on the expressway. Now I was suspected of dealing in the black market and I was going to have to face up to a show and tell. And possibly connected to a murder.

When I arrived home, my wife, Jina, greeted me at the door as I took off my shoes. In Oriental households, shoes are never worn indoors. They always come off at the door and are placed on a mat there. The attire inside the house is socks or bare feet. That's one of the Oriental customs I like very much, because it gives my feet a chance to breathe after being smothered all day in shoes or boots, and there are no corresponding scuffs and scratches in the floor. Not to mention that the floors are easier to keep clean if you're not tracking God-knows-what inside every time you enter the house.

Jina looked concerned. She knew I was on a case, which usually meant weeks on end with rare sightings of her CID husband. But today I was home before 8 o'clock and without a radio. She said nothing, though, knowing I'd tell her when I was ready. Instead, she busied herself in the kitchen, preparing a meal for her unexpected guest.

I stripped off my sweat-soaked clothes and showered. I wanted to wash away the sweat, but I also wanted to wash away the latest turn in a very nasty case — the fact that I was now under suspicion and involved in this thing far more than as just an investigator. Only half of what I wanted to see go down the drain did. I'd still have to go through the investigation, even though I did nothing wrong.

When I dried off, a dinner of bulgogi — marinated beef strips — rice and various side dishes awaited me, as did Jina.

That's one of the things I like most about her. Her patience. It had always been there. In the six years I'd known her, she was always patient about everything. Even though the courtship and meeting her parents had been quite rocky.

You see, Korean people are basically very homogenous. They enjoy the fact that through five thousand years their blood has been "pure" Korean. For a Korean to marry a foreigner took a lot of guts and conviction, because it meant total severance from a family who didn't allow what we know today as international marriages. This was in evidence when I met Jina's parents. They were very much against it. And the fact that I was CID didn't help. Their views of foreigners, and especially foreign police, were limited. They remembered what the Japanese and their police did during the annexation of Korea. There were brutal rapes and murders by the same police who were supposed to protect them. Except back then, the Japanese were only interested in protecting themselves and their interests. Jina's parents feared this was the case with Americans as well. They purposely stayed away from GIs in the nearly forty years since the end of the occupation, when Americans came to stay. That was until about six years ago.

I was stationed at Camp Humphreys then, near Pyongtaek, during my first tour in the republic and met Jina downtown. I was on an investigation in the market area where she was a store clerk. I'd been asking her questions. She wouldn't talk to me at first, fearing her boss would fire her, so I arranged to meet her in a tabang, a Korean coffee shop, after work.

She looked even more beautiful when she entered that tabang than when I spied her behind the store counter. Her walk was graceful and her style was classy, though not snobbish. Her head remained bowed in traditional Korean fashion even after she sat at the table. Under olden standards, Korean women weren't supposed to look men in the eye. This young lady had been taught all the traditional standards. After a few questions relating to the case I'd been working on, however, her eyes met mine and a warm shiver coursed through my body. Those almond-shaped eyes were the most gorgeous orbs I'd ever seen on a face. Her jet-black hair cascaded down the sides of her face, gently framing those eyes with silky strands.

Her voice lilted in the Korean language. It was still lightly singsong when she spoke English. It took my mind through to another place where everything was beautiful and people were kind. Everything about this woman was a joy. We were soon laughing and joking as she practiced her English with me and I asked a few more questions. Those questions were soon behind us and we continued socializing. It seemed like the day had only just begun, as we looked out the window we realized the sun had already set.

Where had the time gone? Jina was worried. She was supposed to have been home hours before, yet she was still here socializing with a foreign policeman. Her family would not be happy if they found out. She told me not to worry, though, and went off to the ladies room. I took care of the bill and, a few moments later, she returned and we left. She hailed a taxi and, before climbing into the back seat, handed me a folded slip of paper. As the taxi drove off under the streetlights I could see a small wave through the rear window.

The note she'd given me was written in Hangul, so I slipped it into my pocket and returned the sedan to Camp Humphreys. I'd get one of the Koreans who worked in the office to translate the note for me in the morning.

I remember the look on his face when he handed me the translation. There was a sparkle in his eyes that told me the note was good news. He patted me on the shoulder and said "good job" as I read. Like many of the Koreans working with the Americans, his view wasn't as narrow as the majority of the population. Though he still preferred that Korean women married Korean men, he was wise enough to know that love knows no national or cultural boundaries. Only this wasn't love yet.

I met her that Saturday at another tabang just outside the post gate in Anjungri. Dressed in jeans with tennis shoes and a light jacket, she looked like a pretty teenager, but I knew different. Her five-foot-three-inch frame, though compact, was very favorably endowed by her Creator. Even though the jeans covered her legs, they couldn't hide the fact that those legs were indeed slender and shapely. The jacket did nothing to hide the roundness of her breasts, which were small, yet firm and well rounded. She was bright and cheery like a teenager, too, but her fun loving attitude and zest for life couldn't cover the intelligence with which she faced life's challenges.

We spent the entire day together, driving over to Sapkyo Lake, where the late President Park Chung-hee had built his summer house. A lakeside resort had sprung up around the estate since his assassination. We watched the tourists, walked along the dikes that protected the area from the sometimes-vicious cruelty of the West Sea during typhoons, and threw food to the fish. We had a lunch of fresh seafood and walked and talked some more.

We met often over the course of the next few months, sometimes going dancing or to a movie. Sometimes we just sat and talked. Our love bloomed in the late summer much like the flowers and trees had during spring and we were doing nothing to stop it, even though we both knew her parents would disapprove vehemently. Even if we finally got past her parents, marriage between people of two nationalities and totally different cultures wouldn't be easy by a long shot. But we were both aware of the complexities and discussed everything before finally deciding between ourselves.

We decided our love could transcend any of these obstacles if we encountered them with patience, understanding of each other, and the determination to succeed. We visited her parents that weekend in Pyongtaek and it went much as we expected. Her mother cried and her father ranted and raved. They both grilled us endlessly, calling in a translator for the job. Then they called Jina's older brothers, who started in on us again.

How could she shame them like this? How was I going to support her? What happens when I leave Korea, as all GIs do, and take her to a strange land? How was their only daughter going to leave Korea and fend for herself in another country? Will I beat her and make her do things she didn't want to do? They didn't expand on that one. They'd heard Americans divorce frequently, while Koreans traditionally keep one mate for life. Was I going to use their daughter up and throw her out?

It was a seemingly endless verbal gauntlet. Jina cried at times, spoke angrily at her inquisitors at other times, but she never gave in. Her family finally quit the heavy hits and got down to the practicalities. Since I lived in the barracks and she at home, where would we live? Do my parents know? Do I make enough money to support her and children? What happens if I have money problems? What happens after an argument? What if the paperwork for her to get married go to the States isn't completed in time before my tour was up? What if she doesn't like life in America or can't get along there? The questions went on, sometimes being asked two or three times.

I don't remember if it was sudden or if they just ran out of questions gradually. All I remember is that deafening silence. Jina came over and sat with me then, holding my hand while the family glared at us. I could understand their feelings. It was hard giving up their only daughter to a foreigner, and a policeman at that. Then the old man's eyes started to twinkle a little. I thought he was finally breaking down into tears and I didn't want to see that. He threw up his hands and said something, a sudden smile spreading from ear to ear. The translator informed me that the father was ordering an engagement party for the next weekend for his daughter and the young American son-in-law. They gathered round and hugged and laughed and all talked at once as Jina cried tears of relief and joy. I just stood there dumbfounded. We'd won.

There were months of paperwork and investigations, which are more extensive if a CID agent is married to marry a foreign national. Jina's family was checked thoroughly for any history of connections with Communist North Korea and dissident groups here in the south. We were both grilled by Korean and American officials as to why we wanted to marry each other. We were finally married in a traditional Korean ceremony at the Korean Folk Village in Suwon.

My young bride and I were dressed in bright new hanboks, traditional Korean dress, as was the entire family. The guests of friends and employees at the village dressed in a variety of hanboks and modern suits. It was a gala, all-afternoon affair filled with traditional ceremony, singing and dancing.

The following weekend we had a western-style ceremony Freedom's Chapel on Camp Humphreys, where Jina was the only person dressed in a hanbok. This ceremony was attended by Jina's family, while the people I worked with attended as my family. My family back in the States couldn't come, but planned to have another wedding ceremony when we got there.

Less than two months after our weddings in Korea, we were assigned to Fort Hood, Texas. It was hard on Jina. Not only was this the first time she'd been to America, but it was the first time she'd been more than a few miles from her family. There was no going home for the weekend from here. Other than the small Korean community, the main population was foreign to her and she had to rely on English to carry out most of her daily business.

Big deal, you say. Everyone should know English. The truth of the matter is, if you were assigned to Korea and had to learn the language just to get around, most American soldiers would be stuck on post and the mission would never get done. Nor would you ever learn anything about Korea. The same holds true for Japan, Germany, Panama or nearly any other foreign country where the military serves. If you stop to think about it, all those countries force their people to learn English for our comfort, while, in America, learning a second language is nearly optional.

Nevertheless, Jina worked her hardest to adapt, depending on me to help her learn better English and by taking an English as a Second Language class on post. She also got a job doing piecework at a local sewing factory owned and operated by members of the Korean community. Her ability to learn quickly and her dexterity soon earned her recognition with her employer as being the fastest and most efficient worker there. She was averaging better than ten dollars an hour by the time we were ordered to return to Korea for this assignment.

As I reflect back on those early days of our marriage, I realize that she always had patience and a very deep sense of commitment to our marriage, as well as to life in general. When things turned rough, as they often did, her intelligence and patience let her sort things out and come up with a viable solution to problems, allowing us to work them out to our best advantage. My beautiful wife had never given up or let things get her down to the point where we became stagnant.

Now as I looked at her, sitting there in her customary dinner chair, I knew why I married her and I knew this problem I was having — indeed, we were having — would pass and we'd survive to become even stronger than we are now. I sat down to eat. Tradition dictated that nothing about work or worries are said during the meal. Instead, I asked her how her day had gone. This too had become a daily custom.

But she felt my tension and worry, even as the cleaning ("the spiders are getting out of control outside again"), food shopping ("the grapefruit isn't quite as good this year"), and other daily household tasks were related. Though she'd had a job in Texas, there was rare and mostly menial work, if any, here in her homeland. Most of the jobs, regardless of ability and education, go to the men. She just basically went about the daily (and very admirable to most Koreans) task of pleasing her lifelong mate.

After dinner, as we cleaned up, I began telling her of the day's events, winding it all up with the ration card with my name on it. After years of being married to a CID agent, she knew the gravity of the situation. She'd seen MPI visit friends' homes. It was always a hassle, creating tension so thick you could cut it with a knife.

There was always the possibility that something would be missing. You either loaned something to a friend or, unthinking, gave it to your parents or threw it away it when it broke. Sometimes you forgot to report its destruction, since that wasn't necessary Stateside and Koreans never had to worry about it, either. When it didn't materialize at the show and tell, MPI would charge you with unlawful disposition of duty free goods — black marketing — smuggling. Rather than CID having to prove your guilt, you were forced to prove your innocence. That was a fact of life in the military overseas.

Louis stopped by just after ten to give me back my radio and badge. He also told me the colonel had lifted my restriction, but that in accordance with policy, I was still suspended pending the outcome of the investigation that had been launched against me. I knew that was the order, because I'd seen it happen to others before me. There was nothing to be done, except help to finish the investigation as soon as possible and forget about it, returning to work at full speed.

Louis and I sat down to a cold beer, which felt really good after the day's events. He confided that the colonel had already called Seoul and an MPI unit would come to Taegu tomorrow. I could expect them here by noon. The boss wanted to get this over with and, God willing, get me back on the case as soon as possible. We were already short-staffed, being twenty percent below the manpower strength required to perform the mission. It didn't help one iota that an agent was sidelined on a case because of the chance coincidence that a false ration control plate had that agent's name on it. I was satisfied the colonel was convinced of my innocence. All I had to do was prove it.

We filled the rest of the evening with small talk as Jina showered and prepared for bed. Louis left by midnight and I was getting quite tired. But sleep didn't come to our house that night. We were both unsettled about the show and tell.

The sun rose the next morning on two sets of red eyes, with neither Jina nor I getting anywhere near a full night's sleep. But we rolled back the covers and started to make the best of a bad situation.

The coffee tasted good and helped perk us up a bit, but it came nowhere close to setting the day right. Jina went out at about ten to get some sodas for our expected guests. When she returned a few minutes later she reported that Mr. Park and Mr. Song were outside the gate waiting for the team from Seoul to arrive. She'd invited them in, but they didn't want any unofficial business with a suspect. They said they'd wait for MPI. They were pure business.

The phone rang at just a little past noon. Louis announced that the MPI team from Seoul just left the office on the way to our house. The colonel was with them. I thanked him and hung up.

I didn't have to tell Jina. She already knew in her heart what the call was about. I just said "show time." We sat down and waited for the gate bell to ring, announcing their arrival. Park and Song would follow closely on their heels like trained puppies when the gate opened. I guessed we still had about fifteen minutes before traffic would allow them to get here, but we couldn't think of one thing to do except wait. It was the longest quarter hour of my life.

Jina buzzed the gate open when the bell rang, allowing them entry without us stepping out of the house. She didn't even pick up the intercom to see who was there. We weren't expecting anyone else and we weren't surprised. They came armed with a sheath of papers that could only be the stacks of printouts from the computer in Seoul and photocopies of the sales receipts.

Colonel Walsh was the first to speak.

"Jim, this is Special Agent Joan Wilkins and her partner Ralph Irwin from the Seoul MPI office. You know Misters Park and Song and you know why we're here. I'll act as witness on your behalf." Then he read me my rights from the Miranda card he pulled from his wallet, making it all totally official. He turned to the striking redhead, Wilkins, who was apparently the chief investigator of the Seoul team. "Shall we get started?" The two Korean chaperones sat as Jina served Korean soda and juice drinks to those who wanted them.

Wilkins did not. She flipped pages until she came to the one she wanted. The look on her face was one of "let's get this over with, hang this guy, and get the hell back up to the civilized world." Most Americans assigned in Seoul thought assignments in the rest of the country were inferior to theirs in the nation's capital, as if upbringing and breeding were considerations for assignment there. Maybe they were right, but I didn't think so. I purposely asked for Taegu because I didn't want to work in the "Crystal Palace," as higher headquarters is often called by those of us privileged to work elsewhere. Some of us privately thought that only the losers got assigned to the "cush" jobs up in Seoul. I guess we're both wrong, really.

Wilkins looked up from her papers after a moment and announced that she'd start with the items bought on the real card. She verified my social security number as she saw it on the page.

Each item was located and verified as she read them off and eventually checked off her list. Refrigerator, gas stove, VCR, TV, Seiko watch, CDs, Osterizer Kitchen Center, the works. It all checked out down to — uh-oh! The last item on the real card.

Where was the stereo? My mind drew a blank. Jina's face screwed up into a puzzled look.

I remembered buying the thing. It was only sixty dollars, but it was over the high value mark of fifty dollars, so it was accountable property. But what did I do with it?

The colonel and I exchanged concerned looks. Wilkins and Irwin were looking like the cats that caught the canary. Things weren't looking so hot right now. Then, with a look of understanding, the colonel raised his finger and shouted, "It's at the office!" Everyone looked at him with surprise. "Isn't that the one you have on the filing cabinet behind your desk?" he asked. Of course. I'd taken it there as soon as I bought it and had taken it pretty much for granted on a daily basis. I'd forgotten all about it being there, even though I turn it on every morning and off every evening.

"We'll go through this other list, then go down there to check it out," Wilkins said, her partner nodding his agreement. The Koreans nodded their approval with a look that made me think for an instant that they might be secretly rooting for us. It couldn't be, but that was my impression. They were likely rooting for that stereo to have the wrong serial number on it or for something from the second list to be found in the house.

Wilkins started in on the second list. As she mentioned an item, her silent partner (Irwin I think his name was) searched the house inside and out to find it. No luck on any of the more than twenty accountable items. When she finished the list, she read me my rights again and announced that I was suspected of unlawful disposition of the duty-free goods listed and not found in my possession.

She turned to the colonel and said, "I think we can dispense with the handcuffs this time if you'll take responsibility." He said he would and we all trouped outside to the waiting sedans, Jina locking the door behind us.

At CID's Taegu headquarters, the commander told Wilkins to use my office for the interview, since it was currently unoccupied for obvious reasons. He reminded her that she could check for the stereo's serial number while we were in there. The customs agents handed Jina over to the interpreter and followed her in for their closed-door session so they could interview her in her native tongue. It was all perfectly by the book and highly professional. Separate the suspects and ask them the same questions, hoping one would slip up or break under the pressure and isolation from his or her partner and confess all.

That was standard operating procedures. I'd seen it before and had even used the tactic myself. This was Jina's first experience at it, though, other than watching cop and robber shows on TV. I prayed her intelligence and patience would guide her through it all, but right now I had to concentrate on my own inquisition.

Wilkins once again announced the charges, slipping a report form into my typewriter as she did so. "I need to ask you some questions," she said. Once the basic information of name, rank, serial number and unit had been recorded, she reached for a tape recorder. "This will record our conversation to avoid any inaccuracies in recording your answers. We'll also review it for any inconsistencies in your story." Standard practice used on every case.

The questioning went on for a couple of hours. Questions were repeated often, trying to trip up any false statements I may have made. Again, standard practice. It just felt totally alien, somehow, now that I was on the other side of the desk, even if I knew it was standard.

Then Wilkins stopped. Even with the air conditioning on she seemed to be hot. I, being under the gun, also wasn't faring so well. I wasn't wearing my suit or shoulder holster, but even the jeans and T-shirt didn't seem to allow me to stay cool enough. It was more or less the stress of the moment for both of us, I guessed, since this office usually felt good even with my business clothes on.

But Wilkins seemed to be wilting in the heat even more than I. She stood and started to remove her blazer, then caught my stare as the garment's descent around her shoulders exposed her holster and standard thirty-eight revolver, then much more. Her breasts strained against the synthetic fabric of her blouse, which was soaked with perspiration and rendered nearly invisible. In a way it seemed kind of funny, even in the position I was in, that a professional woman of her caliber would look like she'd just participated in a wet T-shirt contest. But I didn't laugh. I was more or less in awe. She would have won any of the contests I'd ever seen or heard about.

I could clearly see the black lace bra that stopped just short of covering the nipples, but held the breasts firmly in the position of attention. Just then, as the cool breeze from the air conditioner connected with the warm moisture of her blouse, her nipples reacted immediately by stiffening and nearly poking through the drenched fabric. She must have felt this, because she looked down at them, then instinctively back at me. She hurriedly replaced the blazer and covered that splendid view, blushing as she did so.

"Damned city here is too hot for me," she muttered as she fastened the one button that would protect her body from my eyes. But not my memory.

I'm happily married and wouldn't trade my wife for anything in the world, but women are God's art (they probably say the same thing about some of us, too!). If you buy a painting for the house, it doesn't stop you — nor should it — from admiring the rest of the art in the world. The only difference with the art of women is that you can only acquire one, unless you belong to some certain religious sects. I was very happy with the notion of monogamy, but Wilkins was no slouch in the "art" department.

A few more questions and our session was over. Before she closed out the report, though, she did check the serial number on the stereo. She didn't seem at all surprised that it matched the number on the ration receipt. Although I knew it would, I was still relieved that it was settled. We left the office to see the commander.

"I've done about all I can here, colonel," she said when we were admitted. "Have they finished with his wife?"

"Just did," he replied, adding that she was waiting in the visitors' lounge. "I've signed for custody of you both, Jim. You can go now. I'm sorry."

He knew he didn't have to apologize — I realized that all this was being done in the line of duty to clear up a nagging technicality. It was just a quirk of fate that my name ended up on an illegal ration control plate — or was it? I started thinking about that as I went to get Jina and leave. I'd be interested in checking out some of those other names to see if they matched real people either serving currently or recently in Korea. Once I got this cleared up and got back on the case I'd have to check that angle out. If I didn't get exonerated, I'd at least let Louis in on my idea, if he hadn't thought about it already. Maybe this was supposed to be a classy frame-up or smoke screen designed by the criminal or criminals to keep investigators hopping while they scooted away scot-free. One way or the other I was determined to find the truth in this case.

Jina was pretty shook up. Korean and American laws vary in what can legally be done during questioning. The customs agents told her that if she confessed to black marketing, only I would go to jail for murder. If she didn't, they'd make sure we both spent most of our lives in Suwon, the national correctional facility that didn't bother trying to rehabilitate. They didn't bother to differentiate whether or not we were guilty in truth. They just wanted confessions. They threatened to have her family investigated, implying that they would be jailed even if only caught spitting on the sidewalk, which is a punishable, but not a prison, offense.

But Jina's patience and intelligence prevailed. She admitting nothing, not even agreeing to sign the statement. "You'll have to prove we did something wrong," she told them. They weren't too happy, but they were just doing their job as they saw it.

We rode back home with Colonel Walsh. The car was pretty silent, except for some small talk. We were all deep in thought. I guess the colonel was thinking about what to do next to clear me.

I was giving serious thought to calling Louis and inviting him over. Even under suspension I wanted to keep informed. I knew he wasn't supposed to tell me anything pertaining to the case, since I was suspended, but I figured he would anyway, anticipating my eventual return.

Jina, I found out much later, was having very hateful thoughts about the two customs agents. Most of those thoughts probably couldn't be translated into English in a family-type publication, but if you'd just remember your own thoughts about that IRS idiot who audited you a few years ago, you'd get the general idea.

The commander politely declined a drink when we got home, driving back to the office for "some important work." With time on our hands that we hadn't exactly planned on, Jina and I set about figuring ways to while away time before my name got cleared. I had no doubts that it would. I just didn't know how long it would take. And, of course, there was some uncertainty, especially if it was an elaborate frame job, of which we'd just barely skimmed the surface.

We finally settled on a three-hour drive to Pyongtaek to visit her family and let them know what was going on, if I got approval from the office to leave town for a few days. I called in to check and received permission. "Just be back by Sunday," the colonel had said. Today was Wednesday. That would give us a few days at least. My next call was to Louis to invite him to dinner. After that, Jina called her folks and told them not to go anywhere tomorrow. It was all set. We started the dinner arrangements, deciding on a chicken barbecue that would attract ninety percent of the neighborhood children, as well as some adults. We prepared about twice as much as we'd need, knowing it would be gone as soon as it came off the grill.

Louis showed up at around seven-thirty, nearly making it before half the neighborhood, but not quite. There was still plenty of food left for us all, though. After the children left, hands greasy from the chicken, Louis and I sat down on a couple of lawn chairs near the grill to talk.

"What's going on with the case, Louis?"

"Jim. You know I'm not supposed to confide in you while you're on suspension. They could bust me."

"I know that. But I also know that you don't want to take a lot of time briefing me when I come back."

"Right," he said, looking around to see if anyone was listening. The high concrete walls of the Korean house served to shield us from the view of others, but acted as an echoing board for our voices, so I went inside to turn on the stereo, which would also echo. Louis edged his chair closer to mine when I returned and whispered, nearly under his breath.

"We've cataloged all the cards. There were a few weird names in there, Jim, like Captain John Smith and Benjamin F. Pierce, would you believe." The names were familiar to me, but I seriously doubted that Miles Standish's best friend or a character from a hit TV series would actually be serving in Korea right now. I asked what else he had.

"It seems like all the cards were signed by as few as about two or three people, but they've got to send them to Hawaii for handwriting analysis. The colonel's also sending the ration receipts on your bogus card for the same thing. He's also having them compared to your signature from your records. He wants to get this thing cleared up as fast as he can and get you back to work."

I was glad the colonel had taken that tack, because it would clear me out of this thing right away — I hoped.

"Listen, Louis," I said in the same hushed voice. "Call up to Personnel Command in Seoul and see if any of the names on the cards show up as bonafide people assigned to Korea in the last couple of years, or if any people with those names ever served with Rostock at his former duty stations. I'm curious to know if the use of my name was a fluke or if it's a frame."

He understood immediately and said he'd take care of it. We changed the subject as I got us another beer. By the time he left at about ten, he was armed with a few moves and my in-laws' phone number in case he needed to call. I told him we'd be back by Sunday afternoon.

Jina was up and ready to go before she woke me up at six-thirty. She'd always been good about waking early. I could smell the bacon and eggs cooking as I got ready. The rich aroma of coffee permeated the house before I finished. It all made me hungry. She packed a picnic lunch as I ate, though we'd be there long before we got a chance to get hungry. This was more for the family than for us. It's customary to bring something for the host during a visit.

We packed the basket and the luggage in the trunk of the year-old Daewoo Royale and navigated through the narrow alley to the main street. Then we headed for the expressway that linked Pusan on the southeast coast to Seoul, just twenty-five miles from the North Korean border. We wouldn't be going quite that far, getting off the expressway some forty miles south of its northern terminus.

It was a pleasant day, even if the heat was steamrolling its way up the thermometer before eight. The sun was out and there were just a few puffy clouds floating lightly across the sky. Driving with the windows down would take the edge off the heat. We wouldn't need the air conditioner for this short trip. Jina had braided her hair, knowing what the wind would do if it were left loose. Long hair has that little tendency to dance into unmanageable knots when left in the wind awhile. The last time it took both of us nearly three days to get all the knots out of it. We wouldn't have that problem this trip.

About halfway to Pyongtaek we stopped at the Kumgang Service Area and went for a walk by the river. The recent monsoons had filled the river, making the water on both sides of the dam look the same height. But in the week since the monsoons stopped, or at least took a breather, the river had subsided enough to allow the dam to control the flow somewhat. Attesting to this were the numerous paddleboats dotting the long, thin lake formed there. On the other side of the river was a small outdoor restaurant that usually did a pretty good business during the dry season, but was void of any life today. All in all, the walk was quiet, with the distant sounds of the highway on one side and the joyous laughter of the boaters coming from the other. A temporary sanctuary from the madness that surrounded our lives at the moment. We savored it.

Half an hour later we were entering the expressway, once more headed northward. Experience told me that the ride would be a smooth one hundred kilometers per hour until just about Jochiweon, then traffic would invariably increase and slow us down for the rest of the time we needed to be on the expressway. The only way to get around the congestion on the expressway was to take the scenic route through all the towns, which was a lot slower. The expressway was built to cut the original travel time between Pusan and Seoul down from twenty-four hours to slightly less than six. It worked until the number of cars and trucks on it multiplied at a fantastic rate each year. Now it was nearly gridlocked from Suwon into Seoul, with that final thirty-two kilometers taking sometimes in excess of two hours to navigate. From Suwon down to Pusan, however, it remained a fast drive, save for the slower trucks that had to sometimes crowd both lanes.

We arrived at the family's house just before noon and hadn't even gotten out of the car before her mom began a frantic mile-a-minute conversation with Jina. They walked into the house, Mom grabbing the picnic basket out of the car and Jina taking her make-up case. Dad came out to help me with the two suitcases. It was a nice gesture, but he's under doctor's orders not to lift heavy things, so I waddled them into the house under my own power. Man, I thought, Jina really knows how to pack a mean suitcase. They felt heavier every time we traveled. Maybe I was getting older. I mean, it'll be my thirtieth birthday next month.

As I settled the bags into "our" room, Jina's old room before we got married, Dad floated around me, seemingly oblivious to the fact that I don't understand enough Korean to follow his monologues, though I'm sure he remembered. Or did he?

Anyway, Jina and her mom were in the kitchen, already starting on the night's feast. Korean families put on a big show when family or friends come to dinner.

It's their way of saying welcome, as well as sort of bragging that they have plenty for all — even when they don't. Jina still remembered her youth, when they were so poor they rarely had enough food for the family, let alone guests. But when folks arrived, her parents always managed a big feast, sometimes borrowing from loan sharks at exorbitant interest rates to buy the food. It was a matter of pride for them.

When Jina's grandfather died, a previously unknown wealth was found hidden in the house. Her dad was the eldest son, which entitled him to fifty percent of the take, while his two brothers and one sister shared the other fifty. That, too, is an old tradition. Her dad paid off the bills, bought them the quaint house on the edge of the city, and then paid his "application fee" (bribe is more like it) for a job sweeping the city's streets. The rest of the money went into the bank and has been left virtually untouched since, waiting to provide for Mom and the children after Dad's demise. If Mom died first, the money would be shared as it had for generations before.

We were soon gathered in the living room, the night's dinner simmering away on the stove, the spiciness permeating the air. I knew the dinner would taste good. Mom's cooking always did. But I also knew it was going to play hell with my stomach. I'm glad I went back into the house for the Pepto before we left Taegu. I was going to need it for sure tonight.

But for now the talk had become serious. Mom and Dad were tense as they spoke a barrage at Jina. Something was wrong. Very wrong. Dad, who was usually reserved and all smiles when his American son-in-law came to visit, looked as if the Japanese had returned with their horrific rule from earlier in the century. Mom had become pale as a particularly long narration crossed her lips. Then the talk stopped.

Jina turned from her parents to me. "They've already been here," she said sadly. I didn't have to ask who. Mr. Song and

Mr. Park had apparently already called the Pyongtaek customs office to have them assist in the investigation. They were very prompt, arriving at the house before Dad finished work this morning. They had continued the tirade that Jina had faced from their counterparts in Taegu the day before. They searched the house and grounds, claiming they were looking for smuggled American goods, but left only with a few photographs of Jina's brothers.

Mom telephoned their children right away to warn them that something was up, only she didn't quite know herself what was going on. The agents never bothered to explain when they barged into the house this morning. Upon hearing this I became outraged, but there was nothing I could do about it. Jina had returned to her thoughts about those two men in Taegu shortly after she finished translating for me. She then turned her attention back to her parents, explaining the reason behind this morning's visit. Both of them paled as she related yesterday's events in Taegu. Dad was getting angry.

What a day this was turning out to be. I never really thought the customs version of the Bobsey Twins would follow through on their threat to harass the family, but it sure looked now as if they'd been serious enough. Just then the phone rang and Dad answered it.

"Yoboseyo," he said into the mouthpiece with the customary greeting. His eyes widened. It was all he could do to keep his composure as he muttered an occasional "yeh" through the next five minutes. The man on the other end of the line was talking very excitedly. The type of excited that makes you imagine a very angry person telling someone just what he thought. The rest of us were silent. I was straining to hear every word, even though I couldn't understand them. Tears were falling from Jina's eyes before Dad hung up. Mom's face was devoid of expression and color. This had definitely not been a pleasant phone call.

Dad got up from his customary lotus position on the floor and retreated to the master bedroom, closing the door behind him. He seemed to have been walking very slowly, like someone who'd aged ten years before my very eyes.

A whispered conversation soon began between the women. They were keeping it low so as not to disturb Dad in his moment of obvious pain. Jina was soon crying openly, trying at the same time to translate the phone call and its result to me. As she talked I could feel the blood drain from my face and I felt a little dizzy.

The Bobsey Twins' Bad Boy Brothers had been to see Dad's supervisor. The basic gist of tonight's call was that they didn't need that type of problem and would he mind turning in his uniform shirt and hat, though it hadn't originally been said that nicely. Dad was fired from the job he cherished simply because of a mix-up in a case that I had been working.

I was at fault, even though I hadn't done anything wrong. People near and dear to me were suffering because of my job. I couldn't bear that. As I got up I told Jina to tell her family that I was going to see what could be done to stop this bullshit. I was pissed.

I nearly ran to the Royale and sped out of Pyongtaek and through Anjungri to the Camp Humphreys gate. When I stopped for the ID check at the gate, the MP on duty informed me that Colonel Walsh had been calling and I should go to the CID office to get the message. He asked if I knew where that was and I told him that's where I was headed, anyway. He snapped to attention and waved me through. I drove around the end of the runway, keeping at the posted twenty-five miles an hour speed limit, remembering that the MPs liked to sit near the shoppette with their radar.

A few minutes later, as I entered CID's field office, I was asked if I could be helped. I introduced myself and was immediately handed the message from the colonel. "You're to call him at his office. He's waiting there for you," said the lieutenant, the only person there with a military uniform on. The rest were in the customary uniform of business suits. He ordered the agents to vacate the room and turned to leave, closing the door behind him to afford me some privacy. It wasn't often that someone there was called by Colonel Walsh and they took it very seriously, especially since I wasn't even a member of their office.

I picked up the nearest phone and dialed the Taegu number I knew by heart. The colonel answered on the first ring.

"Glad I got hold of you, Jim," he said, sounding very relieved. "Listen, I faxed some stuff to Hawaii this morning before I sent out the originals. The guys there say it looks like there's no way you could have signed any of those receipts from the false card, but they want to check the 'real thing' before they make it official.

"Look. I'm in a bind. I need you back on duty ASAP. I know you were counting on Louis to help keep you informed, but I had to take some rash steps. Seoul gave approval to send him to Hawaii with the goods so they can get there and be analyzed quickly. I've put the investigation on hold for now. It can wait until you get cleared.

"I know you just got up there, but I thought you should know this and I couldn't dial through to the house. I guess I just don't have the touch for those Korean telephones," he said chuckling.

"Sir, I need some help," I said, sorry to steal from the lighthearted attempt at humor from my boss. I told him what happened this morning in Pyongtaek. He listened intently until I was finished.

"God. What the hell are they doing all that for? It's not like you're suspected of being Communist sympathizers, for Heaven's sake. Look. Let me see what I can do, Jim. I'll have Miss Paek call them right away and ask them over for coffee. I'll let you know what happens. Let the lieutenant there know where you'll be so he can send one of his men out to the house if I need you, OK?"

I agreed and hung up. It'd been less than forty-eight hours since I handed him my badge and gun, yet it seemed like a lifetime's worth of bad had happened since then. This almost thirty-year-old CID agent felt closer to sixty. Suddenly I wondered if I was in the right job. Did my work cause this much grief to the people I investigated who turned out to be innocent? Or were these characters just playing harder because I'm CID? The truth, I came to realize, was that I had no idea. All I knew was that my Korean family was hurt because of something I didn't even do. I had to fix it somehow. I was responsible.

Before I left I drew a map and gave the lieutenant the phone number where I was staying. I also asked him if he knew the local customs agents.

"I know 'em a little," he admitted with a face that told me he didn't particularly care for them. I asked if there was some way he and his men might be able to distract them from their present case for a while, hoping the colonel could put the heat on them from the other end in the meantime so they would leave my family alone. He squirmed a little, then mentioned that he knew something that might help. I didn't bother asking what it was, but thanked him for any effort he was willing to make for the cause. I left to return home and see if there was anything I could do to help out.

I felt better on the twenty-minute drive back, even though I'd gotten caught behind a city bus nearly the entire way after leaving Camp Humphreys. Things might be looking up after all, what with the colonel and the lieutenant trying to work a little magic my way. Maybe it would be enough to keep the heat off for a while, anyway.

Jina and Mom were in the kitchen when I returned, talking in hushed tones still. Dad was outside, standing on the porch with his hands clutched behind his back, staring out across the city. The city he worked for only a few short hours before. He didn't acknowledge my arrival and it would have been impolite to disturb him. I needed to talk with Jina and get the rest of this squared away.

"Can we talk a minute," I said when I could get in a word. She excused herself and followed me out to the car. I told her what happened at Camp Humphreys and what the colonel and the lieutenant were doing for us.

"Do you really think it will help?" she asked when I finished.

"I don't know, sweetheart, but it's worth a shot. Anyway, what's happened here since I've been gone?"

Chapter Two

The dominoes were falling right down the line. Jina's brothers' were visited by the locals and treated very much the same way as her parents. Her brothers weren't any too happy when they called, telling her how much of a mistake it had been to marry a Yankee cop. They had a right to be pissed, but they didn't have to hang up on their sister before she could explain, while it might be my fault, it wasn't because of anything I'd done wrong. Now she was angry and wouldn't talk with them. Mom said she wouldn't talk to them, either. Jina didn't tell her father of the calls, since he was in the bedroom until just about ten minutes before I returned. He was listening to his favorite singer, Lee Mija. He said her music always seemed to comfort him during troubled times. I hoped it would.

Then it hit me. Why couldn't we go to her Dad's work place and tell his supervisor it was all a bad mistake and it would blow over soon, I asked. "They wouldn't care. You're an American. I'm married to an American. They won't even listen," Jina answered dejectedly. All hope seemed lost.

Then I got another idea. "I'll be back in a little bit, honey," I said. "I have to go back on post for something." Her beautiful almond-shaped eyes showed questions, but those questions never passed her lips as she got out of the car. She waved as I drove away. God, she's wonderful, I thought to myself as I headed for Camp Humphreys once more. I hoped this would work.

I headed straight for billeting, hoping Mr. Cho still worked there. He and I had been friends when I worked there during my first tour in Korea.

Cho Young-il was the Korean manager for post housing, answering to the current American manager. While Americans came and went, overseeing missions for a year or two at a time until they rotated back to the States, the Korean civilian work force provided continuity by staying in place. The only way they left was if they were promoted, retired or fired. I hoped Mr. Cho was still there. I needed his help right now.

I was pleased to find him sitting behind the counter when I walked in. "Hi, Mr. Cho. How's it going?"

"Ah, Stewart-shi. Welcome. It has been many years since we last saw each other. How have you been?"

We talked over some old times and I brought him up to date on where I'd been since I returned to the States. Then I got down to the point.

"Mr. Cho, I need your help." I told him my father-in-law was out of work, though I didn't say why. The less said the better. I asked if he knew of any job on post that Dad could apply for. Though Mr. Cho worked in billeting, he kept his ear to the rails and knew of job openings all over post even before the Civilian Personnel Office did. He also knew of a few jobs that weren't hired through CPO. He was, in fact, the unofficial person to see if Koreans needed work on post.

He sat down for a moment, a look of deep thought on his face. This was show, of course, since he knew the information as well as he knew the top of his desk. Then he looked at me and asked, "Would he mind a menial task?" I explained what he did for a living up through this morning and Mr. Cho told me to bring him for a visit. I told him we'd be at the Maxim Club in Anjungri later that evening for a beer.

Mission accomplished. I left for home to bring the good news to the wife who always had faith in me. I hoped I was doing the right thing.

Dad was sitting in the living room, talking with Mom and Jina. It seemed like a calm conversation, so I didn't interrupt, even when my wife looked up and said, "Hi, honey." I nodded to them all and removed my shoes, sitting down cross-legged with them. Korean people appreciate this courtesy from foreigners, even if we don't understand the language. Acting like you're listening intently to their every word makes them feel more comfortable, thus helping them accept the foreigner more easily. I intended, today more than any other, to fit in with the family, though I sincerely strove for that every time we met. I didn't ever want to be an outcast with my wife's family.

Jina turned to me and explained what they'd been talking about. Dad was worried he couldn't get another job with the city, since word of his dismissal and the reason for it would travel fast. Koreans weren't known for keeping secrets. It would be spread as thick as peanut butter by morning. Jina mentioned the possibility of working on post, which her mother readily backed, but her father was skeptical. After all, it was the United States Army that sparked this entire mess. Why would they turn right around and hire one of their victims?

I spoke up then. "I have an appointment with Mr. Cho from billeting tonight at the Maxim Club, Jina. I'd like you to come along and listen to what he has to say." I mentioned that we made a date for a drink. This wasn't lost on her.

When Koreans make any type of business deal, it's formalized by a social gathering over coffee or a drink with snacks (Koreans never just drink — they eat all the while, feeling that this will prevent them from getting drunk). Jina was now aware that I'd already started the ball rolling to get her father employed on post. She thought that was what I had been up to, so she had turned the conversation with her Dad in that direction. Just like always. Without so much as a word between us, Jina and I operated as a finely tuned team. By the time I returned home, her father had already agreed to try, even though his hopes about it were nil.

"I want Daddy to come too," she said, not realizing that was my plan in the first place. I agreed and she translated.

As he was being told what we'd spoken about, Dad's eyes started shining as though he was nearing tears. He looked at me with a look he'd never directed toward me before. That look was always reserved strictly for his Korean children when they'd done something to please him. When Jina finished translating, he spoke and held out his hand.

"I thought you were the demon sent from Hell this morning, but you have proven to be an angel within the family." A lone tear pushed its way down his cheek. Then he surprised me with a hug reserved for his biological offspring. Not only had I been forgiven, but I was finally and fully accepted into the family — a fortune foreigners rarely receive, even though they may take a Korean bride.

The afternoon passed with Mom and Jina chattering away happily in the kitchen, fixing the many side dishes customary to a Korean meal. They acted as if nothing had gone wrong that day. Dad was beside himself, preparing his suit for his evening rendezvous with an employment benefactor. He fussed over which pair of shoes would be best for the occasion, often producing a pair and touching my arm to seek approval or rejection. I'd either nod or shake my head.

After several nods and shakes, he finally settled on a pair of loafers. To him, this wasn't a Korean job with Korean people, or he'd know exactly what to do. This was a job on an American military installation and he felt he was totally unprepared. If only I could have spoken Korean, I'd have informed him that his customs were the way of life for all Koreans, no matter where they sought employment with others of their own nationality.

I chose to wear my jeans and a T-shirt sporting Bill the Cat and touting "The Soju Experience — Party in Korea." Soju is a highly refined sweet potato wine that catches drinkers off guard with its mild taste. People often got very wasted on this national drink.

Dinner was eaten in silence, chopsticks and spoons flying over the table from four different directions. Thanks to Jina's patience, I had learned with some difficulty the art of eating everything from rice to fish with chopsticks. The only thing that can't be eaten with them is soup. Proficiency is the name of the game, however.

Once finished with dinner, Jina changed into her jeans and T-shirt, hers emblazoned with a cute picture of a Korean bride and bridegroom in traditional dress. Her parents had bought one for each of us at the Folk Village after the wedding ceremony. The washing machine ate mine one day. It was now my favorite car wax applicator. We didn't have the heart to tell them about that, though. We'd get a replacement soon and they wouldn't know the difference.

Dad and I climbed into the front seats of the Royale and Jina sat in the back. According to Korean custom, women rarely sit in front with the driver. It took me awhile to convince her that it was OK in American custom. We arrived at the Maxim Club about twenty minutes later and were lucky enough to find a parking space within twenty-five feet of the door. These were usually taken up early in the evening.

The Maxim Club, like all the other Korea Special Tourist Association (commonly known as KSTA) clubs, was there for the sole entertainment of American soldiers and civilians serving in Korea. It was closed to Korean males, except when escorted by an American. We stopped at the door and I signed Dad in. Most times they didn't make us sign our guests in, but they'd been having some recent troubles with Korean youngsters around the KSTA clubs in Anjungri.

In most cases younger people allow their elders first passage in deference to their age, but Dad waived this right because I was sponsoring him. Even though I was much his junior (I never really knew how old he was, though he must have been at least in his late fifties), he stood aside and motioned for me to enter first. As with most KSTA clubs, the music was too loud for my taste even before we opened the cushioned double doors. Once inside, it blasted loud enough to make our eardrums vibrate, nearly to the point of pain. This didn't seem to phase the younger people as they danced on the floor near the go-go stage, some right in front of the gigantic speakers that dwarfed most of the Korean girls.

I was immediately met by Miss Kim, well known among the GIs as the Snake Lady. As she directed us to a table and arranged for a waitress to take our orders, I wondered how she could have possibly gotten that nickname. I allowed that it was possibly because, in addition to being the club's head hostess, she was also the Madame for all the prostitutes working there.

Nearly all the girls working these clubs were licensed as "entertainers," in the loosest sense of the term. Whether they were bartenders, dancers or waitresses, most could be bought for an evening or an entire night of pleasure for the proper amount of money.

As the Madame, the Snake Lady was probably one of the best procurers of human flesh in Anjungri, wheeling and dealing with patrons over some of the finest looking cuties in the area's market. She expected the best from her girls and the proper compensation for their services from the customers. She was a hard bargainer and thus, possibly, the name. She was also about as slim and straight bodied as a snake, having no noticeable figure, but a totally disarming smile on a very alluring face.

No sooner had we been seated at a table near a support beam, that offered us an unobstructed view of the main go-go stage and the rear stage, when the club's owner, Mr. Ahn, hustled over to welcome us.

"Stewart-shi," he said, adding the respected "shi" to the end of my name. "Uhsuh oseyo — Welcome. It has been a long time," he added, signaling our waitress to be snappy with the service. "Please. The first drinks for you and your guests are on me." He then commanded the Snake Lady to have one of her girls get us a plate of anju — a traditional snack dish of possibly raisins, nuts, seaweed, squid or fruit — to eat as we drank. The KSTA clubs usually don't serve anju, but in deference to my Korean guests, Mr. Ahn sent for one. He then left to tend to the bar, while I told our waitress to get him a whiskey-coke on me and handed her the proper two thousand won — roughly three dollars.

She scurried away, returning with our drinks only moments later. We were all drinking OB beer that evening, though I knew Mr. Cho would drink juice when he arrived. Living in Songtan, almost fifteen miles away, he rarely drank when he went out. He usually waited until he got home. As I was thinking this, he entered through the door and made his way to the table.

Mr. Cho knew my wife from my previous assignment to Humphreys, but he'd never met her dad, so introductions went out. We spent a moment admiring the various dancers before getting down to business. When he finally spoke, Mr. Cho got right into it.

"I have checked a few areas of possibilities your father-in-law might be interested in. There are currently a few jobs open, all of them menial labor." He immediately translated this into Korean. Dad nodded his understanding.

"My father is only interested if the work is honorable and will provide for the family," Jina announced with her father's approval. "He is not afraid of hard work," she added, "but that's for you two to discuss."

With that she grabbed my arm and led me off to the dance floor. The music, of course, got louder with each step we took. Some five or six dances later I was bushed, but it looked like Jina was just getting started. I then realized that it'd been years since we went out dancing. I made a vow to take her out at least once between cases in the future. She saw how tired I was and led me back to the table. Mr. Cho had switched to drinking a beer with us.

"We have much to celebrate," he said. "So I have decided to drink OB with my friends. I can take a taxi to Songtan this fine night and get my car in the morning."

Mr. Cho indeed knew where there was a job. Right in his office. One of the cleaning people had left that day and they needed a replacement. Dad accepted the chance gratefully, whereupon Mr. Cho produced the proper paperwork. They had filled it out in Korean while we were dancing. Mr. Cho said he'd type it up in English in the morning.

"Bring your father-in-law to the office tomorrow to sign the papers and we'll walk them over to security and get his post pass. He'll start work right away." It was done. Dad was so happy he bought us all a round, including the owner and the waitress. He also sent for more anju.

Then he reached across the table and shook my hand so hard I thought he was going to take it with him. Best of all, the wages at his new job were a cut above what he did for the city and there was the possibility of tips thrown in for him. He was beaming. I hoped this stroke of good luck would spread over into my case.

In celebration we decided to stay awhile longer, so I switched to drinking Coke, since I'd be driving. Dad, Jina and Mr. Cho stuck with the OB, sometimes taking turns to buy a round for Mr. Ahn, who also took his turns buying rounds for the entire table. We were having so much fun celebrating that even Dad took to the dance floor with Jina a couple of times and once with a go-go dancer. He was in seventh heaven.

It was near midnight when we finally left and I offered Mr. Cho a ride as far as Pyongtaek. I pointed out that getting a taxi from Anjungri would cost an arm and a leg, if he could find one that would go all the way to Songtan that late at night. It was a near impossibility. He agreed and climbed in with us. We waited in Pyongtaek until he was safely in a cab before we finished the drive home. Mom was waiting up for us when we arrived, more food laid out for the celebration she hoped would ensue. We didn't disappoint her, nor she us. The news we gave her was great for her ears and the food she provided was great for our souls.

We all finally went to bed at about three a.m., knowing we wouldn't get much sleep that night.

Mom was up first, preparing a sack lunch for Dad to take on post. It included the normal rice, kimchi and turnip soup. The rest of us woke about an hour later, in plenty of time for me to drive Dad to work. Jina helped Mom with the final preparations. They chattered happily and almost constantly as they worked. It was nice to see Jina having so much fun, as she always did when visiting her parents. The events of the previous day seemed to be a faded bad dream. I dressed and drove Dad to work, stopping by the local field office afterward.

"Ah! Special Agent Stewart. How are you this morning?" The lieutenant seemed to be bright-eyed this morning.

"Fine sir. Have there been any calls for me?"

"Not yet," he said, just as the phone rang. He gave the military greeting and listened for a second. "He's right here, sir. Just walked in. One moment, please." The lieutenant handed me the phone, silently mouthing the colonel's name.

"Stewart here, sir. What's up?"

"How's it going, Jim?" he asked. Before I had time to answer he rushed on. "Louis is at the lab in Hawaii. We should have an answer soon. They told me they'd call right away, but our guys at customs are going to want the written proof, of course. Anything new up there?"

"Not yet, sir. Can you hold for a moment?" I cupped my hand over the mouthpiece for a second and caught the lieutenant just as he was stepping out the door.

"Hey, L.T. Anything on that little diversion you were working on?"

"Yeah. Looks like they'll be off your tail for a few days, but I can't guarantee anything after that," he said

"Thanks, sir." He waved acknowledgment and left as I returned to my conversation with the colonel. "Sorry, sir. Just checking on a little something I had cooking up here before the lieutenant stepped out the door. That'll hold them for a few days. How's it going from that end?"

"Our friend Mr. Park says he'll have them hold off further questioning for us until we get that written report back from Hawaii. If that doesn't clear you, he says he'll have them go ahead at full speed." He then told me that Louis should be on a return flight no later than the next morning. "It's too bad I couldn't give him a little bit of time over there, but he realizes how important this all is."

I agreed with him on both counts and thanked him for all his help. Without his rank standing firmly behind me, people would be able to dawdle forever and the case would be at a standstill, along with the rest of my career.

We signed off and hung up. I crossed the office to the coffee pot. Even though I wasn't hung over I was still mighty tired from the previous evening. The lieutenant returned as I was pouring a cup of coffee.

"Sorry I didn't tell you about that before the colonel called. No time. Hope it all works out for you," he said, returning to his desk and shuffling some paperwork around.

"I hope so, too," I replied, taking a sip of the coffee. It sure didn't taste like the coffee at home, nor like Miss Paek's in Taegu, but it would help screw the old eyelids open. The lieutenant must have seen the look on my face.

"Sorry 'bout that. Guess we're not too good about making coffee. We're used to that, though, since we screw it up the same way day after day." At least he had a sense of humor. I liked that in an officer. I guess he hadn't been in long enough to lose it. Most officers lost it after a while. Then, after they figured everything out, they regained it when it was almost too late to save problems for everyone. With luck he'd keep his like Colonel Walsh had.

"Thanks again, lieutenant. I appreciate all you've done. See you around, sir."

With that I threw the cup in the trashcan and left. There was really no time for a lengthy, unofficial visit to a CID field office, since all the offices in Korea were short-handed. I walked across the street to the ration control office. The civilian clerk was sipping on a Coke while typing something. He looked up when I entered.

"Can I help you?" he asked.

"Not really," I replied, adding that I'd just come from Taegu. "I was wondering if you knew Rostock down there?" I couldn't ask any questions officially, but I could do some innocuous fishing on my own.

"Naw," he said, going back to his typing. After pecking a couple of words on the paper he looked up again. "You CID?"

"Yeah."

"I was told you guys would come around, but I didn't think it would be this soon."

"Don't sweat it," I said. "I'm not on the case now. I was just curious. Have a nice day." I waved and turned for the door.

I left making a mental note that the staff sergeant's death hadn't seemed to affect the clerk one way or the other. Perhaps there was no link between them. Perhaps there was. I walked back to the front of the field office and climbed into my Royale and headed home. Maybe Jina and I could take her mom out to Sapkyo Lake for a picnic. It was a beautiful day, weather wise.

But when I arrived home they weren't there. Jina had left a note saying they'd gone shopping at the Pyongtaek Market. There was soup on the stove and cold rice in the cooker. I realized I hadn't eaten anything since last night and served myself, dumping the rice into the soup to thicken it and moisten the rice. It was spicy but good. I had only taken two spoons full before I started sweating, but I finished the bowl and lay down for a nap. We could still go to Sapkyo if they returned early enough and woke me up. I was asleep in minutes.

It was dark when I awoke and the house was quiet. I looked over in the half-light of the outside street lamp to see Jina sprawled half on and half off the yo. She was in no danger, though. A yo is a mattress laid on the floor for sleeping. It's quite comfortable, especially in winter when the floor is heated by water pipes. The newer houses steered away from the warm gas pipes because of carbon monoxide poisoning. There were still some older types around, but they were mainly in the slums or farmhouses out in the country. It seemed city houses were being replaced at record speed, judging by all the construction going on.

I got up and went to the bathroom to ease the pressure on my bladder. When I returned I noticed that it was nearly four o'clock. I decided to stay up and make some coffee. Mom always kept a jar of the Korean version of Taster's Choice in the cupboard for her American son-in-law. I set the pot to boil and turned the radio on very low to AFKN, the American Forces Korea Network, at Osan Air Base. While the Humphreys station is geographically closer, Osan's signal is much stronger, allowing reception for a distance down the expressway. Humphreys' new station can't be heard much past the main gate of the installation most of the time.

Having a station here is one vast improvement since my first tour in Korea, when the Army here didn't even have an AFKN outlet. It's good that the community at Camp Humphreys had some way of getting its news out to its public without having to time-share with the Air Force station.

I poured my coffee and thought about the case and how everything related to me at this time.

Dead by gunshot, proven by ballistics to be a forty-five caliber round, was Staff Sergeant Rostock. In his rented off-post house were about three hundred illegal ration control cards. One card bore my name, either by coincidence or by design. I was suspended from the case and investigated. My in-laws were shaken down and Dad lost his menial city job because of pressure from the local customs agents.

After more than three weeks, those were all the facts we had and most of them came to light within the last week. Not much to go on yet. And with the colonel calling off the investigation in an effort to clear me, nothing else would be found in the next few days, either.

A door closed quietly. I turned to see Jina's mom shuffle off to the bathroom. A few minutes later she joined me at the table and I fixed her some coffee, making it twice as thick as mine, the way she liked it. When I returned to the table I turned off the radio, since I hadn't really been listening to it anyway. I wouldn't need it now with her here.

"Komap sumnida," she thanked me quietly, respectfully accepting the coffee with two hands. She always spoke formally to me. Normally in Korean circles, men don't serve women. Over the last few years, though, I'd convinced her that I liked to turn the tables a bit every now and then. Jina knew different. It was my little way of thanking her for all the meals she made for us and the general hospitality shown to a foreigner who happened to marry her daughter. Most GIs who married

Murder in the Morning Calm

Koreans supplied their in-laws with some foods and other items from the commissary and PX, but with me being CID, there was no way we could afford, career-wise, to do that. That was still considered smuggling. Archaic, isn't it?

Mom started talking as I sat down. Low tones prevented her from waking anyone up. I didn't know the words, but I received the feeling, loud and clear. She was telling me that everything would be all right and that I shouldn't worry. She was also thanking me for helping Dad get another job right away. A lone tear she wouldn't shed in the daytime slowly made its way down her cheek before she brushed it away. No more followed. Then she reached across the table and held my hand firmly in a gesture of "you're truly one of the family." I was embarrassed enough to stare down at my coffee without saying a word.

Jina appeared just then, rubbing her eyes and looking sexy in one of my T-shirts. She immediately made a cup of coffee before I could get up to make it for her.

"You slept a long time," she smiled. "What time did you wake up?" I told her I'd only been awake a few minutes and we all sipped coffee in unison. Mom got up and started cooking bacon and eggs for me and making lunch for her husband. The women wouldn't eat breakfast until about mid-morning, and that would be rice and kimchi, and possibly some soup. Five o'clock was quite early for them.

Dad was awake when I finished my breakfast. The bacon was a little over cooked and the eggs were cooked over hard. I prefer mine sunny side up, but I wasn't going to complain. Mom was trying hard to learn how to cook breakfast for me and deserved my patience.

I called CID. They'd be just about opening up now after a one-hour stint of doing physical training. Even though they had a small unit here, they had to keep in shape like other soldiers. Suspects were sometimes chased through the streets and Korea was still volatile enough to expect hostile action from North Korean Communism.

Everyone was guessing that Kim Il-sung, the North Korean leader, would have to make his bold move before next year's Olympic Games in Seoul or forever lose his chance. The unofficial word was that he wouldn't have the backing of the Communist world after that, let alone be able to convince any portion of the free world that his actions were just. Everyone south of the Demilitarized Zone was in a high state of anxiety at the thought, especially now that dissident student unrest was on the upswing. Something would have to happen to calm them down before the Games started.

The annual PT Test was another reason for the CID soldiers to keep in shape. It's hard enough for a year-round physical fitness nut to max the test and damned impossible for someone who "crammed" during the last few weeks. I vowed to do some exercising this weekend before returning to work. I needed to make up for missing PT all this week.

The call was answered on the second ring. "Humphreys field office, Special Agent Hargrove." I guess he hadn't figured on helping anyone, because the familiar "can I help you" was left off the greeting.

I introduced myself and asked if there were any messages for me. There were none and I asked him to pass to the lieutenant that I would be out for the day and I'd call when I returned. "If he needs me really fast," I added, "I'll be at Sapkyo Lake with the family." Hargrove said he'd pass the word on and broke the connection. I hung up thinking how his attitude was and how, if he were in the Taegu office, the colonel would straighten out his phone manners.

I must have been standing there looking at the hung-up phone because Jina touched my arm and said, "Yobo," a Korean word of endearment toward a spouse. "Are you OK?" I assured her I was fine and that I was just thinking about something. She looked worried, but I didn't want to concern her over something as trivial as a badly mannered agent. Dad was just finishing with his tie, so I volunteered to drive him in to work, which he graciously accepted. Even though they may work at a menial job, Koreans always dress in a suit and change into their actual work clothes when they get there. It's part of the status game, like needing to buy a limousine when they couldn't afford it and when a compact would be all the family needed.

We walked out of the house together, Dad carrying his sack lunch and I wearing my first suit since Tuesday. It felt strange, but familiar at the same time. I guess I felt guilty for not being at work and not being on leave either. We didn't get too many days like this. I just felt that I had to wear the suit, but I seemed out of place since I wasn't working. I don't know how to explain it any other way. Weird, I guess, but maybe that's just me.

In honor of Dad's first full day on his new job, I played a tape with his favorite songstress on it while we drove to Camp Humphreys. This also hampered any Korean conversation I wouldn't be able to understand anyway. It acted as a type of neutral conversational white flag. Besides, I get into Korean music sometimes, even though I don't understand the words. The tunes do it for me, even with American music. I guess that's why I never got into rap. No tune, just monotone and beat. Heavy metal isn't one of my favorites, either.

I dropped Dad off at billeting, then made my way to the snack bar. Contractors were in the process of constructing a new snack mall, so the only place available, besides the Officers' or Noncommissioned Officers' Clubs, was the lobby of the post movie theater. It was just a group of tables bunched together with a vending area and a small grill and counter tucked away in the corner. I got a cup of coffee that tasted like my socks from yesterday and grabbed a Pacific Stars and Stripes newspaper.

It was the first paper I'd seen since Tuesday morning and I realized how much I missed it. Filled with mostly military news and — face it — propaganda, it was nothing like a Stateside civilian newspaper. Hell, that's all information is, when you come right down to it. Someone wants to convince you about their side of the story. It's all propaganda. But military newspapers go all out. I guess that's why every military unit written about is "the best," and every soldier mentioned is the "most outstanding" soldier their commander ever worked with. Still, it's interesting to find out what other units are doing in their "daily missions."

Years ago, page three had been dubbed "The Pacific Page," featuring highlights from Pacific-based journalists who wrote features about their neck of the woods. Now it was just a conglomeration of stuff. I missed "The Pacific Page." I wondered if anyone else did. Maybe. Maybe not.

Then a headline caught my eye.

"CID Agent Suspected in Largest Black Market Scam."

It had a news service by-line with no name. Could it be the case I was working on? I read the story.

"A new twist in a CID investigation has landed one Taegu CID agent on suspension pending investigation and another missing, according to anonymous Korean customs sources.

"Special Agent James E. Stewart of the Taegu Regional CID office was suspended Wednesday from the case involving the death of Staff Sergeant Timothy A. Rostock, when it was discovered that the Taegu ration control clerk possessed a second card with the agent's name on it. The card was discovered by the suspect agent and his partner while they were investigating the circumstances of Rostock's death.

"This latest event could neutralize the investigation for days or even months, according to the source.

"Meanwhile, two days later, according to the same source, Special Agent Louis L. Linke, Stewart's partner, has turned up missing. Korean police authorities in the Taegu area suspect foul play."

The story stated that there was no comment from the 20th Area Support Group Public Affairs Officer in Taegu, then rehashed what was already known of the case. They didn't miss mentioning that the case had only been in CID's hands for one day before the latest developments occurred. Next to the article was a poor likeness of Louis with the caption, "Linke: Missing."

Murder in the Morning Calm

What a bunch of crap! Who released that? My bet was on our buddies Park and Song. "According to anonymous Korean customs sources," my eye. Just let me get my hands on those two again. I went to the phone next to the door and dialed Taegu, only to find it was a "Camp Humphreys only" line. I took my paper and hopped in the car. Destination: Humphreys' field office.

"Anyone seen this?" I asked as I charged through the door. Their somber nods indicated they had. "Let me use the phone," I said, not asking, as I went to the only unoccupied desk in the office; the lieutenant's. "Where's he?" I asked, indicating the absent lieutenant, as I punched in the Taegu number.

"In Taegu," came the reply. Colonel Walsh had called him at his quarters early this morning with an urgent request to meet. He was flying down via chopper. Probably the colonel's Huey, I thought as the phone rang.

Miss Paek picked it up on the third ring.

"Miss Paek," I said before she could say more than two words of her introduction. "Let me talk to the colonel."

"I am sorry," she said. "He is in meeting with general," I didn't have to ask what that was all about. I knew which general and I knew, or suspected, why.

Headquarters for the 19th Support Command is based in Taegu, with subordinate units scattered throughout Korea. They are the logistical arm of the military services on the peninsula. Though CID doesn't fall under their command, our unit operates on this general's turf. The dead ration control clerk was one of this general's boys and, to him, this must have stunk like some sort of cover-up. If I knew Walsh, he stonewalled the local support group commander and that commander went to the general. There was no way to stonewall Brigadier General Clayton W. Bowles, however. We're talking a star against a lowly silver eagle. I bet Walsh was being dragged across the carpet about now.

Miss Paek's voice came through the fog at me. "But Agent Linke just walk in. You want talk to him?" I told her I would and anxiously waited for Louis' voice to come over the wire.

"Hey, partner. How's your vacation?" he asked.

"Whatsa matter? The geisha houses kick you out before dawn?" I kidded, knowing full well his entire trip was spent on planes and in a cryptology lab. He hadn't had time to find the Japanese pleasure houses in Honolulu, let alone enjoy himself there.

"You're in the clear, buddy. They say there's no way you or Jina could have signed any of those receipts. Wait a minute," he said, covering his mouthpiece so all I could hear was a muffled conversation. When he came back on the line, he cut the conversation short with "I've gotta go now and prove to the commanding general I'm still alive and well. Catchya later." He hung up before I could say anything, but I rest assured that Louis' trip to help Colonel Walsh in General Bowles' office would get that general out of our hair. I smiled as I hung up and left, leaving the resident agents to wonder what that call was all about. I'd had enough excitement for one day. Time to take my two favorite women to Sapkyo Lake.

Chapter Three

Mom and Jina were chatting on the sofa when I got home. I laid the newspaper on the coffee table and asked if they wanted to go to Sapkyo. The flutter of movement into the kitchen to pack a picnic lunch was their only answer, so I went to change into jeans and T-shirt. I wore a nondescript one this time, trying not to imply drinking or frivolity so as not to seem like "the ugly American." We were on the road within the half hour.

Jina sat in the back seat with Mom and I was left alone in the front to concentrate on the many buses and trucks going to and coming from Asan and Sapkyo Lakes. They are both very popular resorts, with hundreds of busloads of people visiting daily from points all around Korea.

The lakes were constructed from the edges of Asan Bay by separating it into three parts, the main bay and two offshooting lakes. The separating lines between the three are very high dikes with a highway built across them. The dikes were constructed by order of the late President Park. Without them, the bay was navigable from the West Sea separating Korea from Mainland China, inland to within a mile of Camp Humphreys, a strategic airfield in time of war. With the dikes guarded by armed soldiers twenty-four hours a day, infiltration was nearly impossible using this route. The two lakes the dikes created became popular as a summer outing location shortly after President Park built his summer home there in the 1970s.

Today was no different than any other day, with buses by the hundreds rushing by in both directions. With all the buses leaving the resorts, there should have been plenty of parking, but by the time we arrived, row upon row of buses stretched out the length of the parking lots. As soon as one left, another rushed in to take its place. And so it went until late afternoon, day after day, throughout the summer months, when the flow would finally trickle to a stop and the resort would empty out shortly after dark.

Bob Warner

Arriving there before noon allowed us to park only about three-quarters of the way across the main lot. The park was crowded with classes of college and high school students and elderly tourists. Most of the middle-aged people were at work during the week. There were a few working class people there, though, taking an early weekend. Mom and Jina raided the trunk and carried the picnic basket together, each grabbing the handle on one side.

We walked toward the water's edge near the West Sea, away from most of the throng so we could be relatively alone — with tens of thousands of people crowded within about a five square mile area, you could never find a place to be totally alone. We talked as we ate, Jina translating for her mom. We didn't talk about anything in particular, but Mom held a keen interest in America, American families, and how they differed from Koreans.

She couldn't seem to comprehend when I explained that American youth came to a period in their lives when they left the family fold to create their own lives. In Korean society the family stays close, even when the sons and daughters marry, with the eldest son caring for the parents after they become too old to work. While that's known to happen in America, it's a given action — almost a family law — in Korea.

We talked and fed the fish until it was time to go, seeing nothing else in the resort except our little spot. We gathered our basket and the remnants of our picnic and walked back to the car, packing everything in the trunk. I didn't see the note under the windshield wiper until I got behind the wheel. I reached out and snagged the piece of paper, pulling it inside. Once I unfolded it, I could see that the Humphreys field office had been looking for me. It was no wonder they stopped at the car, rather than actually try to find us there. That would have been nearly impossible unless they knew exactly where we were. As it was, finding an American-owned car was easy, since we had the standard USFK license plate, which is easy to spot.

"Colonel Walsh called. All is well. Report Monday. Case resumes. Tried to find you. Sorry."

They'd actually attempted to look for us here. They were more foolish than I had originally thought. I read the note again, then let out a big cheer that made Jina jump in her seat and scared the living hell out of her mom. When I explained the note, Jina translated for her mom and we all cheered and hugged in celebration, not even feeling the seats between the front and back of the car. What a day!

The drive back was full of happy chatter and even singing as we tried to keep pace with one of Jina's Korean tapes in the cassette player. Every time I made a mistake we'd all laugh. Needless to say, we laughed all the way back to Pyongtaek. Seems I couldn't get one of those songs right, no matter how hard I tried. But everything else had come up smelling like roses.

We pulled into the driveway as Dad was getting out of a taxi he'd taken home from work. As soon as Mom and Jina told him the news, his eyes lit up and he announced the equivalent of "let's party." We all agreed that something along those lines was called for and the ladies went to make the arrangements. We were off in no time at all, the sun still burning in the western sky as we pulled up in front of the Golden Bell, a Korean nightclub on another edge of town headed toward the expressway.

The music was loud and Korean, but none of us seemed to mind. I paid the one thousand won each for entry and we were escorted to a table. An anju plate of cucumbers, carrots, nuts and raisins was delivered and our order was taken before the rock group finished their song. I had to hand it to these Korean clubs — service was right up there with the five-star establishments in the States, even if it was just a small club, which this was.

There must have been a hundred tables compared to the fifty in an American club of the same size. The dance floor was about ten feet by fifteen, and a series of stand bars filled the edge of the club. Stand bars are individually leased areas where entrepreneurs offer their specialties. The type of order determines who gets your money. The speedier the anju plate arrives, the more money that bar usually makes from the table, since customers tend to stay with the same type of anju plate throughout the evening. Other than the stand bars, the stage dominated the club. There was a flashing light show as the group bellowed its sound throughout every fiber of the club. Nothing, from people to table cloths, went unaffected.

The OBs came for Dad and me while Mom and Jina drank the Korean version of a daiquiri. The beers were somewhat larger than those found in a KSTA club. KSTA clubs generally serve beers comparable to the American twelve-ounce babies, while Korean clubs serve the economy, almost quart-size, beers. We call these "combat bottles."

The light show and music faded, and the stage area went black. An announcer came over a loud speaker system, while a rustle of people and equipment took place on stage. Then it was quiet for a second before a single spotlight highlighted the face and body of a young Korean woman dressed as a Japanese geisha girl. The tune was reminiscent of those played on a mandolin, the twanging of the strings almost pricking the skin as it danced through the mind. The sparse audience applauded the arrival of the special show. The colors of the spotlights changed as the lithe young thing danced through a series of steps possibly familiar to Jina's parents.

Pieces of her costume periodically found themselves no longer clinging to her petite body, having been thrown askance to the floor as she danced. She'd dance around the latest discarded piece for a moment, then swirl away, with another soon finding itself gliding lightly toward the floor. Within a matter of ten minutes she was as unclothed as a swimmer on the beach — a small bikini top and a G-string covered only the essential parts of her body, held together by nearly invisible string. She had definitely emerged as something from a man's wildest fantasies.

The music stopped and the stage once again went black. Then a faint yellow light slowly emerged from the shadows to

Murder in the Morning Calm

show the performer sitting cross-legged on the stage, draped in a chiffon shawl. Sometime during the brief darkness her bikini had also found its way to the floor, leaving her sumptuous body nude behind the shawl. A hint of her small breasts and pert nipples were nearly distinguishable. She slowly rose from the stage as the light grew steadily brighter. Her hands were outstretched above her head, curling back toward her tightly pulled hair. Just her shapely legs seemed to straighten, hauling her lithe body off the stage effortlessly. I couldn't have done that in a million years.

She began to swirl, slowly at first, the chiffon dancing in the air behind her. As the light brightened, she twirled increasingly faster, creating a "now you see it now you don't" effect on her perfectly shaped nude body. A moment later she was off the stage and swirling around to the tables, stopping momentarily to sit on the laps of the men in attendance. I must not have been watching, because there were definitely more people than when we first walked in. She alighted on about twenty men's laps before the single spotlight went black again. They were out only for a second, yet when they came back on, she was nowhere to be found. It was as if she'd disappeared.

A moment of silence ensued as heads turned this way and that in an effort to locate her. Then a thunderous applause rose from the audience.

Before we knew it there were six more go-go dancers on stage with an announcer. "A comedian comes next," my wife whispered in my ear. She'd surprised me so much that I swung quickly around, only to find a knowing smile on her face. She'd seen my reaction to the stripper and knew how that would translate in bed that night. That's one translation I didn't need any type of interpreter for. I realized we hadn't made love since the beginning of this case and I was about to make that up to her.

We took our turns dancing that evening, Jina and I to the more modern music and Mom and Dad to the traditional tunes. The night flowed on slowly while the drinks flowed considerably faster. Jina and I excused ourselves to "go for a walk," leaving

Mom and Dad to party by themselves awhile. We walked around the corner to a small motel and Jina steered me through the door to the desk clerk, whom I happily paid fifteen thousand Won for a room. We strode up the stairs, arm in arm, and spent the next hour and a half in sexual bliss.

We cleaned up and got dressed, wanting to return to the club before her parents considered us lost and went home by themselves. As we got to the first floor landing of the motel, however, we spied them coming from a room down the hallway. We ducked back up the stairs to let them pass without seeing us and gave them a five-minute lead, before following them into the club.

We went back to our table to find Mom and Dad just as we had left them, except with different smiles on their faces. No one talked as we finished our drinks and headed home, each couple in their own rapture. Once home, Mom and Jina prepared a small feast while Dad switched the TV to the AFKN late movie. By one o'clock we were fast asleep in front of the television.

Saturday dawned through the windows, waking me slowly to a beautiful but muggy day. Birds were singing in the courtyard and the familiar weekday sound of construction was silent. My watch said it was nearly six o'clock. Korean construction crews would be getting to work at their respective sites by now if this had been a weekday. Today, however, they wouldn't begin work until about eight. The trash truck was on its route down the street, though, its familiar tune ringing throughout the neighborhood in the dawning hour. They had been hard at work for about two hours by now.

In Korea, trash isn't placed at the curb the night before because renegade youths and roaming animals would leave it scattered over several city blocks by morning. Instead, the offerings are taken out early when the trash truck signals its arrival. Not wanting to wake the rest of the house, I changed to jeans and a jacket, slipped on my sandals, and prepared to do the duty. I went out to the courtyard, found the trash, and carried it outside the main gate to wait for the truck. Several ajumahs standing outside their gates stared in awe at the only American for miles around. They knew their neighbor had an American son-in-law, but were unprepared for the sight of him taking care of the trash. It would be their course of conversation for days, judging by the looks on their faces and the hushed tones in which they spoke to each other.

My thoughts were more along the lines of the case I was back on. Now that everything was cleared up as far as I was concerned, I wanted to get a move on in a positive direction. I decided to tell Jina I'd be returning to Taegu today. I handed the full baskets to the ajushi and they were returned to me seconds later empty. I carried them back into the courtyard.

Jina was waiting for me, attired only in one of my shirts. With the sun glowing through the light material, I could see that heavenly form with the small breasts and their nipples standing firm. Her thin waist accentuated the fullness of her hips and shapely thighs that cascaded out from under the shirt. Her long silky hair waved in the early morning breeze.

I looked around and, seeing no one, took her into my arms, gently kissing her lips while my hands searched the very familiar roundness of her crucial parts. The shirt rose up slowly as my hands roamed of their own volition, revealing her sparsely thatched love box. She adjusted her weight to accommodate my hand. I laid her gently on the steps and we made love there in the morning sunlight.

When we finished we lay there looking into each others' eyes.

"You want to go back today," she said, knowing what I was thinking, as always.

"Yes," I said simply.

"Can I stay here a few days and come back on the train?" I agreed. I never restricted her travels or visits with her family. I owed her much more than that for the love and care she gave me. Besides, we both knew that, being on the case again, I wouldn't be at home too much anyway.

Before I left she phoned a friend in Taegu and arranged for cleaning and cooking every day until she returned. Mom prepared a travel lunch for me and Dad handed me a blank envelope that was fairly stuffed. My eyes asked him what it was.

"Ton issum nida. Kam saham nida."

Jina asked him in Korean why he was giving me money. He answered her with a minute-and-a-half monologue she translated for me. "He says that when he was destitute for a job, his American son found one for him within a few hours. It makes no difference that he lost his other job. That was not your fault. The fact remains that you came through for him in his time of need. He gives you this in thanks." She must have been reading my mind because she added, "It would be an insult to a respectable man if you refused." Her eyes told me to accept the envelope filled with Korean currency, which I did for the moment.

When Mom and Dad put things in the car for me, I gave the envelope to Jina. "Try to give this back without insulting your father. You know why I can't accept it." She knew only too well that the Army's standards of conduct didn't allow me to accept payments for services rendered. In the wrong hands, this type of information could end my career. Even if the money came from my in-laws. She'd heard about other CID agents who worked with me in the past. Their careers were lost for this same reason, after otherwise serving honorably for nearly twenty years. It wasn't worth the risk.

After saying my good-byes I climbed into the car for the three-hour trek southward to Taegu. Traffic was pretty light and I made good time, pulling into the office parking lot at Camp Walker before noon. I went in to report to the duty agent. He handed me a note with Colonel Walsh's home phone number, asking me to call him there as soon as I returned. I went into my office and dialed the number.

"I'm back, sir. How's it going?"

"Great, now that we're back on track," he replied. Then he outlined what had happened and what was to be done next. I told him Louis and I would get on it first thing in the morning and disconnected the contact. He sounded pretty happy that the customs folks had dropped their witch-hunt and I was back on active status. I left word with the duty agent that I would need my sidearm returned at about eight o'clock the next morning, and asked him to set an appointment with the armorer before he decided to go partying. He said he'd take care of it and was dialing the phone when I left to unpack and get ready for the next step.

I called Jina when I got home to announce my safe arrival, then dialed Louis' number to request a meet for later in the afternoon. I unpacked the car and put everything away. It never ceased to amaze me how much hotter Taegu was than any other place in Korea. I know it's because Taegu is situated in a bowl-like valley that collected heat, rarely letting a breeze take it away. Knowing that didn't seem to help any. It was still murderously hot.

The door chimes announced a visitor, so I picked up the intercom to see who it was. A sweet young voice announced that she was Jina's friend, coming to clean the house. I asked her to wait a moment while I jumped into some shorts, then pushed the button to open the outside gate. A moment later a young girl in hot pants and a halter top smiled at me from the doorway. Dressing that way might help her beat the heat, but it didn't help me any.

"Hi, ajushi," she said with a smile, then bounced her way into the kitchen to find the cleaning materials. As she bent over to retrieve a dropped cleaning rag, her round, firm breasts revealed that she wasn't wearing a bra. Unlike most Korean women, this young lady was very well endowed — probably about a 36C. Her hips were also wider than most Koreans, at first leading me to believe she might be Eurasian or Amerasian, which wasn't the case. Also, unlike most Korean women, this beautiful young lady didn't seem to be embarrassed about showing how well endowed she was.

I felt proud that my wife trusted me alone in the same house with this friend of hers, but I wasn't sure I could trust myself. I excused myself, pleading work, and went into my den, closing the door behind me. Out of sight, but not necessarily out of mind. After a few minutes, though, I managed to concentrate on what I was doing when I dug out my notes on the case.

Time went unnoticed until I heard the door chimes ring again. I looked at my watch and realized it would be Louis. As I opened the den door, the sound of running shower water automatically made me look in that direction, only to find the door wide open and Jina's young friend washing her birthday suit thoroughly.

Unlike American bathrooms, Korean facilities may have a tub and shower, but no curtains or fogged glass door. The floor is ceramic tiled with a drain in the middle. Showers are taken on the floor, and the tub is reserved for hot baths. Because of this configuration, I was staring at the unblemished perfection of God's artistry. It was hard to pull my eyes away, even when she looked up and saw me staring. She only smiled, not even trying to cover herself. Like I said, she wasn't shy.

I closed the bathroom door and buzzed Louis in. As I was getting him a Coke I heard the bathroom door open. The look on his face told me what he saw, even though I couldn't see what he was looking at. The full brunt of it hit my eyes, though, as I handed him his drink. There she was with just a towel drying her hair, her large, firm breasts and heavily thatched pubic area totally visible to the naked eye (pardon the pun). She definitely was a sight to behold. I took another towel and put it around her, then introduced her to my partner. I hoped I had her name correct, but I never knew since Jina had so many friends. It was difficult keeping all their names straight.

"Louis, this is Jina's friend, Mihi. Mihi, this is my partner from work." Her smile was bright as she walked over to shake Louis' hand and, in so doing, the towel dropped from her shoulders to rest on the floor. She made no move to pick it up or cover herself.

Louis' chin was halfway to the floor as she spoke. "I'm pleased to meet you. Jina has told me much about you." Then she turned and, bent down to pick up the towel, revealing all her other essential parts, and casually strode into the master bedroom to dress. We were both awestruck. I made it a point, however, not to be home much in the near future until Jina returned.

Louis and I adjourned to the den to discuss the case in hushed tones. Even though she was an innocent, Mihi didn't need to be hearing specifics about the case that weren't known by the general public. We were in there for about an hour comparing notes when a light rap sounded at the door.

"Ajushi. I go home now," Mihi announced. We waited a moment before exiting the den to take up more comfortable positions in the living room.

Louis turned to me and asked the obvious question. "Is she taken?" I shrugged, telling him I didn't really know her status, except that she was a student at Kyongbuk University on the northern side of the city. She went to classes daily by bus, which was about a two-hour ride, and came home the same way, making for a helluva long day. Other than that and the fact that she and Jina were friends, I knew nothing. He asked to meet her sometime when she had clothes on to limit his distraction. I told him I'd see what I could do.

When Louis and I both had the same information and general plan for action we decided to take a break and get some food. We walked over to the main drag and caught a Korean taxi to the ville just outside the Camp Henry gate. They understood English there and catered largely to the GIs stationed at Camps Henry, Walker and George, which were all within walking distance.

The villes in Korea are about the same as just outside the gates of an American military installation worldwide. Vendors sell nearly anything, from trinkets to furniture, car insurance, food, drink and entertainment — everything the GI could possibly want, short of drugs, during his or her off-duty hours. Sometimes even drugs were available. Part of my job was to stop drug sales to Americans every chance I got, so some "vendors" in the ville didn't care for us CID guys very much. The legitimate ones, however, treated us well, aside from the attempt to gouge our paycheck before the sun set on payday.

The taxi let us out in front of the Camp Henry gate and we dodged the traffic to cross the street. It didn't matter if you were in a crosswalk or not. Once you stepped off the curb in Korea, you might as well be wearing a target painted on your shirt. We fended our best, though, and finally made it. Then we walked the half block to a restaurant near the Texas Club that served just about everything.

About an hour later we finished eating and I found a PX taxi. I gave him the address and we were off, trying to fit into the flow of traffic and navigate over toward the back gate of Camp Walker. The ride took about fifteen minutes and I was home sweet home after paying ajushi and giving him a small tip.

I unlocked the outside gate and went for the house door, only to find it already unlocked. I cautiously opened it to check inside, trying all the while to remember if I'd inadvertently not locked it. As it slowly swung open the smell of several Korean dishes assailed my nose. I peeked in to see Mihi cooking.

"Hi, ajushi," she exclaimed when she saw me. "I go home, then shopping for your dinner. When I come back, you gone. But I find Jina's extra key and come in to cook. That OK?"

I told her it was all right, making a mental note to ask Jina not to leave the key in the same place anymore. When I came out from the den, I told Mihi to keep the key until Jina returned because I wouldn't likely be here too often to let her in. She agreed. At least she was dressed in a little more this time, wearing a T-shirt that went almost down to her knees and a pair of skin-tight Bermuda shorts that went down to a point about an inch below her kneecaps. I think she was also wearing a bra, but I wasn't going to get close enough to find out.

She talked as she cooked. "I will meet friends tonight, so I cook for you, then I go. I will wash dishes tomorrow morning, OK?" I said that was all right too, and thanked her for her help.

It would have been an insult to let her know I'd already eaten, but if she was leaving as soon as I was served, I could eat a few bites, then put the rest in the fridge. That would save her feelings and I wouldn't have to spend an hour explaining.

I switched on AFKN to see if anything was on while I waited for Mihi to finish up and leave. Don't get me wrong. She's a likeable girl. Maybe too likeable. I just didn't trust myself. As much as I truly loved my wife, I was still a man and I was still fallible. There's only so much temptation a man can take before he gives in. And I don't like temptation to be so close without wifely or friendly protection.

After a couple of commercials into a program I wasn't really watching, she brought dishes and dinnerware to the table. As she bent to her task, I noticed I was wrong — about the bra, that is. She wasn't wearing one. I closed my eyes until she left. As she was setting some things in the sink she said, "Don't wash dishes. I do tomorrow, OK?" Only after I agreed to those terms did she say she was going out on her date. She sashayed out of the house, singing a popular Korean tune, and closed the outside gate behind her. Whew!

I took a few bites of the dinner she worked so hard on, but really couldn't eat any more, so I placed the rest in storage dishes and put them in the fridge, as planned. I'd take them to work tomorrow for lunch, but right now she needed to see dirty dishes in the sink when she returned. The food had to be gone.

I wasn't tired so I looked for something to do. I rummaged through my videotapes to see if there was something I hadn't watched five times already. I thought I'd have to visit a Korean video store and rent one, when I found a tape Louis loaned me about a week before we were put on this case. I hadn't seen Top Gun yet, and I guessed now was as good a time as ever. The reviews sounded good.

It turned out to be as good as the reviews said and I think I dreamed of Kellie McGillis in a leather jacket, miniskirt and spiked heels all night. Then the sun filtered its way through the window to announce to my eyelids that a new day had begun. I got up and donned my suit and holster and a pair of comfortable shoes.

I'd just dug last night's dinner out of the refrigerator and zipped it up in my gym bag look-alike when the doorbell chimed. I picked up the intercom to hear Mihi's singsong voice announce that she was here to cook breakfast. I buzzed her in, but explained that I would be eating at the mess hall (they want us to call it a dining facility now) with my partner, Louis. She didn't understand why I wouldn't let her cook breakfast, asking if last night's dinner had been OK. She opened the refrigerator door to see if I'd stuffed it in there. I assured her the dinner had been wonderful, and that this was a business breakfast. She understood.

Mihi assured me the house would be cleaned and dinner would be ready by five o'clock. "Do you bring your chingu (friend, this time meaning Louis) with you tonight? I must know to cook," she said. It was more than that, I thought, because there was an impish smile on her face.

I thought Louis would like that, but I also thought it would be better to have Jina here when they formally met. I could keep Louis under wraps, but this beautiful young creature was another story entirely. I told her Louis would be working late, but she could meet him again sometime soon. She seemed a little put off, but content with that, and started cleaning the dishes from the previous night's meal, which would actually be today's lunch. I grabbed the food from the refrigerator and spare fan out of the den and went out to my trusty Royale.

Louis and I headed for the office after a quiet breakfast. We'd pick up our weapons and radios before heading over to Rostock's house, where we'd hopefully get a jump on the two customs guys. Maybe we could get something done before the crap hit the fan again.

I parked the car and locked it in a vacant lot just around the corner from the victim's last address in life, bringing the bag in tow. Louis was armed with the fan as we trooped to the house. The outside gate lock was getting rusty without daily use. We'd have to bring some WD-40. But the house door opened easily. Louis set up the fan while I stashed our lunch, bag and all, into the refrigerator.

We started searching the house from top to bottom, each of us doing separate rooms, then changing places. Personal letters. Notes. Anything MPI might have missed that could give us a clue to Rostock's killer and why he had all those ration cards. Six hours of searching produced only the photo of a young Korean woman. It looked like it had been taken near the front door of the MVP Club. That wasn't far from the restaurant where Louis and I ate the night before. I put the photograph in my pocket, and Louis and I went back to Walker to write up our daily log and turn in the hardware. I gave him a ride back to the barracks and we agreed to meet for PT the next morning. Then I drove home.

I remembered the photo of the young woman when I got home and laid it on the table. Even with the fan, six hours in that house was enough to make me feel as if I'd been swimming in sweat all day. I checked my watch. It was a little after three o'clock and I estimated it would be nearly another hour before Jina's brazen young friend would show up to cook dinner. I had time, but took a pair of gym shorts into the bathroom with me and locked the door, just in case. As I started the water, I heard the outside door open and the familiar singsong "Hi, ajushi" rang through the house. Thank God I'd been cautious.

I could smell the aroma of dinner filling the house. A spicy chicken soup the Koreans always made. I was ready for it, spices be damned. I hadn't eaten anything since breakfast. We'd been concentrating on finding clues in Rostock's house and forgot to eat the dinner-lunch I'd packed. We'd better eat it tomorrow, for sure.

I came out of the bedroom and saw Mihi bouncing back and forth between the refrigerator, sink and stove, busily preparing a meal Jina would, no doubt, pay her generously for. I had to admit that she was a hard worker. The house had been cleaned to within an inch of its life and food was being prepared every day, as requested. I'd have to be careful about how I praised her work with Jina, however, since Korean women tend to be overly jealous, no matter how innocent the situation.

I slipped a pair of jeans over my gym shorts and donned a T-shirt, then switched on the TV. Nothing good was on, but I let it stay on just the same. It would keep me company and help keep my mind off Mihi while I studied the photo on the table. She came over just as I picked it up. There was a strange look on her face. She almost seemed angry.

"You know her, ajushi?" she asked. I knew now that she could be angry at the thought of her friend's husband screwing around. She was pointing at the photo in my hand, but looking me straight in the eye. She would require a detailed answer or she'd bug me until Jina came back.

"No. I don't. Louis and I found this photo in our investigation today," I said, explaining the meaning of investigation and, finally picking up an English-Korean dictionary off the shelf to help explain some of the other words she didn't yet understand. The next half-hour became somewhat of an English class. Words that Jina already knew and readily accepted were new and strange to this young lady. But she finally got the gist of it before the dinner burned and the six o'clock news came on. My wife had apparently clued her in about not disturbing me during the news, because she remained in the kitchen, coming out only during the commercials.

Commercials on overseas military television networks have a different meaning, for sure. In the States they're exactly that — commercial advertisements. To a GI, especially overseas, they're a period during a program when he can go to the kitchen or bathroom and return before missing any of his show. Since the Department of Defense can't appear to endorse any commercial ventures, advertisements are substituted with military-oriented spot announcements, such as security, theft in the barracks and energy conservation. Some are pretty craftily created, while others are so dorky that you can't believe they'd actually air something like that.

It was, during one of these program breaks that Mihi came in with an announcement that caught my full attention.

"Ajushi. I know the woman in the picture. She was my friend before university. Do you and Louis need to speak to her?" When I said that we did, she quickly smiled and said, "I will try to find her for you tomorrow." Then she returned to her duties.

Dinner was served right after the CNN sports program, and I chowed down heartily. It wasn't five o'clock, but a little late isn't all that bad occasionally. She sat across the table from me, her chin cupped in her hands, watching to see if I made a face that would tell her she had failed. After I tasted everything on the table and issued a smile of satisfaction for each item, she happily returned to the kitchen to begin cleaning up. With tomorrow being a class day she apparently wasn't going out tonight.

I brought my dirty dishes to the kitchen under a disapproving scowl from my cook and cleaner. "That is the woman's job, ajushi," she said scornfully, hands on her hips and beautiful chin jutting out. She looked cute like that. So I didn't offend her further, I left the remaining dishes on the table and retired to my den to review my notes. I was accustomed to helping Jina clean up and found myself looking for things to do. I finally decided to return to the table and watch TV as she worked. Why should I feel uncomfortable around my own house?

She was done cleaning by nine o'clock and sat down for a moment, watching AFKN with me. That lasted only for a few minutes, however, and soon she was up and getting ready to leave. "I will return in the morning. Do you want breakfast?" she inquired. I said that would be nice, adding that I needed to eat before seven thirty in order to be at work on time. I told her what I wanted for breakfast and what time I thought she'd have to arrive to cook it in time. I would just be returning from PT to shower and change and wouldn't have much time at all to eat. I didn't feel the need to tell her that I usually didn't have breakfast on PT mornings, since I'd already spurned her breakfast offer this morning. She left looking as if I'd just given her a big compliment about a pretty dress or something, singing as she went out the door.

I prepared for bed and set my alarm for four thirty. It was going to feel strange getting back into the swing of things.

I realized on my way to pick up Louis the next morning that I hadn't done any physical training in a week. My promise to exercise this last weekend had fallen through with the good news that came. This was going to cost me in the physical arena. By the end of the day I'd be sore all over, not to mention the next morning. I'd just have to make the best of it. I lagged behind a bit in the two-mile run, but otherwise kept pace with the unit. A sharp look from the first sergeant had me catching up as fast as I could. He wasn't a man you wanted on your ass because you couldn't keep up. He knew how to make your life miserable. I'd stay with the company, no matter how painful.

Mihi arrived at the house just as I parked the car, smiling and issuing her daily "Hi, ajushi!" We both entered the house under the scornful look of a neighborhood ajumah who would no doubt tell Jina all sorts of stories when she returned. Most of those stories would probably be fabricated in her mind between now and then.

Mihi cooked breakfast, surprising me by preparing the eggs exactly the way I liked them. I had to admit that Jina briefed her well. I noticed as I sat down to eat that she was wearing full jeans and a blouse that covered everything. She was also wearing a bra, probably because of the university dress code. She must have read my mind because she almost blurted out, "We must wear underclothes to school or be punished. I hate to wear them, but I must study." She fell silent and I think we both blushed. I quietly wondered if "underclothes" meant panties as well, and hoped she couldn't really read my mind.

I finished eating as she cleaned up, and we both left at the same time. I offered her a ride, but she politely declined, explaining that her friend would meet her at the bus stop. I offered her some money for bus fare until Jina returned, but she refused, saying it wasn't necessary. "I enjoy doing things for you," she said, disappearing hurriedly around the corner. She was gone from sight by the time I'd backed the Royale into the alley.

I retrieved Louis from the barracks and we headed for the office to meet with the colonel for a case update. He started the meeting before we even had a chance to sit.

"The commanding general wants to see you and me, Jim." He then briefed us on what had happened while I was in Pyongtaek and Louis was in Hawaii. "After you both left, Park and Song figured they had to make brownie points with their boss, so they informed him you'd been relieved pending investigation. They didn't bother to tell him that you were probably innocent. In fact, they made it look as if you were confirmed guilty as hell. I'm sorry about them calling in the Pyongtaek crew to jump all over your in-laws."

I knew it wasn't his fault and told him so. I explained that I'd found Dad a job on post and that things would iron out after this case was locked up. The colonel said he'd check on him periodically to make sure he was treated right, then went on with the briefing.

"The general got really bent out of shape when that news story hit Stripes, though, I gotta tell you both. Seems Park and Song came in looking for Louis here. I told everyone not to mention to anyone where he'd gone or why. That must've gotten them thinking we'd buried him for a while. When they told their boss about you, Jim, they also mentioned that they couldn't find Louis. They issued the story to the Korean Associated Press who sold it worldwide. They started looking for you in the States until I called the Pentagon to have it dropped. You two had better call your folks.

"Anyway, the general called me in after the support commander had a meeting with him. You both should know that Colonel Butch doesn't have any love for me. He cried to the general that I was trying to ruin his record by covering up a big crime ring within the CID on his turf. The general, being concerned, of course, hauled me in and chewed my ass. We cleared up Louis being missing as soon as he returned from Hawaii with the report that cleared you. Now he wants to hear your version of the story. Just tell him the truth, Jim."

We let this sink in as Miss Paek entered with coffee for all three of us. The colonel went on after she left.

"What've you guys got so far?"

Louis and I briefed him, with me discussing the photo from Rostock's house. I told him I had a lead on the girl and Louis and I would try to follow it up this evening. "Will we have our Korean chaperones from customs today?" Louis asked.

"Not those two," the colonel replied. "They'll attach two others to us when they get settled. The oil hit the fire when they found out that Park and Song left out some very crucial information from their report about you two." He smiled and I sensed there was no love lost on that particular front either.

"C'mon," the colonel said, standing up. "Let's all go over to Henry to see the old man. Maybe if we're early we can hurry up and get our butts chewed, then get back to work."

General Bowles was much more amiable after he realized everything was well under control and that the colonel hadn't breached any regulations. He asked only to be kept informed to the best of our ability during the remainder of the case. He finally realized why we hadn't informed him before we moved the last time. He wanted us to try to find out why customs acted the way they did with the false report and the news release to the Associated Press.

The colonel assured him that we'd try to find out everything through channels, but if they wanted to keep this under wraps, he might have the United Nations Command commander-in chief put pressure on the Koreans through government channels. We knew that would cause bad feelings for a time in certain political circles, and I secretly wondered if this case was really worth that type of effort.

We left the general's office and the colonel offered Louis and me a cup of coffee at the snack bar. It hadn't gotten hot yet, so we walked past the sedan and crossed the parking lot to the snack bar. Some kids were playing video games, but the only other patrons were a couple of sergeants drinking coffee at separate tables. It was like they were armed with CID radar because they both stared at us when we entered. It must have been something about CID and FBI agents. Even without a uniform, people seemed to spot us right away. I self-consciously checked to see if my shoulder holster was exposed as we walked over to the coffeepot.

After coffee and a little small talk, we went back to Walker in the colonel's sedan. Before we got into our own car the colonel said, "Crack that baby wide open. I want to know everything as soon as you've got it. We've got other cases to get busy on." We nodded and I got behind the wheel as Louis slipped in on the passenger side.

I backed out and pulled onto the street. "Where to?" Louis asked.

"Where else?" I replied, pointing the sedan out the gate, headed toward the late ration control clerk's house. Even though we'd searched it from top to bottom, we might still find something new there. The only lead we had was the girl in the photo, and Mihi wouldn't be able to help with that until she got out of class later in the afternoon. Besides, our lunch was still in Rostock's refrigerator.

It was funny. MPI had gone as far as to clear Rostock's personal possessions for shipment back to the States. The movers were scheduled to come in today. Inventory would have been completed last Friday. But finding that box and its contents had frozen everything in place. The only people who could have had access to any of it were Louis and me. Without us, the colonel couldn't get in there now, unless he decided to relieve us of duty. The Korean customs agents weren't even allowed access without us being present, though they thought they had all the importance in the case. The fact is, Louis and I controlled everything here. That was quite a responsibility for "lowly enlisteds like us," as we like to say.

I parked the sedan in the familiar vacant lot and we locked the doors, then walked up the alley to the front gate. Louis took a can of WD-40 out of his bag and sprayed the lock, smiling in my face while he did so. "Bet you forgot," he sneered. I shrugged, knowing I had. Louis was good about things like that, helping make us one of the best teams the colonel had at the moment. I appreciated his attention to details throughout every case we'd been on together.

We went to work as soon as we opened the door and turned on the fan, not even stopping for a break until about noon. I dug our lunch out of the fridge and we sat down on the doorstep to eat in the breeze and try to figure the case out. Right now, we decided, we had a body, three hundred illegal ration plates, and only one small clue in a house still full of personal possessions. That didn't sit too well with us.

We finished our lunch in silence, neither of us even noticing what we were eating. It must have been good, though, because it was gone almost before we knew it. I had to hand it to Mihi. She'd make someone a nice wife someday. I instinctively looked at Louis for a moment with that thought. We covered the dishes and placed them back in the bag, zipping it up and returning it to the refrigerator. As I closed the door, I noticed a number written on the rubber door gasket in pen. It looked like a phone number, but I couldn't be sure. I pointed it out to Louis who copied it down in his notebook. "Let me have that before we split up for the day," I said. "I'm going to have Miss Paek call that number in all the provinces to see if it leads to anything.

"Why don't we just have her get a written record from the phone company of calls made from Rostock's phone number. That would be easier, and it would have the area codes as well," he said. I stopped and looked at him. Of course he was right, but I couldn't let him get away with that.

"You're right," I replied. "Glad I thought of it." He faked a stomach punch and laughed.

"Right on, dude," was all he said. We closed up Rostock's house and decided to turn in the sedan and hardware, then go back to my place. The colonel OKed it, since we'd be out late checking on the woman in the photo. We told Miss Paek what we wanted before we left and she got on the phone immediately. I told her I'd call back in an hour.

My watch said it was two o'clock. We hopped into my Royale for the trip out the back gate. When we got to my place, Louis asked to use the shower and take a nap. "Good idea," I said. When he was showered I let him use the master bedroom, then I jumped in for a rinse and lay down on the sofa.

About an hour later Mihi arrived to cook, waking me up when she came in the front door. "Hi, ajushi. I wake you?" I rubbed my eyes, reassuring her it was time for me to get up anyway, and her concerned look evaporated as she began the dinner preparations.

I remembered Louis as I splashed some water on my face and asked Mihi to cook for three people. She gave me a quizzical look and I explained that she and Louis were invited to eat with me. "OK," she said rather emphatically, rushing about to add the extra ingredients needed for the company. She seemed happy to have been invited. I mean, what the hell. She was here cooking and cleaning for me. She should be invited to partake of some of the goodies, right? Besides, Louis was here to chaperone me, and I him. I guess that works out right. Or does it?

I woke him up so we could run over our plan for the evening. As he was shaking the sleep out of his brain, I asked Mihi what she knew of the girl in the picture.

"Her name is Lee Juhee," she started. "Like I told you, she and I were friends before university. When we finished high school she disappeared for a while, but I saw her in the market about two months ago. I heard that she was working in one of the American clubs near Camp Henry, but when I asked where she'd been, she just told me she had a boyfriend. Probably an American boyfriend, eh, ajushi?" I guess she didn't really want an answer, because she rattled on about the chatty type of conversation they'd had as Mihi walked home with her.

"Where did she live?" I asked, ready to compare notes. She thought for a second as she minced up some green onions, then stopped, describing directions from the market to Rostock's house. Louis and I looked at one another, confirming what we already suspected. Louis was really awake then.

"How old is she, Mihi?"

"I think she's twenty-three," she said, guessing that she and her friend were about the same age. Not wanting the conversation to sound like an inquisition I nudged Louis and nodded toward the den. Mihi caught us in mid-flight. "I have asked around, ajushi. She worked at the MVP disco club. Some people say she's not there now, though. They say she left about two weeks ago. They haven't seen her since then."

We thanked her, then went into the den and closed the door.

"We might get lucky," Louis said. "Maybe she came back or someone there might know where she went." I agreed and we decided to visit the MVP to ask questions. They'd open about eight o'clock or so, but nobody would be there until about nine. We planned to leave the house about nine. We went into the living room and switched on the TV, sitting down to watch whatever was on.

"You will not find her," Mihi said from out of nowhere. Louis and I looked at each other again. This was starting to be a habit, I thought.

"Why not?" Louis asked her.

"Because everyone knows you are CID and that you are investigating, I think the word is, something wrong. They don't want to be a part of something wrong. But I think I can find out where she is," she said, returning to her cooking.

"What do you mean?" I asked.

"Well," she started thoughtfully. "They won't talk to you, but they might talk to an old school friend. I could go in there dressed like they are (like a prostitute) and let them think I work another club. They might talk to me." Just then I remembered Miss Paek and the telephone listing from Rostock's house. I nearly jumped across the room to grab the phone, taking everyone by surprise. I asked about the list, which she said could be picked up on her way home from work that night.

Mihi reached for the phone as soon as I hung up, calling her mother to say she would be meeting with friends later. She assured her mom that she'd be OK for classes the next day, and that she'd be home to change clothes as soon as she was done here. No, she wouldn't need dinner. She'd be eating out. She smiled as she hung up the phone.

"All set." I couldn't help but wonder what would happen if her mother found out the entire truth. I called Jina in Pyongtaek and let her in on what was happening, rather than letting her hear about it later in a not-so-good light. Her tone changed just before we hung up.

"Take care of her, Jim. She doesn't know that kind of life. You know the GIs. See that nothing happens, OK?" I assured her I'd take care of everything with Louis there to help. We hung up, passing kisses back and forth, which set Louis and Mihi to laughing uncontrollably.

Mihi was serving the dinner as I hung up. It was very tasty and we ate until every dish was empty, then sat back to relax awhile. Mihi was already feeling like she was a part of the elite CID, so Louis and I filled her in on what not to do.

She listened, then laughed and said, "Don't worry about me, big brothers. I have you there to protect me." She got up to remove the dishes from the table. "I clean dishes tomorrow," she said, grabbing her handbag and flying out the door, singing a popular tune as she disappeared.

Chapter Four

We parked the car on the street and sat for a moment. "Now remember, Mihi. You're not a kyungchal," I said, using the Korean word for police. "You go in, ask for your friend, maybe have a few Cokes, then come out. Louis and I will do the same, keeping an eye on you the whole time, OK?" She agreed and exited the car. We watched her all the way to the door.

With her attire, she clearly outfoxed any of the women I'd ever seen in the clubs. The high heels and leather miniskirt accentuated her pear-shaped buttocks and shapely legs. The skin-tight fabric of her thin white blouse accentuated the black bra that didn't quite conceal her nipples, but slightly camouflaged them. Her black hair fell straight down her back. She had come to the house in jeans, asking to use the bathroom. She came out twenty minutes later, dressed and layered with makeup. She looked exquisite. When I asked where she got the clothes, "a friend" had to suffice for the answer. She volunteered no more. I wondered what her parents would think if they saw her dressed like that.

I shot a glance over at Louis, who looked as if he was going to drool all over the dashboard. I couldn't have that and handed him my handkerchief, which he pushed away without taking his eyes from her. I knew exactly what he was thinking. I tried to evict those same thoughts from my head by reminding myself what a wonderful wife I had. Damn! I wish she were here now.

A couple of minutes after Mihi entered the MVP, followed by the stares of the male population on the sidewalk and driving by in cars, Louis and I locked the car and followed suit.

The MVP Club is one of Taegu's newer clubs, sitting a few doors farther down from the Camp Henry gate than the others. Situated in the basement of a four-story hotel, it sits across from Henry's barren cinder block walls. Its claim to fame is virtual non-stop disco, playing loud enough to be heard through two sets of closed doors and out onto the busy sidewalk, even with

Taegu's traffic at its noisiest. In the summer the club is cooled by two huge air conditioners located next to the dance floor. The DJ's booth, of course, is right next to one of the cooling units.

Some fifty tables are placed so close together that people jostle to get in and out when the place is full. It usually fills up between eleven at night and two in the morning on weeknights, and is often overflowing on Friday and Saturday nights. A few of the waitresses and bartenders earn extra cash now and then by taking a customer home for a night of pleasure. Other prostitutes also frequented the club to attract business while having fun.

Then there's the "downtown" clientele — the bank tellers, secretaries and whatnot who came in to dance and meet Americans for a lark. Most would come in groups and leave the same way, but occasionally one would go astray. It was to be expected wherever young men and women congregated. While most of the other clubs offered eloquently dressed or scantily clad "hostesses" to attract customers, many of those same people often came to the MVP to see and dance with real Korean girls. Even the younger men were getting tired of the hookers.

A few older customers were perched atop bar stools, while another twenty-five or so younger ones sat around at tables, some in groups. The waitresses were fairly busy, since only a few had showed up for work at this early hour. One, however, sat at the bar in deep conversation with a customer. Another who had apparently just delivered drinks to a table was laughing and bouncing a tray lightly off her knee, listening to something funny from one customer who was clowning around a bit.

We chose a table near the back of the club, as far away from the speakers as we could get, and ordered Cokes. We spotted Mihi sitting at a table with a GI, engaged in attentive conversation. We tried not to look as if we were watching her, though we took turns watching and scanning the club.

About the time our sodas came, Mihi excused herself and approached a waitress. They talked for a moment, then Mihi went into the ladies' room. The waitress followed her a minute later after dropping her tray off at the bar. We sure as hell couldn't keep an eye on her in there. Since everyone knew we were CID and on duty (I still wondered how they could tell), Louis and I just sat, drank our Cokes and watched, waiting for Mihi to reappear. When our waitress returned with a second round, I pulled the photo from my pocket and asked if she knew the girl.

"Yes," she said over the din. "She was a waitress here some time ago." When I asked where she was now, she shrugged and offered only that the girl in the picture had an American boyfriend. "She don't need come here any more." She turned and left to wait on other customers. I returned the photo to my pocket and leaned over to tell Louis what little I'd found out. He nodded, still keeping his eye on the door where Mihi had last been seen. A minute later she and the waitress both appeared, laughing as if they'd been friends for life. Maybe they had. I don't know.

Mihi looked around, not overtly showing anyone she was looking for us, then asked a GI if he wanted to dance. It was comical. He got up so fast he almost knocked the table over. I chuckled and sat back to enjoy the show.

They lasted about eight dances before that poor soldier looked like he'd been dragged on a ten-mile run. Mihi, on the other hand, looked fresh and ready to go another eight. She was really enjoying herself. Louis and I made our way to the door just as he begged off dancing again, and Louis made for the men's room while I stood at the door to wait and watch. That was her signal. She excused herself to leave and received about five minutes of "when will I see you again," then pried herself away to walk past me through the double doors. Louis popped out of the rest room just as the doors closed, and we pushed through them together and climbed the stairs to the sidewalk. We met Mihi just outside the door at the top of the stairs and got into the car, driving away before talking.

"She went to visit her aunt in Kangnung," Mihi said as we turned the corner to head toward Camp Walker. "Here's the address and telephone number there," she added, handing Louis a slip of paper.

"Your house," was all he told me after he read it, and I made a straight shot of it.

Louis handed me the note when we got inside the house, and I compared it with the note in my pocket that had the number from the refrigerator door gasket. They matched. Except this one also had the area code. I'd bet a month's pay that it would also match at least one phone call from Rostock's house, if not more. We'd see in the morning.

Mihi was sitting on the sofa, repairing her makeup. "This is fun, ajushi," she said, plying lipstick to her sensuous mouth. "Can we go out again?" I reminded her of her classes the next morning.

"Besides," Louis added. "You did a wonderful job tonight. You need to sleep now." I picked up the phone and dialed Pyongtaek to let Jina know we were home, safe and sound. I put Mihi on for a minute, then hung up. Mihi headed for the shower. She couldn't be caught going home with makeup on and smelling like a brewery. Louis and I retired to the den, remembering the last time she'd used the shower in our presence. A "good night, ajushi" signaled her departure a few minutes later and Louis and I went into the more comfortable living room, both silently wishing we hadn't been the ones to introduce her to the GI clubs.

"Now we know where that number leads," Louis said, looking at the paper again. We went to the map and located Kangnung on the northeastern coast of the republic, very close to North Korea. The two well-traveled routes would either take us through Pohang, on the southeast coast, and up the coastal highway, or up the expressway through Suwon, and eastward over the mountains. Neither was good if you counted time and safety into the equation. We opted to ask the colonel for a chopper to Camp Long in Wonju, and a car from there to Kangnung. We'd still have to navigate that mountain road, but it was better than doing so after four hours of highway driving.

We headed to Camp Walker to get Louis back to the barracks for some sleep. We'd ask the colonel for the Blackhawk in the morning. He'd also set up the car and the interpreter-guide for us. The colonel was good about that type of thing. He'd make sure we had whatever we needed to accomplish the mission, even if it put him out a little. He was a real soldier's boss. I headed back home as soon as I dropped Louis off, then hit the sack. Surveillance really takes it out of you, no matter how easy it looks in the movies.

Mihi came in early the next morning and I rushed to get a pair of shorts on. She giggled, holding a hand to her mouth. Maybe I shouldn't have let her keep that key. That was a close call. When I was presentable, I came out of the bedroom and told her I'd be gone for a couple of days and wouldn't need cooking for a while. She gave me a forlorn look, as if I was taking away her livelihood. I didn't know if it was the cooking or her minor part in the investigation, but I felt sure it was the latter.

I called Jina in Pyongtaek, although it was only a few minutes before seven, and told her about the trip. She issued the standard "be careful" and we hung up. Breakfast was ready, and I noticed Mihi had cooked enough for two. She was sitting in front of one of the plates, waiting for me to sit down. It didn't upset me, but I was more than a little surprised. I sat and picked up a fork, which, in Korean tradition, gave her permission to begin eating. She took a few bites before saying anything.

"Ajushi. Did I help last night?"

"Yes," I said. "You helped a lot."

"Then why do you go away?" she asked, not realizing, I guess, that we were going to Kangnung as a result of last night's efforts. I explained this to her, and she volunteered to help there as well.

I told her we were going by chopper, because it was faster and safer than driving. She began to understand once I explained what a chopper was. I assured her we'd be all right and would be

Murder in the Morning Calm

back in a few days. After a few bites of her breakfast, she spoke again, this time apparently not feeling as sure of herself.

"Bring Louis back safe, OK?" That was it. It wasn't the cooking or her playing CID. It was Louis. I promised her that Louis would return safe and sound with me. I can't really complain. Americans are usually assigned to Korea for only one year before returning to a Stateside unit. This is a country where you must fall in love quickly if you wish to marry a foreigner, or lose him forever. After all, that's what happened to Jina and me. Mihi was silently cleaning as I left the house. I felt sorry for the kid. Not because she was hooked on Louis, but because she wanted to see more of him and I was taking him away for a few days.

On the other hand, Louis wasn't known for being the one-woman type. He did his share of "butterflying," as Korean women called it, and then some. I realized that Louis could break this young woman's heart if he wasn't ready to be tied down. I tried to push those thoughts out of my mind for the time being so I could concentrate on my driving and the tasks at hand for the next few days. There was time to square away this relationship once we returned safely from Kangnung.

I locked up my car and went inside the office to meet Louis. We wouldn't need our radios for this trip because we'd be operating too far away from any U.S. bases. Miss Paek issued us Korean pay telephone credit cards so we could keep in touch. She included long distance dialing instructions.

The standard travel orders were issued, and we were on our way to the helipad, the colonel giving us a lift in his sedan. We briefed him fully about our plans in Kangnung on the way. He issued us his standard good luck wishes. The chopper was warmed up and waiting when we arrived, its rotors swirling lazily in the hot sun that baked the flightline.

We boarded and got our luggage and ourselves strapped in for the forty-five minute flight to Camp Long. The bird took off, lifting over the city and circling northward from the takeoff pattern to head up the expressway. We'd cut over, following

Route 4 to Wonju, finally landing at the Camp Long helipad on the hilltop next to the post chapel. Then it would be a two-hour jaunt through mountains that usually hide in the clouds, the road switchbacking around countless times.

Half an hour later we could see the outline of Seoul to the north, as we turned east on the final leg of our flight. The skyline was barely visible through the haze. Of Korea's forty million people, more than a quarter of them live in Seoul. Those ten million plus people always seemed to be on the go, filling the streets in buses, taxis, cars, trucks mopeds, motorcycles and bicycles. Pushcarts were also a standard traffic hazard. The vehicles zigzagged to fill the most minute spaces left by inattentive drivers. Koreans were the masters of driving four abreast in three traffic lanes. One jokingly told me that the painted lines were meant for foreigners, not Koreans. The general populace seemed to agree with that notion. To me, driving in and around Seoul is a nightmare.

The capital city disappeared in the haze and I looked down. The cars looked like little elongated dots as they drove along the highway a thousand feet below. If they were just slightly bigger, I thought, they'd look like Hot Wheels cars. We landed at Camp Long about fifteen minutes later, where we were met by our guide and interpreter. He normally stayed in the Long CID office, translating for the local agents but, at the colonel's request, he was attached to us for our trip.

"Hello," he said, first bowing to the waist, then offering his hand. "My name is Mr. Park from the CID office here. I will tend to your needs on your journey." I jokingly asked him if he was related to the Mr. Park in the Taegu customs office. His face turned dour and he denied any relation to the man. He immediately got into the driver's seat of the sedan and motioned for us to climb in. I thanked God he was driving through the mountains instead of me. I sat up front and Louis slipped in to the back seat. Mr. Park waited until we were out the gate and headed eastward on the highway before he spoke again.

"I am sorry about my manners," he started. "The Mr. Park you refer to in Taegu is no friend of mine. He comes here often. Not to Camp Long, but to Wonju City. I often see him in the coffee houses and mokkolli houses." A mokkolli house is a place that serves a cheap, creamy, somewhat bitter rice wine of the same name. It's the cheap drink for people who can't afford an inexpensive bottle of soju. It tastes OK, I guess, after the first couple of cups, but it leaves a helluva hangover and a bad smell on your breath.

"I think his visits are not always for legal purposes. I even tried to find out things about him, but his associates are quite closed-mouthed about him. When I try to follow him, he loses me before he gets to his destination. Of course, this is my own private investigation. I am not a trained investigator like you agents are," he said, looking over at me with a toothy smile. Mr. Park's final statement stuck with me. "He sometimes seems to act like a gangpeh," he said, using the Korean word for gangster.

On a whim I took out the photos of Rostock and the girl and asked if he'd seen either of them. "Oh yes," he said emphatically. "I remember her." He thought for a moment before speaking up again. "She was here talking with some of the same people your Mr. Park spoke with. I never saw them together, but they seem to have some of the same associations. Him," he motioned to the photo of Rostock, "I don't know. All you Americans look alike to me," he smiled, then concentrated on his driving.

We were getting into some curvy areas now and Mr. Park needed to focus all his attention on the road. I was convinced he hadn't seen the dead sergeant before, since he'd readily opened up about the other two. We sped along in silence until we got to the highest point on the road, which was marked by a service area and a tourist overlook. Mr. Park pulled in.

It was a gorgeous sight. A set of steps at the end of the parking lot was led up to the top of the ridge and a towering monument. Beyond them to the east, we looked over the smaller mountains and rolling hills leading to the East Sea, between

Korea and Japan. To the left we could see occasional glimpses of the road we would soon be on, winding downward through the mountains. The sign said we were about a thousand meters — roughly three thousand feet — above sea level. Though nothing compared to the view of the Pacific from the mountains in California, this was impressive in its own right. We forgot about the case for a few moments as we luxuriated in the beauty before us.

"Down there," Mr. Park said, pointing slightly to the left, about where the road might go, "is Kangnung. That is where we are going. It is a nice city that does not see too many Americans. Please forgive the people who will stare at you. You will be almost unique in their lives." Then he pointed more northward as our eyes followed. "That mountain top is in North Korea. At the foot of it, just to the south, is Sokcho. It is a wonderful resort in South Korea."

I wondered for a moment about a resort directly under the eyes of communism. Didn't the vacationers feel ill at ease? Didn't the Communist peons feel as if they'd been lied to by their dictating leader, seeing those people having fun in the sun right under their very noses? The answer to that lay in Kim Il-sung's doctrine, which claimed that areas close to the Demilitarized Zone were wrought with capitalist lies. What you saw was not what you got, he told them endlessly. He said the people in the south were ordered by western capitalist warmongers to act as if they were having fun under penalty of death. He ordered them not to succumb to this capitalist lie. Yet, they must sometimes wonder if they are getting accurate information about what their eyes see.

An hour later, after we'd eaten, we were careening down the mountain. Mr. Park seemed to take great pleasure in seeing the looks on our faces as he veered six inches from one ledge and a foot from the next. The trees at the bottom of the ravine looked like fuzzy-topped toothpicks stuck in a dervish, and each curve made me think that we would land squarely on top of one. But we made it safely down to Kangnung and entered the heavily guarded city, then wound our way through the streets to the Daeho Hotel in Kyungpo. It was impressive, to say the least, with a beautiful view of the ocean.

Mr. Park translated, even though the desk clerks knew nearly perfect English (they must be certified by the Korean government before working in a tourist establishment). A bellhop grabbed our bags and escorted us up the stairs to the fourth and top floor. Elevators are rare in buildings less than five stories tall in Korea. I noticed the room was fully furnished, complete with a mini-bar stashed inside the compact refrigerator. Anything missing was replenished on a daily basis and added to the final bill at checkout time.

There was an array of soft drinks, as well as Korean and imported liquors in the shot-size bottles. There were also fruits and nuts in vacuum-sealed plastic containers for those who get hungry or just like to eat while they're having a drink. But the prices were sky high, as attested to by the menu glued to the door of the small refrigerator. I could eat a full meal in a local restaurant for the same price they charged for a Coke here.

I changed clothes, planning to get something to eat at a local Mom and Pop restaurant. I figured Louis was doing the same. I had no idea about Mr. Park. We were on our own when it came to non- business, unless he volunteered.

The door chimes rang as I was shaving, sounding like a chickadee having a heart attack. I leaned out of the bathroom and unlocked the front door. Louis came strolling in, looking like the fox that'd found the chicken coop. "What's up?" I asked, as the blade gouged another acre of skin from my chin.

"Found a nice place to eat," he said, smiling like the devil. "I described what Mihi cooked for us last night, because I couldn't remember the name. The man at the check-in counter came up with a joint less than a mile from here. It should be easy to get to."

"And what makes you think I want to eat the same thing two days in a row?" I asked, dabbing another piece of toilet paper on yet another wound. Would it ever stop bleeding, or was this a North Korean blade in the razor the hotel provided?

"Relax, man. I just want to see if they can cook as good as she does."

I stopped for second and looked at him. There was a strange look on his face, one I'd never seen before. Could it be? Nah! I went back to hacking up my face (sure wish I'd remembered to bring my Norelco), then cleaned up as best I could and got dressed. It looked like a toilet paper blizzard had hit my face full force, but I was hungry. Let 'em laugh, I thought.

"So why the thoughts of Mihi, old chum?" I asked as I was slipping on my jacket. "What happened to 'butterfly man'?"

"Hey," he objected. "All I wanna do is compare. What's wrong with that?" I let the subject drop and we left, locking the door as we went out.

But I knew. That was enough.

I peeled toilet paper off my face as we walked down the steps, making little deposits in ashtrays on each landing. Maybe I was marking the trail so I could find my way back.

We stepped out the front door into a sweet evening breeze. The decorative palm trees were swaying lazily in the waning light. Though still early, the sun was falling behind the western mountains that had been eastern mountains this morning. The haze was clearing over the ocean as night made advances on this side of the mountains. A lone boat crossed the expanse of water from north to south, probably on its way home after a day of fishing.

The driveway to the hotel bent and sloped down about a hundred yards to the road. Must be a real bitch trying to come back after a night of partying downtown, I thought. We set out and took a left at the main road, heading toward the small town. It was peaceful. You couldn't take a quiet walk like this in Taegu, that was for sure. The traffic would mow you down if you tried.

We passed beachside vendors selling everything from food and drink to T-shirts and photo albums, all marking Kyungpo as the only place in Korea to spend a vacation. We came to a small open-air restaurant and Louis pulled out a slip of paper from his pocket. "This is it," he exclaimed, after comparing the Hangul markings on the paper with those above the entrance. He stepped inside like he owned the place and I followed, wondering what I was getting into.

As soon as I sat down, I found a picture on the wall of a dish I liked. It sure wasn't the same thing we ate last night. Louis waited in bliss for the waitress to arrive, holding another slip of paper in his hand. It was obviously a note written in Hangul, saying what he wanted to eat. When she finally ambled over to our table, Louis handed her the note, which she immediately understood. She nodded, then turned to me. I got up and pointed to the picture of the dish I wanted, then simply said "OB" to add a beer to the list.

"OB opsoyo," she said. When I looked as if I didn't understand (which I didn't), she rephrased the reply. "OB. No," she said, shaking her head. I asked for a Crown Dry, and she agreed, then trotted away to the kitchen to fulfill our culinary desires of the evening.

A moment later she reappeared with Louis' water and my beer, then scurried off again. It wasn't more than a few minutes before she brought our dinners. The service was fast. We wolfed down our meals in silence. We'd both built up quite an appetite coming down that mountain. Fear had probably frightened away all the lunch calories we'd amassed at the scenic overlook, because we ate as if we hadn't seen food in a week. We finished and strolled up and down the street until we found a club that looked like it would suit our needs.

It was a Korean club that relied on disco to attract the younger vacationers. The music was deafening, but we took a table near the dance floor, anyway. It was almost empty at this hour, so we ordered a couple of Cokes and waited. It wasn't long before crowds were attracted by the music and started streaming in. Whether they came alone, in pairs or small groups, they stopped to look at the Americans "invading" their club. They sat at tables well away from us.

The club filled to near capacity within the next couple of hours and we were getting tired. There was no sign of Miss Lee, and there was a good chance she wouldn't even show up in this club. We agreed to wait for another hour, but when time expired with no results, we finished our drinks and escaped into the warm summer breeze outside.

We stopped on the sidewalk to adjust to the relative quiet and the lack of strobe lights. That's when we saw her.

She looked much better than she did in the picture, but then, who doesn't? Especially a vibrant young woman, now clad in knee-high boots, denim miniskirt and white blouse buttoned to the neck. A dark blazer, open at the front, completed the ensemble. She had a sleek build, with curves where they ought to be, though with slightly smaller than American features. Her hair was cropped just short of touching her collar and her sloe eyes could melt hearts at fifty paces.

She walked toward us from across the street with the grace of a model. It was difficult not to watch her, as attested to by the many turned heads for more than a block in either direction. I could see why Rostock fell for this bundle of charm. She gave no hint of knowing us as she climbed onto the sidewalk, turned slightly and passed next to us, her perfume wafting on the breeze she created. It had a warm fragrance of peaches ripening under a gentle summer sun.

She entered the club next to the one we had been in. We waited a moment, then followed, paying a cover charge at the door and suffering the glares of hundreds of Korean men and about ten young women seated within. On the three stages dotting the far wall were go-go dancers undulating or wriggling to the music. They were in G-string outfits and high heels, or wore high-heeled boots that stretched either up to their knees or mid-thigh.

One dancer on the left was rather skinny and tall, with jet black hair flowing down to her ankles. The hair was clearly her most attractive feature. Center stage held a shorter version, still skinny, with hair cropped close. On the right was a full-figured version of the girl we'd followed into the club. She had very shapely legs and thick hair that stopped just short of her buttocks.

We spied an empty table next to the stage and made our way through the crowd, with hundreds of eyes following our every move. We sat with our backs to the wall so we could take in the entire club without turning around and being obvious. The waitress produced anju and beer, which we'd agreed to since they only sold Coke mixed with liquor. She poured the drinks while we started nibbling the fruits and nuts on a plate. The apples were carved delicately into swans. Cute. That was one way to sell a perfectly good twenty-five cent apple for a buck and a quarter, I thought.

Our picture girl, Lee Juhee, appeared a moment later, coming out of the ladies' room and looking around. I hoped this wasn't just a pit stop for her before she moved elsewhere. I hated to think we'd gotten established here at the cost of nearly seventeen dollars, just to have her go to the bathroom and leave right away. It would be a pity to leave everything on the table, but that's exactly what would happen if she moved on. She conferred with a passing waitress who, standing on her tiptoes, finally pointed in our direction. Was she seeking a place to sit, or looking for Americans? Or maybe she knew we were CID agents. Either way, she nodded her thanks to the waitress and made her way through the crowd toward us. Even in the low light of the club she attracted the attention of every male in the place. It was almost as if there weren't any dancers on the stages, because no one looked in that direction. This little lady was definitely a showstopper wherever she traveled.

"Excuse me," she said in a light voice we almost couldn't hear above the music. "Would you mind if I sit here?" We nodded our assent and she sat down. In a hooker bar near the gates, that would have meant the customer was obligated to buy the woman a drink. But as Miss Lee lowered herself into the chair, removing her blazer to reveal a sleeveless blouse, she said, "I will pay for my own drinks, Americans. Do not worry." She turned her attention toward the stages and ignored us for the most part.

There was still no hint that she knew who we were, but she could very well be playing some sort of game. A waitress brought her a cream-colored drink in a high glass, with crushed ice topped by a miniature umbrella. She began to sip slowly, pursing delicately glossed full lips around the tiny straw. It was very sensual to watch. She noticed our eyes on her and smiled gently, then turned once more toward the go-go dancers. It looked as though she was evaluating their performances.

As the music ended, the three girls on stage bent to pick up piles of clothing discarded at their feet. They rushed off the stages toward the dressing rooms near the front door next to the bar.

The next event took us off guard. When two other women got up to take their places on stage, so did Miss Lee. "Street clothes" came off and the three were clad in G-string outfits as the music began. The two dancers farther away looked similar to the girls who'd just departed, but Miss Lee was a cut above them, both in looks and dancing style. Louis and I watched with great appreciation, keeping in mind that we were here on business. I leaned over and asked him to call Mr. Park. "Have him bring the sedan, Louis. We might need it." He playfully gave me a hateful look, but rose and made his way to the door, returning a few minutes later.

"He'll be here in about ten minutes," he announced as he sat. He mentioned that he may have woke our friend up, because Mr. Park didn't sound too happy, even though he said he'd be here right away. I nodded and returned to my "surveillance." Louis gladly joined me at that duty. When Mr. Park arrived he, too, sat in quiet appreciation. Shortly afterward, the fifth song ended and Miss Lee gathered her clothes and dashed off to the dressing room. We briefed Mr. Park on what was happening. He'd already made the connection between the dancer and the girl in the photo. Pretty good, considering he'd just been roused from his sleep.

Miss Lee returned about fifteen minutes later, dressed in a hanbok, traditional clothes usually worn in a club only during the holidays or for a special show. I knew of no Korean holidays that day, nor were any of the other ladies dressed up, so I suspected a show. I leaned over and asked her about it.

She nodded as she sipped. "I am hired as a stripper," she said simply. I nodded and sat back. Talking with her would definitely have to wait. If she went haywire, the management wouldn't appreciate losing their star attraction. They might not mind missing a go-go set or two later, but the main show was a different story.

Three dancers took to the stages at the end of the set. When they finished, they exited toward the dressing room, and the lights dimmed to nearly black, save for the glow of the table candles. Nearly a minute later, a solitary white spotlight illuminated Miss Lee's face on center stage.

An old Korean tune came over the loudspeakers, the familiar Oriental twang providing the only rhythm for her movements. The light slowly expanded in breadth, showing the entire stage. A long, nearly see-through log shawl covered her hanbok. She took it from her shoulders, spun around, covered her face for a moment, then let it drop to her shoulders again. The second time, the shawl floated to the floor of the stage when she was done with it. The spotlight slowly changed from white to yellow, then green, red and blue as she danced. Near the end of the first tune, Miss Lee untied and discarded the top of her hanbok, revealing a pure white undergarment.

She started spinning wildly to the applause of the audience as the second tune came up. The music was much faster than before, with more of a rhythmic drumbeat. When she stopped spinning, she danced gracefully about the stage, slowly loosening the bottom outer layer of her garment, then slipping the shoulder straps down her arms. The colorful fabric floated to the stage to rest on the top piece. The undergarment now hung freely in layers from her shoulders, billowing out to reveal her near perfect legs occasionally as she danced. When the music reached its end and the light went bright red she lowered herself to a cross-legged sitting position on the stage, as the final note spilled from the gigantic speakers.

She remained motionless as a much slower tune began. The light slowly changed to green. It must have been her cue, for she raised her arms slowly above her head, then slowly rose herself from the stage. She dropped her arms and the hanbok's undergarment fell gently to the stage, her foot pulling it off as she stood. This revealed that the only remaining clothing consisted of a G-string outfit that was much skimpier than before, the cloth barely doing its assigned job. The bottom patch, in fact, was severely underequipped for the mission, not quite covering the entire thick thatch. When she turned sideways in her dance the fabric stood noticeably away from the skin, pushed by the curly hairs that seemed to strain in an attempt to escape from this small prison.

A minute or so later, she retrieved the shawl from the stage and draped it loosely from her shoulders, pulling the snap from her skimpy top in the process. The top slipped out from under the shawl and dropped gracefully to the floor. She danced and swirled and spun for a minute, dancing lightly in the wind to teasingly expose her well-rounded breasts. On one spin, the bottom of the string outfit sailed to the floor, revealing the heavily thatched area beneath, which seemed to play peek-a-boo as the shawl fluttered around. The lights played in blue, green and red, but strategically avoided the white. When the yellow light shone, the audience could easily discern what lay beneath the light shawl.

The lights eventually dimmed to near darkness as the music ended. She dropped the shawl and pranced around the first few rows of tables, raising a leg here for a second, sitting on a lap there for another and generally raising the ambient temperature within the club. Some men waved money to entice her over for a visit. She collected her tips as she visited.

One older gentleman got the treat of his life. She grabbed his head in both hands and, standing between his legs on the chair, pushed his head between her legs for a split second. Then she jumped to the floor, snatched his offering, and sailed to other tables, pulling another man's face in between her breasts. He must have taken a playful bite, because she yelped and quickly danced away smiling.

When she got to our table, she stepped up on the chair she occupied earlier, then hopped onto the table. I had to admit that, up close, her body was almost as nice as my wife's. I felt a strong pang of guilt until I rationalized that I was here on duty and that this was a potential suspect in my case. I sat back to study the evidence before me.

The guilt totally disappeared when she toyed with Louis' hair and stroked Mr. Park's cheek with her foot. The guilt came raging back, however, when she squatted in front of me on the table and opened her legs as wide as they'd go, revealing her love box in all its intimate beauty just inches from my face. I think I began to sweat a little because she snatched my handkerchief from my hand (how did it get there?) and placed it squarely between her legs with a false expression of modesty dancing across her face. The crowd was in an uproar. She took the handkerchief away and blotted my upper lip with it, then placed it on my head. The audience went wild with approval.

Still squatting in front of my face, she reached for my change, about six thousand won, and picked it up. She put the money between her legs, then flashed it in front of my face before she rose and jumped off the table. She'd just gotten to the stage and I'd gotten my hanky off my head when the music died and the lights went black. When they came on again, she was gone and the audience was issuing a standing ovation in my direction. I was really embarrassed this time. I smiled and took a sip of beer to help regain my composure.

Three other go-go dancers jumped up from their tables and filled the stages with their struts, their street clothes rapidly dropping to the stage floors. Mr. Park leaned over to get my attention.

"She's good. But I think it would be better if we took her out of here to talk. Why don't you ask her to eat? She seems to like you best." He was smiling and I knew what he was thinking. But he also had a point about talking to her elsewhere. Time was of the essence, and trying to talk here wouldn't be right. I nodded and we waited for her return from the dressing room.

After about a half-hour, she sat back down at the table and I issued the invitation, which she readily accepted. "Dancing like that makes me hungry. Thank you," she said, then went to arrange it with the manager.

I could believe what she said. When her order arrived at a small restaurant next to where Louis and I ate earlier, she wolfed it down in only a few minutes. I wondered if she'd eaten anything else today. She pushed the dishes aside and pulled a glass closer, pouring soju, then mixing in some Coke.

"How long did you know Rostock?" Louis asked when she seemed comfortable with us. She stiffened slightly and glanced around warily. By this time we'd already casually introduced ourselves as CID. "It's OK. We found your picture in his house."

"I know him about a year. Why do you ask this?"

We explained that we were assigned to the case and that we weren't here on vacation, but as part of the investigation. "When did you leave Taegu?" I asked.

"About two weeks ago, just after he died. I did not kill him." She looked adamant in her denial.

"Do you know who did?"

"No." She sipped her drink. She was nervous, but didn't look worried. I believed in a way that she didn't kill him, but I wanted to know what other information she might have.

"When did you begin to live with him?" Louis asked. We didn't know for sure that she had, but we strongly suspected as much.

"About a week after I met him," came the answer.

The story unfolded. She knew he was the "ration man" when she agreed to share his bed, but that wasn't her motivation. She claimed to know nothing about the ration cards that were found, or any illegal dealings.

She answered questions for about an hour, seeming not to worry about the club or her manager. Maybe she'd arranged to take off for the rest of the night, but I really didn't think so. Mr. Park reached into his pocket and showed her a well-worn photo of our Taegu customs man. This caught me off guard. Speaking in Korean, he asked if she knew him. She nodded.

"How well?" I asked.

"He used to come to the house sometimes on the weekends and drink a little with Timmie. Sometimes they would go outside and talk in whispers. Sometimes they would go into another room and talk. Sometimes Timmie would tell me to go to a friend's house or go shopping for a couple of hours when he came. About a month ago I heard them arguing. I could not tell what they were saying, but I knew they were very angry at each other. This man left and Timmie just walked around the house, hitting the walls and screaming bad talk. He never told me what they talked about and I did not ask."

She acknowledged seeing the metal box we'd found the cards in, but claimed she didn't know what was in it. It was always locked, she said. "Every time he opened it, he would close the door to the room and tell me to stay out." She was looking down at her soju glass now, the fifth refill almost gone.

"Why did you leave Taegu?" Louis finally asked. She took a moment to compose her answer.

"I was afraid," she said lowly. "I thought the person who killed Timmie would try to kill me. When I found him, I called the KNPs, then left to go to my friend's house. I wasn't there when they arrived, because they would have taken me to jail whether I did it or not. That night I climbed over the wall and took all my things." That must have been before MPI started investigating, because no women's clothing was found in the house, according to their initial report. Not even one jar of makeup. She had been pretty thorough about getting everything out of there. "I planned on staying in Taegu somewhere, but then I got worried that they could find me there and kill me. I don't know why Timmie was killed, and I don't know why they would want to kill me, but I was afraid. Even here." She waved a hand around the room, but meant the entire city. "I am afraid they will find me, but there was no place more far away for me to go."

I looked at my watch and expressed concern about her work. "Yes," she said. "I must go and explain to the manager that I became ill and can not work the rest of the night. Will you give me a ride to my room in Kangnung?" She looked hopeful. We agreed to drive her, but it was more than a personal favor. We needed to know where she lived in case we had more questions — or needed to arrest her. That made it official business. She returned a few minutes later with her bag, and we left for the half-hour drive. It was nearly one o'clock in the morning. I was glad we'd had Mr. Park come with the sedan.

Her room near the Kangnung train station was in a seedy rooming house that rented by the hour, night, week, month or longer. The room had a thin mat on the floor for sleeping. Other than that, her small wardrobe took up the remaining space. The communal shower and toilet was outside. There was no running hot water. That luxury meant putting a kettle on the charcoal stove. What a meager existence. Korean people usually took it in stride if they had to survive this way, but I hated the sight of it. There was no way I could live like this. It was just too transient for my tastes.

We saw her into her room and gave her a hotel business card with our room numbers on it in case she remembered anything new. It was nearing two o'clock as we turned the car in the direction of Kyungpo and our hotel.

Mr. Park was the first to bid good night, using a tone heavily implying that if the hotel wasn't on fire, he'd rather not be disturbed. We agreed and waved as he went through the doorway, into the lobby, to claim his key. Louis and I strolled down the driveway until we were out of earshot of any casual passersby.

"What do you think?" I asked him.

"I dunno." He paused before continuing. "I don't think she killed him, but I'm not 100 percent sure she didn't know anything about the cards. You heard what this Mr. Park said about her being in Wonju. But that info about the Taegu Mr. Park adds an interesting twist. What about you?"

"About the same. I wonder, though. Could this be why Mr. Park stepped on it? I mean, it looks as if he was acting a little overzealous about implicating me. He sure was hasty about alerting his boss that you were gone. He totally failed to give his superiors a slight — but critical — piece of information in his report. And he went overboard on the attack against my in-laws. Now this information about him and Rostock, which he also failed to mention."

"Something stinks," we said in unison.

We agreed to call it a night and went upstairs. I couldn't sleep, though, and soon went out for a walk.

It was peaceful down on the beach. I could hear music from the many clubs blaring down from the main street about two hundred yards away, but the gentle slapping of the waves could also be heard. I passed a few couples, but was otherwise alone as the tide rose, then began to fall. I watched the sun come up over the ocean, then headed back to the hotel for breakfast. There was a message with my key. It gave a phone number and Miss Lee's name. I decided to use an outside pay phone rather than the one in my room, just in case her worries were justified. I headed out the door again. I dialed the number at the first phone box and, when the rooming manager finally answered the phone, asked for her.

"Something I remember," she said when she got to the phone, a little out of breath. I guessed she'd run all the way from her room. "That ajushi your friend showed me in the picture. He had a shopping card, you know?" When I said I didn't understand what she meant by a shopping card, she went on.

"The card you Americans use to go shopping in the PX. I saw him with one before Timmie told me to leave the room. He took it out of his wallet and was shaking it at Timmie. That's all I remember. I just thought to myself that he's not a GI, so he shouldn't have one."

A Korean customs agent with a ration control card? Not legally, that was for sure. I thanked her, set a "date" for lunch and hung up. Returning to my room, I thought about this new information, then called Louis' room to wake him up.

I told my groggy partner to meet me in the restaurant in ten minutes and I'd buy him breakfast for his troubles. He muttered an obscenity and hung up. I knew he'd get up though. He was a total professional and usually knew something important was cooking if I woke him up.

I dressed and descended the stairs to the lobby, then turned left and went into the restaurant, taking a table near the window. There was a scattering of people among the tables. The main crowd would start trickling down in about an hour. I ordered coffee and waited for my partner to arrive and cuss me out in person.

I was nearly finished with my first cup when he arrived, so I ordered two coffees this time and told the waiter we wanted menus. He gave a curt bow and left to do our bidding.

"Now what did you want to go and wake me up for?" Louis asked, the sleep still clouding his eyes and slurring his speech. His brain was probably in the same neighborhood. It was time to wake him up.

"Our friend, Mr. Park in Taegu, had a ration card in his possession at least once while Rostock was alive," I told him. I was right. The cloud left his eyes and a very alert attentiveness took over his entire being. He kept quiet, though, as the waiter returned with the coffee and menus.

We both selected omelets and allowed the waiter to run off before taking up the conversation again. I explained the tidbit of information Miss Lee had given me over the phone earlier. Louis was all ears and wide-awake. Once I was finished, however, Louis felt I needed to explain why I was out all night. I let him indulge, though he was hoping for a little more than a walk along the beach. I hated to disappoint him.

"So. You're buying, huh?"

"I said I was."

"Great," he said with relish. "I might have two breakfasts. Last night kinda took it outta me."

The waiter returned with our food. He placed everything on the table, stepped back, bowed, then turned and left. We ate in silence, paid the bill and left, heading back upstairs.

"It's your turn to call in," Louis announced as we were climbing the stairs. "I did it all day yesterday."

"Right. My turn today, then we'll split the duty tomorrow." It looked as if his mind was going back to sleep, so I let him go. I'd wake him up in time for the meeting later. I brushed my teeth and headed out to find a calling card phone to call the office.

Our Camp Long Mr. Park was sitting in the lobby reading the morning paper when I returned. He jumped up and threw the paper on the sofa when he saw me.

"Stewart-shi," he called. "I tried to call your room this morning but there was no answer. I did not think you would be awake this early after last night."

"To tell the truth, Mr. Park, I never slept. I went down to the beach for the night."

"Ah," he responded, probably wondering what occupied me from two o'clock until now. I didn't bother to explain further. His face brightened after a moment and he invited me to breakfast in the restaurant. I told him I'd just eaten with Louis, but that I'd be honored to go and drink some coffee while he ate. This seemed to please him no end and we marched into the restaurant. We engaged mainly in small talk for the next half-hour, discussing families and the like.

He was a war orphan with six brothers and three sisters. He was the youngest, only a year old when the Communist soldiers under Kim Il-sung invaded Seoul in 1950. The first day of fighting in the city claimed both his parents, so he never really knew them. All he had were a few vague memories.

The family photos were left behind as he and his siblings raced out of harm's destructive path. They finally made it down to Pusan before the Communists were halted along the Naktong River, just outside the city limits of Taegu. They stayed there until the war was over, begging food and candy off the GIs who passed through, heading toward the front.

They didn't believe it when soldiers told them the war had stopped in July 1953. They waited another month before they ventured northward, finally ending up in Seoul about two months later.

"What we saw there made us cry," he said with a shaky voice, even after all these years. It appeared as if he was reliving the experience. "I remember that everything around me was broken. The buildings. The roads. Everything. As children, how could we rebuild? But the Americans there helped us. They were kind. We owe our lives and livelihood to Americans. All of Korea does."

I solemnly wished that all forty million Koreans thought that way. But for the many who were born after the war, there were no memories of Americans fighting and dying to save their freedom. There was a new dissatisfaction rising. That mood brought about such questions as "What have you done lately?" and "Why are you really here?" They also blamed America for dividing the country so communism could grab the northern part of the country.

Some of these questions were easy to answer; other points were difficult to get across. The dissatisfaction kept rising.

"That is why I work with the Americans," Mr. Park said. "That is why I volunteer for all extra assignments, even though they don't always have the money to pay me for the overtime or some trips. I spend my own money sometimes. Don't get me wrong. I don't mind. I would work for the Americans for free if life didn't cost so much," he said with a sincere smile. I actually believed he would.

We finished our chat and left. As we climbed the stairs, I told him about the lunch date with Miss Lee and asked if he would attend. He said he would and we went to our rooms to relax. I reached into my bag and dug out the latest Alfred Hitchcock Mystery Magazine. It sometimes helped me forget the case I was working on and even gave me hints on how to proceed in some cases. I relaxed with the magazine next to the window until Miss Lee arrived.

We waited for her at a table near the window that had a view of the vacationers playing in the surf. The lunch crowd had come and gone for the most part. The few remaining stragglers were sitting far away. We welcomed her, then ordered and ate, waiting until after we'd sated our appetites to discuss the case. Louis opened the conversation.

"You say the man in the picture had a 'shopping card'?" Louis asked.

"Yes."

"Could you describe it?" I asked, pulling out my wallet. If she had any trouble with the description, I'd show her mine for comparison.

She thought it was plastic, though she'd never touched one. It was a mixture of browns and reds, she said. Then she demonstrated with her hands that it was about the size of a credit card. I showed her mine, which was red, white and blue — the new design issued to all soldiers and dependents in U.S. Forces Korea.

"No," she said. It was definitely brown, but the rest of the design looked similar. She was certain of it. I asked her to excuse us for a moment, and she made a pretense of having to use the restroom.

"She's talking about the old card," Louis said. We agreed that, when she saw it, the transition was taking place from the old to the new. We surmised that Mr. Park had been there to ask for a new card. But how could he use it? Korean civilians weren't allowed in the PX or commissary unless they worked there. He needed a GI contact or a GI's wife to do his shopping for him. He'd give his contacts the card, and they'd shop for him using it. An inattentive cashier could have let it slide by accidentally. Bribes weren't out of the question either. Those were the only methods that would have worked. Miss Lee returned as we finished discussing this new item.

Mr. Park opened the new inning. "I saw you in Wonju a few times talking to people. Who were those people and what did you talk about?" She explained that they were people she'd heard Rostock mention. She went to prove to herself that what she was doing wasn't wrong. By the time she left Wonju, she was sure he was into something illegal, but no one would talk to her about it. When she returned to Taegu, Rostock was angry with her for talking to the people in Wonju and he kicked her out of the house for two days. One of them had apparently called him while she was on the train. She never pried into the matter again.

Mr. Park wrote all the questions and answers down like a pro. When we were finished, he handed her the paper and made her read it to make sure it was exactly as she'd said. When she agreed, he asked her to sign it and certify it with her thumb print.

We took her back to Kangnung so she could get ready for work. On the way, she asked if we would be at the club that evening. I hesitated, which gave Louis a chance to get us in trouble.

"Sure," he spoke up. That did it. We were committed. There was no way either of us would go to the club alone, and he knew it. I decided to settle that with him later.

"Of course we will," I acknowledged when she looked at me, adding that we'd be leaving for Taegu in the morning. I gave her a card with our Taegu phone number. I also wrote my home phone number on the back and told her to ask for Jina if she had any other information we might be able to use.

"You are married?" she asked, looking totally shocked. I held up my ring finger with the gold band that hadn't come off since day one. "I am sorry. I did not see that," she said, blushing.

"It's OK. You were doing your job. Besides, it was fun, but don't tell that to my wife," I said jokingly. We laughed and she seemed to be happy absolved of any wrongdoing.

"Anyway," I added, "if you remember anything at all about that man or about Timmie, call us at once, OK?" She said she would and exited the car, running all the way to her seedy hotel. We turned the car around and headed back to Kyungpo in silence. Our work was completed here, but afternoon was no time to be heading west over that treacherous mountain road. We stopped on the way and I phoned the office. The colonel ended the conversation by saying his chopper would be waiting for us at Camp Long by noon the next day.

I climbed back into the sedan and announced to the guys that they'd better rest up once we got to the hotel. "Looks like it's going to be a long night," I said, and we laughed, telling jokes on the way back. We were happy about the progress we'd made in the case, however slight, and were gearing ourselves up for a night of general partying. We had the right to celebrate. I'd just have to get a cash advance off my VISA card to show Louis and Mr. Park how much I appreciated their help.

Chapter Five

We climbed aboard the chopper the next day almost exactly at noon. Louis didn't look so good, so he sat directly in front of the open sliding door, just in case he needed it. Mr. Park looked a little rough around the edges, too, when we shook hands goodbye. Luckily, he'd earned the right to go directly home to bed. Louis and I had our flight and reports to write before heading for the sack.

I probably didn't look too pretty myself. It had been a rough night. We invited Miss Lee to the table and ate and drank and joked until about four o'clock. She did her dances, this time singling Louis out twice. He liked that. You could see it in his eyes, even through the hangover. The chopper lifted off and I made a mental note to have the colonel send a letter of appreciation through the entire chain of command to Mr. Park. I'd compose it later. Right now it was time for a nap. Next stop, Taegu.

The world was shaking when I woke up, making my head swim. I opened my eyes to see a smiling Colonel Walsh shaking my shoulder. "OK, Jim. Last stop. Time to get off. Wake your partner up and let's hit the road."

He went to give the chopper crew the rest of the day off while I got Louis moving. The chopper's engine had already been shut down and the rotors were close to stopping. Helluva nap, I thought to myself. We got into the colonel's sedan and headed away from the airfield, back to Camp Walker and the cool office. Boy, I thought, it's hot down here. I already missed those cool ocean breezes.

"You must have had a fun night last night," the colonel said, not really expecting an answer. We grunted in unison anyway. In an effort to get the cobwebs out of our brains we threw some water on our faces before going into his office for the briefing. We'd need more than water, we both realized.

When the briefing was finished, the colonel told us to write up reports for the two days we were gone. "Then go home and get back into shape. You guys look like hell," he said, chuckling.

We got up to leave and, when Louis had left, I turned back to the colonel. "Sir, Mr. Park at Long. He needs a good letter." He told me to draft it up and give it to Miss Paek for typing. I left to join Louis in the tedium of the reports. When we finished, I left Louis at the barracks and drove home. Sleep. That was all I could think about at four-thirty in the afternoon.

What's that they say? Something about the best laid plans of mice and men? Jina was already home when I arrived, having caught the noon train from Pyongtaek. She'd arrived only a few minutes before me. I realized my pent up frustration was getting the better of me, so I took the phone off the hook, disconnected the door chime, locked the door and grabbed her. We headed for the shower together. The next stop was the bedroom, but we weren't interested in sleeping right away.

We made wild and passionate love, then rested while I told her about Kangnung and Kyungpo. Then it was time for a mellow lovemaking session, much softer with a lot of gentle caressing. After that, the only thing I heard was the alarm clock signaling a new day. It was Friday, but I wasn't ready to go in for PT. I dressed for the ordeal anyway and headed out the door. I had to wake up Louis before dragging him out to the car. If I had to suffer through it, he damn sure would, too.

And suffer we did, but we both made it through. I dropped Louis back at the barracks and dragged myself home for some breakfast. Jina was cooking when I walked in. It was going to be a muggy day. I was already sweating like a hog.

I suggested inviting Louis and Mihi over for dinner, followed by an evening out. Jina liked the idea instantly and reached for the phone. "I'd better call Mihi before she goes to school and makes other plans," she said with a smile. I left for work.

Louis was already in by the time I arrived. "I filled out our temporary duty travel vouchers. Sign yours and I'll take them both over to finance. We'll get the money tomorrow afternoon." Louis would be refunded all the money he spent on the trip, but I wouldn't fare so well after bankrolling that party. That was one thing I was going to have to explain to my wife. I signed my voucher and Louis scarfed it up, heading for the door.

"By the way," I said, making him stop before he got outside. "Jina's back and she's invited you to dinner tonight. Be there, because Mihi will."

His eyes glazed over as he turned to the door slowly, then fell through, jokingly "falling" in love. I hoped he'd catch his balance before he hit the pavement. I went to my desk to see what had accumulated during our absence. Nothing much. Just the usual baloney from the company and a few memos from people saying they'd witnessed crimes that they thought we should investigate. A day wouldn't be complete without those anonymous letters and notes. It was usually some girl who was pissed at her boyfriend for standing her up, or someone who thought their groceries weren't bagged correctly at the commissary. "That joker must be on drugs," and, of course, drugs weren't allowed in the military. "You should get right on this!" But one envelope caught my eye. Addressed to me personally, "EYES ONLY" was stamped in bold, black letters, meaning only I should see the contents. I opened it.

The note wasn't signed, but it started out "As a concerned citizen..." The stamp proved it was someone with access to a military office, which meant a GI or Department of Defense civilian. I doubted it was a Korean worker, because the English was near perfect with good handwriting. Koreans weren't too adept, for the most part, at writing script English, though there were a few exceptions in the workforce. I read the note.

"As a concerned citizen who knows you're working this case, I think you need to know that I saw a Korean man give a ration card to a lady. I think she was a dependent wife. I followed the lady to the PX. She bought a stereo, then took a PX taxi and met the same man, giving him the stereo and the card. He put the stereo in a brown Kia Concord, license number 3738. I don't know what the first symbol was, 'cause I don't read Korean."

That eliminated the Korean workers. This was definitely an American. The note went on to illustrate what the writer thought the symbol looked like, then ended with "Good luck!"

"Miss Paek," I said, handing her the note. "Are there any symbols like this in Hangul?" She looked at it for a moment, then wrote down a few possibilities. "Call the KNPs and ask them to run a check on that number. It's a brown Kia Concord, probably from around Taegu or the neighboring province." She immediately reached for the phone, adding the 3738 to the end of each symbol she'd written out. I went back to my desk to search the rest of the pile. That's when I remembered Mr. Park's letter. I called the office at Long and got his full name and his Korean ID number and sat down to draft the letter.

I was on the second paragraph when Miss Paek said the police would call us as soon as they found out who owned the car. I thanked her and continued with the letter.

When I had five paragraphs of praise lavished around what he'd done during our trip, I handed it to Miss Paek, asking for her assistance. "You know all the right things to say to help Korean people get promoted," I said. "Could you fill this out, type it up final, and give it to the colonel?" She looked it over, then smiled up at me.

"Of course, Stewart-shi. I will take care of it." She fed a sheet of paper into her typewriter and, in less than twenty minutes took the three-page final letter into the colonel's office for his signature. It was sent out before noon. If it didn't get him promoted, it would at least secure his job. The Korean upper-echelon placed great importance on letters endorsed by American generals, which this would be. I was just getting down to my notes from the past few days of the investigation when Louis returned. We grabbed some coffee and retired to the lounge to discuss tactics.

I showed him the note I'd received and told him what was cooking with the information it contained. I also told him that the colonel had sent an inquiry to customs concerning Mr. Park — the Taegu one. It normally wasn't our place to question customs office practice, but this involved the death of a GI and we had every right. Then I mentioned the letter to Mr. Park at Camp Long. He agreed it was worth at least a letter, probably more.

"By the way, old buddy," he said, "how much do I owe you for that party the other night?" I waved him off like it was nonsense, but he pressed, so I told him I had spent nearly two hundred dollars. I thought he was going to faint, but he pulled out his wallet and dug out some twenties, shoving them at me. "Here's part of it. I'll owe ya the rest." I protested, but he stuffed them into my jacket pocket and walked to the other side of the lounge.

A moment later, we were running over the facts, fiction and rumors we had so far on the case. We needed more, but probably weren't going to get anything until we heard from the Korean police. We decided to clear some of the minor bullshit off our desks in the meantime.

The call came in at about four that afternoon. Most of the license numbers were non-existent. The final one belonged to Mr. Park Young-gil. The police gave Miss Paek the address, adding the fact that the listed occupation for Mr. Park was with Korean customs. Louis and I looked at each other. Another report that this gentleman allegedly had unauthorized possession of a ration control plate, and this time with a direct lead to a purchase, albeit anonymous.

We marched into the colonel's office and were back out in less than ten minutes with authority for a stakeout. If we were lucky enough to catch him in the act, apprehension of the suspect was included in the authorization. I called in four more agents and had them report to us in the lounge. We briefed them on what we were looking for, in what general area and why. They were out the door to change into jeans and T-shirts before I could say "take off." Louis and I scrambled to do the same and met at Camp Walker's main gate within the hour.

Walker had two access gates: the main gate, which carried most of the traffic in and out of the compound, and Gate 2, which was the closest to my home. The CID office was also near Gate 2, which is why I had located a house there, rather than on the other side of the compound. The PX, on the other hand, was closer to the main gate, so most of the traffic entered and exited there. Most of the vendors and clubs that depended on GIs and their families for their existence were also located outside the main gate.

Radios in tow, Louis and I staked out the gate, while two other agents went to a point outside the PX. The last two stationed themselves inside the PX. Since the man we were staking out knew Louis and me, we got permission to do our surveillance from rooftops on opposite sides of the street, just a few buildings down from the gate. We used binoculars to get a clear view of everyone who came and went. Ten minutes later, I ordered a radio check and every agent involved responded. We were set and in position. All we had to do now was wait.

It was hot up on the roof, but a slight breeze helped ease that a little. Even in jeans, a T-shirt and baseball cap, I was sweating up a storm. "Good," I thought. "It'll help me sweat out some of that beer from up north." But we weren't on the roof long enough for that. Louis' voice was jumping out of the radio at me.

"Brown Concord coming. Wait. License ends in 3738. It's down at the end of the airfield." I couldn't see it from my position. "He's stopped," Louis' voice shot at me again. A pause. "He's just sitting. Stand by." The four other agents reported that they were standing by and ready for anything that might happen. I dropped my binoculars, their weight jerking me forward slightly. Why couldn't they make powerful binoculars in a lightweight body, I wondered. I picked up my radio and changed the frequency to one that was monitored regularly in the office.

"Charlie Delta One, this is Sierra Alpha One."

The duty agent responded, and I told him to get word to the colonel that our rat was out of the hole. We signed off, and I switched back to the frequency we were using between teams. "Colonel's informed," was all I said when I keyed the mike. Louis nodded from the other rooftop and brought his binoculars back up to his eyes. I did the same, even though I couldn't see anything yet. About twenty minutes passed and the breeze had all but stopped.

"Green Chevy with SOFA plates stopped next to rat. Looks like they're talking. Can't see much movement. Stand by." All units acknowledged. We waited a little more, then Louis' voice shot out at us again.

"Green Nova. Female. She's moving. He's not. She's coming in. License ends in 1294. Asian. Green blouse. Ready."

After she passed us, the units at the PX would take over. I tracked her from the time she left Louis' line of sight until she was inside the gate. The units stationed outside the PX would then track her until she went inside. The inside units would take over there. The two guys outside the PX would have a better description of her once she exited her car. They'd radio to the two agents inside, who would verify what she bought and took out the door. While she was inside, the outside guys would verify the license number and vehicle identification number, then notify us when she left the parking lot. We had a very good idea where she was going when she left.

The agents inside would leave the store in front of her once the purchase was verified, while the two on the outside would follow her. Louis and I would pull up the rear, acting like GIs out shopping, hats pulled down low enough so Mr. Park couldn't see our faces.

Everything went according to plan, and soon Louis and I had stuffed our binoculars in our bags and were checking our weapons. We rushed down to street level and started walking as she left the lot with her undetected escort. Our rat hadn't moved an inch since he parked.

The team to her front faked car problems about thirty feet beyond Mr. Park's car, propping the hood up and bending over the engine compartment. No doubt they could see between the separation of the car and hood. The woman pulled up next to Mr. Park's car, got out and opened her trunk. Park popped the lid on his trunk and got out, too. Louis and I were about forty feet away, still meandering and looking in store windows, but watching them from the corners of our eyes. The team following her pulled in just in front of us and got out of the car, talking and laughing. We walked up alongside just as Park pulled a new TV out of her trunk and placed it in his. He wiped his forehead and pulled out his wallet, counting out a lot of bills. He handed them to the woman and took the ration card. The arrest was made without incident, catching both offenders very much by surprise. We took them back to CID headquarters, where Park cried that we had spoiled a six-month investigation he was closing up.

The colonel was waiting at the door for our "guests." He took personal charge of Mr. Park, soon-to-be-ex-customs-agent, and ushered him handcuffed into the interpreter's office. They'd already called customs to ask for official assistance. When we informed them who we had, the chief inspector personally came. They were going to be especially hard on him and he deserved it. Not only a cop gone bad, but one who'd tried to dirty an honest cop along the way. It made little difference that I was an American this time, and I rather liked that attitude. Park was going to get his just due.

We typed up the report concerning Mrs. Kyung Stenberg, then called her sergeant husband in to take custody of her, after we informed him of her actions and after she had her turn with the interpreters. Park was our big fish for the day, though, and would be first. Mrs. Stenberg spoke English rather well and understood what was going on. We confiscated the fake ration card she'd gotten from Park at the scene. We also confiscated her card once we got to the station. It would be up to her husband's company commander to reissue the card if he thought it was wise. Until then, Sergeant Stenberg would have to do the shopping for the family.

She didn't speak at first, except to answer our questions on the basics of the report. She wrung her hands out in her lap, remained silent, and waited for her husband.

Mrs. Stenberg was a pretty woman, twenty-four years old, with soft facial features, looking almost meek and shy. Her clothes were neat and clean, but not expensive. Just a mix of Korean and American in them. Her hair was pulled severely back from her face into a ponytail. Her green blouse was long sleeved and buttoned at the wrists, despite the heat. Its looseness largely hid what was beneath. She wore gray and white slacks, almost a plaid design. They hugged her hips and thighs while she sat, but hung loosely from the belt when she stood. I could tell her hips and legs were probably quite shapely, though that was mainly a guess.

Her husband arrived about half an hour later, driving over from Camp Henry. He worked as an administrative sergeant in the military personnel office at 19th Support Command's headquarters. He was not a happy camper. He stood behind his wife's chair as we briefed him on what we had and what would happen next. His knuckles turned whiter with each sentence. When we were done, he lay his hands loosely on his wife's shoulders and spoke very quietly — the sound of a very angry man trying to hold his composure. Her eyes stayed with her wringing hands as he spoke.

"I warned you about black marketing, didn't I? You know that could ruin my career. But you had to do it, didn't you? Why? Don't I make enough money for us?" Few of us in the military do, I thought to myself. He continued. "Now you're involved in a murder investigation, too. This won't help us stay in Korea any longer, like you want."

That was true. Even if they weren't involved in the murder, the black marketing charge would bar any hopes of him getting an extension. The soldier was ultimately held responsible for every action taken by his family members, whether or not he did anything wrong himself. The charge could also hurt any upcoming promotions. He went on, talking in the same low voice, letting her know the disappointment he felt with every word. She was crying quietly now, still saying nothing.

When Stenberg was done, Louis advised him to telephone his office to let them know he wouldn't be back to work today. We also let him call his company commander to inform him, rather than having us do it officially. It would be better than reading about it in Monday morning's official blotter report — at the same time his commanding general did. Meanwhile, the colonel had already briefed the old man about the bust, specifically mentioning Mr. Park. He later told us that the general was so elated that he'd called the Commander-in-Chief of the United Nations Forces, who'd been on his case about the newspaper article in Stripes.

After Stenberg called his commander, we asked him and his wife to sit in the lounge and wait for the interpreters. I told him it would probably be awhile as he walked out the door, with Louis escorting them so they wouldn't get lost. We didn't actually worry, though, about them leaving the building before we were done. If they did, Stenberg's career would be finished, and he knew that. He had nothing to gain and everything to lose if he couldn't escape to America. There was no point in running because we could seal the ports with a simple phone call.

The interpreters finished with Mr. Park just as it started clouding up outside. Maybe a foreboding to his future. We were going to get our first afternoon thunderstorm since the end of the monsoons. The thunder rumbled distantly, like cannons on the horizon. Louis collected the Stenbergs, directing her into the interpreters' office and him into mine. Time for a chat.

"Sit down, Sarge," I said, standing up behind my desk. The impression of looking taller sometimes helped during questioning.

He was in his mid-twenties and stood nearly six feet tall, probably weighing in around a hundred eighty pounds or so. He was dressed in the Battle Dress Uniform — BDUs — that had arrived on the military scene just a few years before. The old olive drab uniforms would be but a piece of history once their final "extension" ran out in October. His hair was cut very short, making him appear more like an infantry soldier than an administrative sergeant. I walked around to the side of the desk, stopping just in front of his chair, then started in.

"You realize I have to read you your rights," I said, then waited for him to acknowledge. I recited the lines to him, stopping between each one to make sure he understood. Once I was sure he did, I got down to brass tacks, pulling no punches.

"Sergeant Stenberg. Your wife was caught by six CID agents in the act of illegally disposing of a new television set from the PX. She allowed transfer of it from the trunk of a green Chevrolet Nova," I said, picking up the report off my desk for effect. "That Nova is registered to you. She caused that TV to be transferred to the trunk of another vehicle not registered to an American, then accepted money from the Korean National male who had been driving that vehicle.

"Prior to her apprehension, she was seen talking with this man. Then she drove to the PX, bought the TV, and returned straight back to this man at his car. At the time of apprehension, she had in her possession a ration control plate issued to you, and she'd been seen seconds earlier giving another ration control plate to the Korean male. The name on that card was Stella Tolbert. That's not even close to her name."

I let that sink in for a moment. His eyes widened as he grasped the complexity and totality of the matter. "The TV was purchased under that possibly fictitious name." We were still checking to see if any of the names on the three hundreds confiscated cards were real.

I returned to my chair and sat down, folding my hands on the top of the desk. This was cause for a pause before dropping the entire load on him. He didn't say anything.

"The charges so far include unlawful possession of an RCP that's not hers, use of that RCP to purchase a controlled item —

the TV set — at the PX, transferring that TV to a Korean National not authorized to shop in the exchange, and possibly accessory to the crime of murder, either during or after the fact.

"Without the implication in the murder, the rest of the charges will stand alone. The proof is there and it's concrete. There were six agents involved in the apprehension. Let me tell you what's going to happen."

He looked at me across the desk in expectation of hearing the worst. I gave it to him.

"The Korean customs people will levy a fine against your wife for the taxes that would have been received by the government for the legal sale of that item. If there are any more items attributed to her transfers, they will also be taxed. With six witnesses, she's automatically guilty in their eyes. There'll be no court. Just sentencing by customs. You may as well get the money together, 'cause they'll collect.

"On the other side of the coin, your wife will probably not be allowed access to the PX or commissary during the remainder of your tour in Korea, if that isn't cut short as well. Your purchasing power will be cut dramatically. In some cases, the family is only allowed to purchase a hundred dollars worth of necessities a month, while you now have at least seven hundred dollars. You won't be able to buy any controlled items, including alcohol and cigarettes, nor any single item costing over fifty dollars. This may be lifted later with an appeal through your commander to the support group commander.

"I can almost guarantee that any planned extension in the Republic can be forgotten as of this very minute. I can also almost guarantee that your commander will initiate a show and tell at your quarters, to be conducted by MPI. They, along with a team of Korean customs agents, will be searching for all the high-value items purchased since your arrival in Korea. They will also check for items listed under that false card. On that, you'll be bitten either way.

"If you have any of those goods, you'll be charged with possessing two Ration Control Plates in an effort to circumvent the ration system. If you don't have any of them, you'll be charged with unlawful disposition of whatever duty-free goods are listed under that card."

Stenberg couldn't accept that. "But what if she didn't buy anything else on that other card, but someone else did? I mean, if he let her use that card, he probably let other people use it too."

"That's understood. Right now, though, she's the only person connected with that card besides him. She'll be held responsible until we can get a handwriting analysis that says otherwise. Customs will try to hang the whole lot on her, and you two don't have a chance in hell of fighting it without us to help clear her of some of those items. We'll do what we can."

He did accept that, so I continued. Now it was time for the Coup-de-Gras.

"She's also being investigated by us in a conspiracy to commit premeditated murder."

His eyes shot up, even though he knew it was coming. He looked me straight in the face to see if I was kidding even the slightest bit. I wasn't, though, and he knew that. I didn't give him a chance to speak either.

"Investigation only," I emphasized. "She's not being charged at this time. The recent murder of Staff Sergeant Rostock is still unsolved and your wife's apprehension was made directly in the course of that investigation. There is strong reason for us to believe that she and the Korean National male may have been involved. They are the only two suspects we have at the moment, and we're looking into it from there."

I stopped. He was obviously distraught, as well I'd be if I were in his position. This morning everything goes right, then WHAM! Out of nowhere, someone rains on your parade. The thunder clapped heavily outside, shaking the windows, and buckets of rain started falling. It had to be a coincidence. Didn't it?

Stenberg just sat there. I rose from my chair and turned to look out the window for a moment. I didn't turn around until he spoke.

"What if she knows something and cooperates?" he asked in a small tone I almost didn't hear. I turned and leaned on the back of my chair.

"We might be able to put in a good word to make things easier," I said, making sure it didn't sound even remotely like a promise, but rather a "maybe — if." He nodded his understanding.

"I never knew Rostock," he said. I waited for more. "I saw my wife talking to him once in the NCO Club over on Camp Henry though. They were near the slot machines. She likes to play those things, even though there isn't a chance in hell of any sizeable win."

The slots. Damn those things anyway. They took everyone's money and offered only a small payout (the club system said the payout was 96 percent but, from what I'd seen, it just wasn't close to being likely). The players just knew they were going to hit it, though, so they borrowed and lost — borrowed and lost again — and again.

Suddenly players were deep in debt, and they'd lost all their husband's money too. The next step, most of the time, was the black market. They rarely told their husbands about their debt or their black marketing, knowing what would happen if they did. I'd bet that if they got rid of slot machines in overseas clubs, half the black marketing would disappear with them. All we'd have left would be the profiteers, who would be considerably easier to round up. Maybe MPI and CID would finally catch up on their workloads.

"Anyway, I didn't know what they were talking about, because he left before I got within earshot. When I asked her about him, she said he was just a friend of one of her girlfriends. I accepted that at the time. Maybe I shouldn't have."

"How many times did you see them together?" I asked.

"Only that once."

"When was that?"

"About a month ago."

There was a chance that she was just Park's new recruit and maybe the TV was the only item she had bought and sold. That's how it would turn out if they were lucky. I didn't hold too much stock in that, though.

Louis opened the door before we could talk more.

"Excuse me, Jim. Stenberg's first sergeant is here and would like to speak with you." I excused myself, advising Stenberg to stay put, and walked out the door, closing it behind me. I met the top in the lounge.

"Good afternoon, first sergeant. I'm Special Agent Stewart. It shouldn't be much longer now. How can I help you?"

"What's he in for?"

"He's the sponsor. His wife was apprehended during a black marketing sting in connection with a murder," I answered. "She was picked up while transferring a TV to a Korean National." As with Stenberg, I saw no reason to tell the first sergeant that the Korean was a customs agent.

"How serious is it?"

"She had a second card on her that will probably prove to be a false name. We're checking it now." The look on his face soured. I think he lost all hope of getting the Stenbergs out of anything.

"Are they being questioned now?"

"Yes. The interpreters have Mrs. Stenberg in with them. He's in my office."

"Mind if I sit in with the sergeant?"

"Not at all. C'mon," I said, leading the way. I opened the door and let him enter first. Stenberg was sitting right where I'd left him. He looked as if he hadn't even breathed since I left. I offered Top a chair behind Stenberg, then took my seat behind my desk.

I recapped what had already gone on. "I already read him his rights and we were just wrapping this up." I looked at my notes again.

"You told me you saw your wife and Rostock together near the slot machines in the NCO Club about a month ago, and that you have no idea what they were talking about?" Stenberg nodded. "Can you remember exactly what day it was?" I pushed a calendar toward him, which he took in his hands and studied, but came up with nothing positive. "What day of the week was it?"

"Wednesday," was the reply. "It was bingo night. But I don't remember for sure what week. It didn't seem real important at the time." I could understand that.

"Have you ever seen your wife with two ration cards?"

"No, sir."

"Did you ever see her buy anything that you don't recall seeing at home later?"

He thought for a moment, then shook his head.

"Have you ever had visits at your home by strangers, especially Koreans, say, in the last few months?"

"No, sir," he said, then, "Wait! There was a man. He wore a suit. It was about eight in the evening and he seemed pretty mad about something. This was the day before that guy was found dead. That's the only time I remember seeing him, though."

The first sergeant's eyes opened wide.

"Could you recognize him if you saw his picture?" We'd placed several "ringer" photos in the mug book for this occasion, and Mr. Park's was the newest addition. We got it from the pass and ID section.

"Maybe. I'm not sure, but I'll try."

I told them I'd get the mug book and be right back. I knocked as I passed the interpreters' office and leaned in to tell them not to release Mrs. Stenberg yet. They agreed to keep questioning her. I got the book from the files and took it back to my office, laying it on the desk in front of the sergeant. He started leafing through it, taking long looks at each page of photos. I crossed the office to the coffeepot and poured a cup, offering some to my two visitors, who both declined. I walked over to the window behind my desk and stared out into the steady rain. It looked like the monsoons had returned. About five minutes passed before anything was said.

"That's him," said Stenberg, pointing at the center of the page as I turned around. The first sergeant got up to look too. I looked closer and saw our good friend, Mr. Park. I made note of the page number, the location on the page, and the name under the photo. I made the first sergeant verify that it was the photo Stenberg had identified, then pulled it out of its sleeve. I took it to the interpreters' office and announced the finding. The interpreters started firing a new line of questions at Mrs. Stenberg.

I returned to my office.

"I'm done for now, Top, but I'd like them available in case I need them again." The first sergeant nodded. I finished by asking for a copy of the Noncombatant Evacuation Operation map that showed directions to their off-post house.

"You'll have it in about twenty minutes," Top said, picking up the phone. He spoke a few curt sentences to his clerk, then hung up. "It's on the way." I nodded and told them they could wait in the lounge for Mrs. Stenberg. They left, closing the door behind them.

What a series of developments we had here, I thought. Louis stepped in a moment later.

"How'd it go?" he asked. I handed him my notes and he sat down to read them. "Ah hah!" he said as he returned them to my desk. "The plot thickens." It sounded like something from Sherlock Holmes. I typed up the release forms that the first sergeant would have to sign for the Stenbergs and took them into the lounge. We'd soon be done for the day, and I wanted it all tied up.

"All we need is your signature, Top, and you'll be free to go as soon as his wife has completed and signed her statement." I handed him the forms and he looked them over, scribbling his signature on the required lines.

"Any idea how much longer?" he asked as he handed them back.

"Let me check," I said, exiting with the signed release forms. I returned a few minutes later with news that they were wrapping up and she'd be ready in a couple of minutes. They both nodded and I returned to my office to complete the day's reports.

Louis and I were out of there just a little after six. I waited in his barracks room, reading the latest Penthouse while he showered, shaved and dressed. We decided to bash around ideas at the house while the women got dinner in the works. After we sat down to eat, there'd be no more discussion about the case throughout this evening. We dedicated that time to the two women who helped us get this far.

The afternoon thunderstorm had died down by the time we left the barracks. The waning sun reappeared intermittently, creating little steam clouds that danced upward from the pavement as we drove to the house. Jina had cleaned the house from top to bottom and was busy dicing vegetables and slicing meats. We were greeted with a warm smile, and I got a healthy kiss.

"Mihi will be here in about half an hour," she announced. "Dinner will be ready at nine." Louis and I retreated to the den for a while to milk the brain cells for our next possible move. We heard Mihi enter as we were getting started. Jina recruited her to help with the dinner, and told her we were in conference. They both giggled wildly. The two could be heard scurrying around in preparation.

Louis opened the session.

"I vote that we review what the interpreters got today as soon as we're able to tomorrow." I knew what he meant. We probably wouldn't be up too early after a night of partying with the girls. We'd already informed the colonel that we wouldn't be in until sometime in the afternoon.

"Right you are," I replied. I mentioned that it looked like one aspect of the case was sewn up. "I don't think Mr. Park will be disturbing the investigation anymore."

We discussed the possibility of having his former partner, Mr. Song, investigated as well. We'd make the attempt, even though it would probably be nixed. Since Mr. Park had gone down, though, a secondary request to have a new team paired with us was likely to be approved. We made a note to approach the colonel on those two ideas.

We bounced around other ideas about Mrs. Stenberg's involvement, weighing the possibility of another multitude of as yet undiscovered false cards. It could be quite staggering.

We realized we'd need intelligence from customs when they were finished with Mr. Park. They usually weren't too happy about sharing their findings with us, but they might be more willing in this case, in an attempt to make amends. Park had given their entire organization a black eye and they wanted that wiped away as much as possible. They'd probably bend over backward to help us on this case now, and we were willing to take advantage of that unusual twist of fate.

One thing they wouldn't help us on, and we had no jurisdiction to even ask for, was in searching Mr. Park's house. That would be entirely in their hands, and we'd have to trust that they would do an unbiased job. Louis and I figured they would, though, just to keep the slate as clean as possible.

And there was much more out there that was yet to be found. We just had no idea how much there was or how we'd find it. We didn't really have any more leads unless the interpreters' reports held something new. We needed a real big break in the case, but we didn't know where it would come from or when.

The session ended when we were hailed for dinner. We left the den and the case behind for the time being. It was time to clear our heads of the entire thing for a while. That sometimes led to clearer thinking when we got back to it.

Mihi objected to Louis and I helping clean up the dishes after dinner, but Jina soon convinced her that it was an American custom for men to help if the meal was pleasing. I jokingly told Louis what he'd have to expect when he got married and we all laughed. Louis didn't object this time, as he normally did at any mention of marriage. I caught that immediately and shot him a look, which he returned with a mere smile, then returned his gaze toward Mihi. He was really hooked, by George.

The girls went into the bedroom to get ready for the evening out, and we could hear mile-a-minute chatter through the door as they giggled almost constantly. Mihi had brought a rather large bag that she'd taken into the room. They came out some time later, dressed to the hilt and looking like twins.

Their hair was done up in buns, positioned on the backs of their heads. They both wore black blazers with white blouses buttoned at the collar, and skirts that ended just above the knees. Mihi reached into her bag to bring out a pair of black high-heeled boots that climbed to a position just below the knees. The effect was rather stunning, allowing only a few inches of each leg to be observed. Jina reached into the cabinet to retrieve an identical pair and put them on. The effect on both Louis and me was uncanny.

We stared at the beauty of God's art for only a moment before regaining our composure and rushing into the bedroom to change. Jeans and T-shirts with running shoes wouldn't be the order of dress tonight with these two beautiful women. Luckily, Louis and I were about the same size, so I was able to provide him with one of my suits. He selected the dark blue, while I opted for the black. We presented ourselves about fifteen minutes later for inspection. We must have passed because the women gave each of us a kiss on the cheek. I dug out shoes for both of us and we followed the women out the door to grab a cab. This was going to be a party and there was no room for drinking and driving.

At Mihi's request we started at the MVP club, where she had gained valuable information that sent us up north. Her GI friend was there and he tried to get a dance with her, but she politely refused, holding on tightly to Louis' arm. Louis grinned like the cat that ate the canary and took her out onto the dance floor himself. I had to hand it to him. He kept up with her all the way.

We went to a Korean club next, somewhere down in the heart of Taegu. It cost a mint to get us all in, but they featured comedy shows, singers, disco, go-go girls, double DJs and a live band. It was really a show. To cap off the evening, we headed for another Korean club around the corner from our house. We returned home just as the sun was rising.

Louis graciously accepted an offer to sleep in the den after we escorted Mihi to her door. We would have let him accompany alone, but Korean custom frowned on that for the first few dates. They seemed to get along well the entire evening, but now it was time for some shuteye. I don't think any one of us had hit our pillows for more than a few seconds before we were dead to the world.

It seemed like only a moment before Louis was rapping quietly on the bedroom door, calling for me. It was afternoon though. I could tell by the location of the sun through the window. I got up and went into the living room.

"We'd better get a move on," he said. "It's almost two." I started some coffee and went back into the bedroom to retrieve some clothes, then splashed water on my face. We headed for the office after we polished off the coffee.

There was a message waiting on my desk. Seoul's MPI office had picked up a soldier using a false RCP in the commissary. The GI was assigned to a unit there, but the card was of Taegu origin. They knew about the dead ration clerk, of course, and also about our subsequent investigation into several such cards. In fact, one of their agents had conducted the show and tell at my house when a card showed up bearing my name.

The message alerted us to check the fax machine, which Louis did right away. At the top of the sheet, an MPI report on the incident, the words "good luck" were written in bold letters. The signature at the bottom was "J. Wilkins." That's why we had received it so fast. She was the agent who'd conducted my show and tell. They'd picked up the soldier just the day before. Normally we wouldn't get the report for about a week — in the mail. I sat down to read it.

Specialist Rogers had entered the commissary at Yongsan and showed his ID card and ration plate to the ration control monitor at the door, an undercover MPI agent. He made several purchases of what we termed suspicious items. They wouldn't normally be considered suspicious if bought with other regular household purchases. But they were quick movers in the black market and when bought by themselves, they became suspicious items. Every military policeman, MPI and CID agent watched for those types of purchases.

When Rogers handed the clerk the RCP to be anvilled (just as a credit card was anvilled under the receipt in the older credit card machines), the agent took a second look at it. He noticed it wasn't the same one presented on entry, nor did it match the nametag sewn on the soldier's uniform. The MPI agent placed the card back in the machine and waited for the transaction to be completed, then apprehended Rogers. Rogers was taken directly to the MPI office, where he claimed to know nothing about the false RCP or how it got into his wallet. He thought it was his, he vowed, since he only had one. The false card was confiscated, along with his real one, and his commander ultimately signed the custody form for his release. An investigation would follow. End of report.

Interesting.

I handed the report to Louis and dialed the Seoul MPI office.

The duty agent said that Wilkins was in earlier, but had left about ten minutes before I called. Damn. I left word for her to contact me Monday morning, when I knew we'd both be in, then hung up. Copies of the interpreters' reports on Mr. Park and Mrs. Stenberg were on my desk, so I read them before passing them on to Louis.

They didn't contain much more than we already knew. Among the unanswered questions were how Park had gotten that card, how long Mrs. Stenberg had been buying for him and anyone else, how many other people had false cards, how many cards Park may have had, and if Rostock was the sole supplier. The questions were asked, but definitive answers never came. There was a mountain of other questions as well to answer, especially who killed Rostock and why, but these would have to hold me for today. They might even lead to the other answers.

I hate to think of death as simple, but cases were relatively easy to investigate if murder was the only crime committed. But when that turned into an investigation of several hundred other crimes, the problems were compounded. I say several hundred, but there may have been several thousand or several hundred thousand crimes committed in direct relation to Rostock's murder within the last two years. I wondered if we'd ever really sort it all out.

Louis and I spent the next couple of hours thinking about questions for Rogers up in Seoul. We'd fax them to the local CID office there, ask them to interview him, then return the answers by fax. I got them out as soon as we were finished, complete with the official request. They wouldn't be too overwhelmed and could get to it Monday if we were lucky. Then we started thinking of questions to ask Mrs. Stenberg, her husband and Mr. Park. We could interview the Stenbergs ourselves, but we'd have to request that customs ask Mr. Park our questions. They could either comply or shrug it off as something they didn't have to help us with. We wouldn't actually do anything over the weekend, but we'd get right on it first thing Monday morning.

When we were finished, Louis suggested that we contact the other installations throughout Korea and remind them of the need to closely check all ration cards, especially those issued from Taegu. We ginned it up and sent it out by fax to all Army, Air Force and Navy investigative offices. They, in turn, would alert the commanders and ration control offices under their respective jurisdictions. We hadn't notified the public affairs office yet, because we didn't want to alert any criminals still on the street that we'd uncovered the false card scam. We'd wait until they were all recovered and would deal with the criminals accordingly.

Any commander could authorize a ration card check or a room search at his or her discretion. That would take care of the barracks people, but the off-post folks would be slightly more difficult. House searches in the ville weren't authorized unless an MP and a Korean National Policeman were present, and there had to be probable cause for each search.

Commissaries, PXs and liquor stores would have to be alerted as well, with hopes of cooperation. They usually employed Korean workers who weren't too interested in helping the authorities. For the most part, they seemed to believe that black marketing wasn't a criminal offense. They usually didn't want to help either side of the case. We requested local support group and installation commanders to order their civilian workers to assist. That usually got results.

The sun was setting as we finished up, so we locked up and I took Louis back to the barracks.

"See ya for breakfast," he said, waving goodbye as he exited the car. "Why don't we meet at the 19th Hole at about nine?" I agreed and turned the car around for the drive home. I was tired.

Jina and Mihi were sitting on the sofa, talking animatedly, when I arrived. I guessed they were talking about last night and I didn't interrupt. I went straight for the fridge and grabbed a cold Bud. A little hair of the dog, so to speak. I felt like I had a little hair of that dog in my throat that needed to be washed away.

Jina finally turned to me. "Honey. A Miss Lee called from Kangnung. She asked me to have you call her. Why?"

I told her who Miss Lee was, and that satisfied her. It was apparently the same thing Mihi had told her, because they started talking again. As long as the stories matched, I was all set. She turned to me again and asked why Miss Lee would call the house. I told her that she might have more information pertaining to the case. She dialed the long distance number in Kangnung, then handed me the phone after asking to speak with Miss Lee. She sat back down and renewed her conversation with Mihi.

Miss Lee sounded breathless when she got to the phone. She must have run all the way from her room again. She definitely got her exercise.

I asked what information she had, and she told me she remembered Rostock worrying about someone only a few days before he was killed. She thought it was some type of policeman or something, but maybe she was mistaken. She was sorry that she didn't have a name or anything, but hoped it would be some use to us. I thanked her and was about to hang the phone up when she asked how Louis was. I said he was OK and she asked me to relay a "hello" to him. She said goodbye and hung up, and I replaced the phone in the cradle.

"Why did you tell her Louis was OK?" asked Mihi.

"Because she asked."

"Did they do anything together?"

"No," I said. "We were there for work." She seemed to accept the answer, but sulked anyway. Louis was going to have some explaining to do the next time he saw her. I regretted saying his name over the phone, but I was tired and hadn't thought about it at the time. Besides, he'd talk his way out of any trouble. He was innocent, after all.

I sat at the table and hit the TV remote for AFKN. Maybe there would be something interesting on before I hit the sack. The girls started talking again and I heard my partner's name mentioned more than a few times. I think my wife was defending him, but I couldn't be sure. A little later she woke me up and shuffled me off to bed. Mihi was gone.

The alarm woke me at seven and got ready for work. We weren't going to be in the public eye, so I dressed in jeans and T-shirt. I carried my holster and radio belt holster in my gym bag, along with a jacket, just in case I needed them. I drove to the golf club restaurant and bought a newspaper, then sat down to wait for my partner. The 19th Hole was usually crowded with golfers on Sunday, and that day was no exception.

Louis arrived and, before he even had a chance to sit down, I greeted him with "Boy are you in trouble." His face blanched as I told him the conversation surrounding Miss Lee. The waitress brought the required coffee and menus and we ordered. Once she left, Louis inquired, "How mad is she?"

"I dunno. She looked more depressed and perplexed than anything else. I think you, Jina and I can swing her around though." He regained his composure somewhat, but remained sullen. I really think he's falling for her, I thought to myself. I picked up my paper and started reading it, handing Louis the sports section. That usually cheered him up. He took it without a word and set himself to reading it. Our food came a few minutes later, and we pushed the paper down into a chair and chowed down, then headed for the office.

A string of faxes was running out of the machine when we arrived. The requests for assistance that we'd sent out the day before had been received and acknowledged. A few had even been acted on already. It was going better than we'd planned, so far. We could only hope and wait. Maybe something would turn up to give us more leads.

We tried to think of more questions for Park and the Stenbergs, going over the information we already had repeatedly. We finally exhausted that angle and decided to call it quits for the day. The phone rang as we were walking out the door. The duty agent was in the next room, so I picked it up.

"I thought I might catch you in," said a female voice at the other end. I tried to figure out where I'd heard it before.

"Excuse me," I said apologetically. "I know the voice, but I can't seem to place a face with it."

"Wilkins. MPI. Seoul. Does that connect?" she asked with a husky laugh.

"Yeah. Hi. What's up?"

"Got your message. What can I do for you?"

"I just wanted to thank you for that report on Rogers," I said, letting her know I'd received her fax from the previous day. "Could you keep me posted if any more come up?"

"For you, no problem," she said. Was I hearing things or did her voice just become a bit huskier? I decided against asking and thanked her again.

"Look," she said, "the next time you're in Seoul, why don't you stop in? Maybe we could share some information." It sounded like she was implying something more than the words that were spoken. My mind's eye flashed back to the scene in my office when she'd removed her blazer. The view had been spectacular, to say the least, but I was happily married. I tried to keep the conversation on a professional level.

"Look, we were just heading out the door. Why don't I give you a call tomorrow morning to see if there are any new developments?" She agreed and we broke the connection. I turned to Louis, who was smiling strangely.

"Looks like you have the same problem I do," he said. Then he turned on his heel and headed out the door. I followed without saying a word, knowing that it could very well be true. What a sobering thought!

Chapter Six

Monday morning PT was its usual painful self. Things were a lot tougher after a weekend, even if you worked both days. Maybe it was all in my mind, but it sure didn't feel like it. I gathered the new sheets from the fax and started reviewing them just before the colonel arrived. He got settled and called Louis and me in for an update. We gave him what we had, which wasn't much, then cleared the way for the other teams to report on their cases.

One team wrapped up their case over the weekend and was given a new one surrounding a missing weapon. It had been reported missing Saturday, but the company commander thought it might have been gone before that. He'd been away on leave, and his executive officer had failed to conduct an arms room inventory the previous month. It could have been missing for nearly two months before its disappearance was finally discovered. I asked the colonel for copies of anything on that case, since the missing weapon was the same type used in our murder. He made sure the team working the case understood and they promised to provide me with anything that came out. The meeting adjourned and I returned to my desk, as did the others.

I called Stenberg's first sergeant and asked that the soldier and his wife come to the office for additional interviews. I also invited him if he wasn't busy. He declined, but said he would have them here any time I needed them. It was set for one o'clock and I hung up. I dialed Wilkins' number in Seoul. She answered on the first ring, identifying herself very professionally.

"Oh," she said after I introduced myself. Her voice changed dramatically. I decided I wasn't previously hearing things after all. "Hi there. How was your weekend?"

I told her it was a normal working weekend and she laughed. "Look, did you come up with anything new?" I wanted to get this phone call over with before anything else happened, or before she got any ideas.

"Nope. Nothing yet, but we're still working on it. Listen, why don't you give me your home phone number so I can call you right away if anything breaks during the evening?"

I told her that wasn't a good idea and reminded her that I was a happily married man. She slammed the phone down without even saying goodbye. I smiled and replaced my handset in the cradle, hoping that the process of quelling that little brush fire I hadn't ruined anything in our professional relationship. I needed her help in this case, even if only to gain information from Seoul. I might have to call her back later and apologize, even though I hadn't done anything wrong. Something came to mind about the wrath of a woman scorned. Louis and I left to check out Rostock's place once more.

We returned to the office around noon with nothing new, and Miss Paek got up to go to lunch, then hesitated. "Do you still need this list of Rostock's phone numbers," she asked, holding up a sheath of papers, "or should I file it with the rest of the things for the case?"

Louis and I looked at each other and answered in unison. She handed the stack to us and continued on her way out the door, giggling as the door shut behind her. Louis grabbed a notebook and we retired to the lounge so we wouldn't be interrupted. The duty agent would take care of incoming calls.

We worked the lunch hour away, noting that there were many calls placed to only a few numbers throughout the month preceding Rostock's death. We wrote these numbers down for Miss Paek to trace as the duty agent informed us that the Stenbergs had arrived. I asked him to have them brought to the lounge, and he turned and disappeared. They came in a minute later.

I introduced Louis and again informed them of their rights. They agreed to answer what questions they could.

"What's your home phone number?" Louis asked immediately, looking down at the list. Stenberg rattled it off, and the look on my partner's face told me the number was there. He was counting the number of times that number showed up on the list. "Staff Sergeant Rostock telephoned your house thirteen times in the month before his death. Who did he talk with?"

A long moment later Mrs. Stenberg muttered, "Me." Her husband turned and looked at her, the color draining from his face. He didn't say anything. I asked her why the calls had been made.

It came slowly at first, then flooded out as she went along, telling how Rostock tried to blackmail her into having sex with him. She consistently refused, crying through many nights as her husband slept. She didn't know how long she could hold him off. Stenberg looked as if he was going to be sick. She continued.

"He said he'd tell my husband about me buying things if I didn't. I told him I only bought one thing before. He said that was enough."

I interrupted her to ask what she'd bought before the TV. There was no statement about another purchase in the report from the interpreters.

"I bought a small stereo. Under fifty dollars. I didn't have to use a ration card. But he said he would tell, and that scared me." She turned to her husband, tears in her eyes, and said, "I'm sorry, honey. Please don't be more angry." She bowed her head in shame.

"Did you know about any of these phones calls?" I directed my question to the sergeant. "No," he said, adding that if he'd known what was going on, Rostock wouldn't have lived as long as he did. I advised them to see the staff judge advocate's defense lawyer as soon as they left, and let them go. They were now prime suspects. They definitely had motive, as did Mr. Park. Nor could we rule out Miss Lee in Kangnung. She claimed innocence, true enough, and it seemed so. But veteran agents will say that the innocent looking suspects are often the most deadly when cornered. There were probably also hundreds of other prime suspects we hadn't yet uncovered. It was nearing time to check all those phone numbers on the list.

We returned to the outer office, giving Miss Paek the remaining phone numbers. "Please find names and addresses for all of these, Miss Paek." She got right to work, shunning the reports she'd been working on. She was quite possibly the most efficient secretary I'd ever had the pleasure of working with. Louis and I went for lunch. The dining facility was closed by now, so we headed for the 19th Hole again. Their lunches were even better than their breakfasts.

We ate heartily, putting the case behind us for the moment, then returned to Rostock's house one more time. We both knew he had to have kept a list of his "customers" somewhere. We needed that list to wrap up the black marketing end of the case, at least, and we weren't stopping until we found it. What a tedious job investigating could be, but we loved it because of the ultimate good feeling we got when we finally pieced the puzzle together in the right places.

A message from the support group commander awaited us when we finally returned at the end of the day, empty-handed once again. He wanted to know when the dead soldier's personal property would be sent to the States. If we didn't have a definite answer, he was going to give the man's family our phone number and have them call us.

It was late, but I figured I'd call anyway to see if he was still in. He was and I told him I'd call the family if he'd give me the phone number. He was happy to get rid of that task and hung up. I delayed the call until it was evening on the east coast, and morning in Korea. Louis and I came up with a few pertinent questions to ask while we had them on the line, then went home to get some rest. Tomorrow would be another day.

Mihi was at the house with Jina. After the "Hi, honeys," Mihi said, "I want to talk to Louis." I asked if it could wait until the next evening, because I'd already dropped Louis off and we were both bushed. Jina stood up for us and finally convinced Mihi that we'd have Louis over for dinner the following day.

She reluctantly accepted that, then stormed out the door. Kangnung was eating at her, we concluded, even though she hadn't told Jina why she needed to talk to Louis so urgently. Jina prepared dinner as I told her about my phone conversation with Agent Wilkins in Seoul. She laughed.

All the women want you two, don't they?" she asked jokingly. At least I hoped she was joking. I smiled. Dinner was ready soon and I ate. Then I hit the sack as Jina tuned in to a drama show on MBC. I was fast asleep in minutes, still aching a little from PT. I dreamed strange things that night, and woke up just as the alarm was about to ring. I shut it off so it wouldn't wake Jina, and headed to the kitchen for coffee.

I stalked through the house, dressing and sipping my coffee in silence. I had no idea what time Jina went to bed, so I didn't want to wake her before I left. I slipped out of the house not realizing I was an hour early. It finally hit me when I approached the dining facility doors and found them locked. I went to Louis' room instead and woke him up just moments before his alarm rang. What's good for me should be good for him, too, I thought.

"What's this?" he asked, opening the door to let me in. He was in his briefs, walking back into his room and rubbing his eyes with both fists. "Personalized service?"

"Thought you might like to help me out."

"How?"

"I gotta make a rough phone call and I need some moral support."

"Bullshit. You've never needed moral support on those phone calls before," he said, pulling on his trousers. "Where are we eating?"

The dining facility was the cheapest place around, I told him. "Besides, they don't screw up eggs too bad." We both laughed and he finished dressing, then packed his electric shaver in his bag.

"I can shave on the way in," he said. He zipped up the bag and we headed downstairs. The dining facility wouldn't be serving food yet, but we could go in the back door and have coffee until then.

We headed straight to the office after breakfast and dialed the number in the States. We composed ourselves and got the questions ready. The connection could be broken at any time. Military phones weren't the best for overseas calls.

Chapter Seven

I explained to the dead sergeant's father why his son's personal belongings were still in Korea. I didn't mention that Rostock, himself, was coming up in a very bad light. That would have devastated the family, since we couldn't yet prove, beyond doubt, that is, that he was doing anything criminal before his untimely demise.

"Honest, sir. We'll release his effects as soon as possible and send them along. In the meantime, did he send any large amounts of money home?" I asked. When he questioned my question, I realized I couldn't keep the truth from him any longer, though. I outlined the investigation we were conducting into his late son's life.

"That's why we need some help, sir. We think his killer may have been tied up in this scheme with him, and we've got to get all the facts to see who they might lead to. Please help us."

He paused for a few seconds, then let out a sigh. "Tim sent home money every month for about twelve years. It wasn't much, but I knew it wasn't hurting him. We banked it for his retirement years. About six months ago he sent us money orders totaling more than ten thousand dollars. He sent another ten grand about a month after that.

"I wrote, asking where he got all this money he was sending, but he never answered. I tried to telephone, but was always told he was out. In the last three months before he died, he sent more than fifty thousand dollars. It's all in the account. We haven't touched it."

He told me the name of the bank and gave me the account number readily, saying he wanted to clear this matter up and put it behind him forever. I thanked him and assured him his son's possessions would be forwarded as soon as we got the case settled.

I filled Louis in on the details, then offered to buy coffee at the 19th Hole. The dining facility food might be cheaper, but they didn't have good-looking waitresses.

We returned to the office just as Colonel Walsh pulled up. We exchanged pleasantries and went in together, Louis and I following him into his office.

"We need to freeze a bank account, sir," I said before he even had a chance to sit down. His look told me I definitely needed to brief him, so I did. He said he'd have Miss Paek type up the request as soon as she got in. It would be faxed to the military installation nearest the bank, and they'd get the district attorney there to freeze the account until the investigation was complete. We'd also review any banking history on Rostock, his military finance records and his spending habits to see if we could determine how much money was obtained by illegal means. I was gambling that all the money would go to the Korean government for taxes and fines before this was finished.

The colonel asked what else had transpired, and we told him about the phone calls from Rostock's house. "Other than that, sir, there's nothing to report. If they don't turn up anything, we'll be hurting for clues again." He told us the standard "keep plugging" and we left. Time for a cup of coffee while we sifted through whatever came in the mail and over the fax.

Miss Paek came in at eight thirty and handed me the list she'd picked up at the phone company. It contained the names that belonged to the phone numbers called from Rostock's house. One call was made to Mr. Park's home, while another was to Park's former office at Taegu's customs headquarters. Other numbers had Korean names attached to them, while the rest were American.

We called the postal locator to obtain duty phone numbers for the Americans on the list, and wrote them down next to their names. We started calling and making appointments after we had all five of them. Louis and I had to cover all the interviews ourselves, so we spaced them apart to cover the entire afternoon. We retired to the lounge to coordinate our plans and efforts.

We'd have spouses brought in tomorrow morning if we needed them. By lunchtime we had the entire afternoon strategically mapped out, so we headed for the NCO Club on Camp Henry for a bite to eat.

When we returned from lunch, something dawned on me. I picked up the list and it hit me like a sledgehammer. I passed the list to Louis and asked what he saw. It took him a minute, but he finally realized what I meant.

"Amanda Compo?" he asked. I nodded. One of the people on the list could be the wife of an MPI agent. In fact, the same agent who worked this case before it was handed over to us. Louis got on the phone right away to ask postal locator the question we felt we had already answered.

It panned out. Specialist Amanda Compo was married to the agent. I checked the list again. There were five calls to the Compo home from Rostock's number during his final month on this earth. It could be tricky, though, so we retired to the lounge again to plan the contingencies for this particular interview. We didn't want to alert them prematurely if there was a connection deeper than the phone calls.

Since Compo was MPI, we wanted to catch them red-handed so there'd be no questions and no way out. I hoped we were wrong. No one likes a dirty cop. Louis called to cancel Amanda's interview after a short discussion of the matter. We had to brief the colonel before we took any steps, but he'd already left for the day. We made that top priority on the list of things to do the next morning. There was no sense bothering him at home right now. We decided we'd done all we could for the day and got ourselves out of there, too.

It was still early, so Louis and I hit the gym for an hour before heading back to my place for dinner. Louis was going to have a long evening convincing Mihi of his innocence, and we wanted to clear our heads of the case before going home. Exercise allowed us to do that while we kept in shape at the same time. It also let us get rid of some pent up stress much more cheaply than by punching holes through walls. We both vowed to be calm this evening, no matter what hit the fan.

We also promised not to laugh, but that was mainly to keep Louis on an even keel. He couldn't afford to get uptight about the entire thing if he really wanted to win Mihi's heart. Coupled with her natural fear of his running around, this was like a test — to see how he'd perform under fire. I still go through that occasionally, but my wife has mellowed a lot in the past six years.

The ladies were sitting on the sofa, deep in conversation, when we arrived. That stopped when they heard the outside gate open. We entered without stopping, as if nothing was out of the ordinary. We said our hellos while removing our shoes, and sat down at the table, leaving our gym bags by the door.

"Tell me about your Kangnung girlfriend," Mihi said with a fiery opening shot. Round one had begun and it would prove that Fort Sumpter was only child's play in comparison.

Louis survived with only a relatively mild case of emotional mauling. In fact, we were all joking about it by the end of the two-hour session and he and Mihi are doing great as a couple now. He'll be meeting her family this weekend, so Jina and I will have to prep him on what to expect from that encounter. It shouldn't be quite as bad as ours, because her family generally didn't disapprove of Americans, though they didn't heartily endorse one becoming a member of their family either.

But that, of course, will have to be sidelined to the hours we're not on the case. With the new information we'd received, we hoped to have some time to help him with his personal needs.

The other four interviews at the office went smoothly enough. One person said Rostock had only made harassing phone calls to his number, so we asked him to bring his wife in the next morning. He claimed to know nothing else. Two of the remaining soldiers knew he'd called at least once, but didn't know why. Their wives would come in with them, too. The other had a second card in his wallet. We noticed it when we asked to see his ration card and the false one fell onto the floor.

We and went into full questioning mode. He was the final interview of the day, so we double-teamed him.

The young soldier blanched when he saw Louis pick the card up. He knew we'd caught him. "Where'd you get this?" Louis asked. We'd already read him his rights when he first walked in. He was searching frantically for a story that would save his career, but we wanted only the straight and skinny. We weren't interested in any sort of fiction.

"I asked you a question, Private Dobbs," Louis said very firmly, emphasizing the young soldier's lack of rank, since it would be the only rank he'd ever hold.

The price for holding an extra ration card, used or not, is time in the slammer and a bad conduct or dishonorable discharge. Many commanders didn't have the forgiveness within them to overlook this. Soldiers were briefed on the consequences as soon as they got off the plane at their new assignment in the Land of the Morning Calm. In the collective mind of the military, there was no exception whatsoever. I usually agreed, but a private deserves a second chance sometimes. Hell, he'd only been in the Army for what — a year or so?

"Look, private," I said in a much softer tone than Louis'. "We don't want to cause problems, but there's a dead staff sergeant connected with that card. Right now you're in a helluva mess, because this one holds accessory to murder along with the ration card offense." I let that sink in for a moment or two.

Louis sat down on the sofa to his side, with the ration card moving between the fingers of his left hand. His right hand remained free in case he needed to go for his weapon. It rarely happened within the confines of the office, but you could never tell. One of these days someone could very possibly go berserk.

I started in again after Dobbs regained some of his color. "A month ago a staff sergeant was killed. He was the ration control clerk. You heard about it on the news, didn't you?" He nodded. Of course he had. There wasn't a person in Korea who hadn't. Hell, it even made the Korean news channels and papers. "Now you pop up out of nowhere with an extra ration card. How do you think that will set with the brass?" He was fidgeting, but made no move to run. I gave him another moment to think things out.

I knew he was probably thinking of a way to get out of this, but there wasn't one. The phone rang. I picked it up and Miss Paek transferred a call from Dobbs' supervisor. I identified myself and asked how I could help.

"No. We're just asking Private Dobbs about some phone calls made to his house last month." I looked at Dobbs, who stared at me in disbelief. "No, sarge. We're not charging him with anything right now. There's nothing to book him on. We're just trying to get a little information is all. Right sarge. No problem. Any time." I hung up and looked at Dobbs. Just in case he didn't already understand, I lined it out for him.

"Look. We need some information. You're a private. Maybe you deserve a second chance. Maybe you don't. But we want you to tell us what you know about Rostock and his dealings. Open up."

He started stammering, but the information flowed faster and smoother as the story unraveled.

Rostock knew Dobbs was in Korea on a singles tour — no family at the government's expense. His 19-year-old wife was in Korea, though, at Dobbs' expense. He also knew that she wife was pregnant and they'd need money for the new baby. Since Dobbs couldn't buy baby formula in the commissary or PX, he'd have to get it on the black market — at about 250 percent above cost. This would ruin his paycheck, and he wasn't due for promotion in the near future. On top of that, Dobbs' pay wouldn't allow him to send his wife back to the States, even if she was medically cleared to fly. She was about five weeks from delivery, if all went smooth. Dobbs was in a hurt and Rostock knew it. Like a wolf closing in on a wounded deer.

Rostock first approached Dobbs when he signed for his ration card, but Dobbs refused, the lectures about the black market still fresh in his frightened mind. The ration man persisted, apparently discovering his family problems through friends or some other avenue. It wasn't hard for someone who knew where to look to get information. Rostock kept offering Dobbs a fifty percent profit on any order he bought, but that wasn't enough to change the young private's mind.

Then Mrs. Dobbs got sick and doctors said she wouldn't be able to breast-feed the baby. That was the last straw. Dobbs agreed to do Rostock's bidding.

After he'd finished I picked up the phone to verify the illness with the dispensary. She was indeed in poor shape. I called his unit's orderly room to ask why he hadn't been issued a temporary baby food exception because of the pregnancy. They informed me that it had been taken care of about two months earlier, but apparently the card hadn't come in yet. I asked Louis to check the list of cards we'd found to see if Dobbs' was in there.

"It seems for the present that you might be on the up and up," I said after the door closed. "But if you'd asked the company, they'd have told you that you'd be able to buy the baby things you needed legally." He looked like he'd been hit with a boulder labeled "stupid." I shut off the tape recorder so he could see the motion. "What did you buy for Rostock?"

The movement wasn't lost on him. He opened up readily.

"He wanted mostly cigarettes and alcohol. Then he started asking for rice and cheese and other simple stuff like that. Sometimes he'd ask me to buy meats."

"Is that all?"

"For the most part. But he did ask me to buy a camera once. They wouldn't let me get it, though."

"Who?"

"The commander. When I applied for a letter of authorization to purchase it, he said I didn't make enough money for a camera like that and disapproved it. Rostock was angry as hell, but what could I do about it? Two days later it was on the news."

"What was?"

"His death. I didn't know it was murder until a few days later."

"OK," I said, and took him into the lounge. "You wait here." I left him and went back to meet Louis in my office. He was already there and the look on his face told me that the card was in the lot confiscated from the house. I called Dobbs' company and told them to reapply for the card, saying that the card had come in but couldn't be issued.

That convinced the first sergeant and he promised to have a new application ready by mid-afternoon. I told him I'd send Dobbs over to sign it and we hung up. I called Dobbs back in and he sat on the edge of the chair.

"Didn't you sign another ration card application?" I asked. He admitted that he did, but Rostock told him it was disapproved. There was a knock on the door, and Dobbs' commander came in. He introduced himself, but I didn't let him get any further than that. "Good. We just finished. You can take him back to sign his new ration card application, if you would, captain." Stunned at the suddenness of the brush-off, all he could say was "OK." I handed Dobbs his identification card and real ration card, and told him I'd call if I needed to talk with him again. He nodded, thanking me with his eyes, then followed the captain out the door.

'What's this? Be kind to privates week?" Louis asked with a smile when we were alone. I responded by offering him a home-cooked lunch, and called home to set it up. It was close to one now. We left in my car.

We mulled over what we'd learned so far during the week, which wasn't much. At this rate, we wouldn't finish the investigation until we each had a foot in the grave. We had to turn over a big piece of the puzzle rather soon. We were only getting minor bits and pieces each day, and none of them led anywhere solid.

The only large chunk we had was the anonymous note that led to Mr. Park's apprehension. But even that hadn't led anywhere closer to the circle we were aiming at. We needed to wrap up the black market end, which would surely produce our killer. We were sure the murder and the false cards were very closely connected.

We returned to the office after lunch, just as stumped as when we'd left, but we'd decided on one thing — to watch Compo rather closely for the next few days. That might produce something — we hoped. We thought it might be best to brief the colonel as soon as we got back, since we'd be investigating another law enforcement officer.

Walsh cleared us for whatever we thought was best after we told him about the connection between the MPI agent and the dead ration control clerk. We developed our plan over the next few hours, and went home to change for the next phase of the operation. That would take at least the better part of the weekend. I'd have to cover it alone while Louis spent a few hours with Mihi's family, but that would be OK. The meeting was set for Sunday evening, after the exchange and the commissary closed. It would be just a tail job by that time — following them around in a rental car. We wouldn't chance using the sedan since the MPI agent could probably pick it out on a busy street.

I drove around the MPI building, since it was on the route from my house to the office, to see if Compo had driven in or if his wife had taken the car to her office at Camp Henry. It wasn't there. I met Louis at the barracks and drove him to the PX, where he'd wait to see if Compo showed up. I went over to Henry to wait for Amanda Compo to finish work and see where she went. If they met at the PX, Louis and I would team up and follow them. If not, I'd follow them alone until they got home, then I'd swing back and pick Louis up. We had our radios so we could keep in touch through the entire episode in either case.

All the planning in the world wouldn't help beat the heat and humidity though. The car's air conditioner was on the fritz, and it was a good twenty degrees hotter inside the car than out. Even with the windows open. I left the car to sit under a small tree nearby. It wasn't much of a tree, really, standing only about eight feet tall with sparse foliage, but it had more leaves than the open parking lot. I was rewarded at about four o'clock with a view of Specialist Compo leaving for the day.

It was a good hour before the end of the regular workday, but that didn't mean much on a Friday. Soldiers and civilians often left work a little early, as in the civilian world, to grab an early start on the weekend. You couldn't really blame the soldiers. Their duty day began at a quarter to six in the morning, three days a week, and often stretched into the early evening. And there was no overtime pay. An hour or two on a Friday was just a bit of compensation, when you got right down to it.

I pulled out shortly after she did, and maneuvered in behind her Dodge wagon as it was going out the gate. I let a car or two get between us, then pulled out into the traffic to follow at a distance, while alerting Louis over the radio. He reported that he'd seen nothing of her MPI agent husband yet, but vowed to keep his eyes peeled. I told him that could hurt, then signed off before he could reply.

We made the final turn toward the front gate of Camp Walker about twenty minutes later and I keyed the mike to alert Louis. He reported that husband Ernie was just getting off the bus and heading across the parking lot to the PX. When Amanda pulled through the main gate, I told Louis we'd meet in fifteen seconds, since her destination was also the PX. I told Louis to watch the agent closely. They might have been shopping separately, or just not realize the other had been going to the PX.

"And we'd better not talk over the radio anymore until we're both out of there," I said. We turned the units off and stuffed them inside our gym bags.

Specialist Compo turned the station wagon into the parking lot and searched for a space close to the main entrance. I picked one across the lot, near the florist concession, so I would be out of the car first and still be able to follow her into the store.

The ration control monitor properly checked her identification and ration card before allowing her to enter. I spotted Louis in the back of the store, near the stereo equipment.

I showed my ID, ration card and badge to the monitor, informing him that my gym bag contained equipment necessary for the job I was performing. That was enough for him, and he let me in without depositing my bag at the door. I wasn't about to leave it there with my weapon and radio in it.

I followed the agent's wife through the ladies' section, where she chose a few innocuous items of underclothing, then over to housewares on the opposite side of the floor. I noticed Louis and his suspect slowly heading for hardware as I crossed through the aisles. The Compos met near the check-cashing station. They exchanged a few words, then he cashed a check while she went through the checkout to pay for their combined selections.

There was nothing in the cart that would suggest black marketing, so I waited in the mall area for her. A few minutes later, the agent came out to wait for his wife, while Louis grabbed a pack of gum and entered the line behind Amanda. He saw me outside and knew Compo wasn't in a hurry to go anywhere without his wife. He'd follow them out, so I went to wait in the car for the procession.

The couple exited the PX mall and got into their car, heading off post. We followed them to their house with no intermediary stops. We were in surveillance position within half an hour of leaving Camp Walker. We'd wait until one or the other moved, then switch off. Louis would tail the agent while I stayed with his wife the first time up.

By nine o'clock, all the lights in the house were out, save for the TV. A half-hour later that, too, was extinguished. We waited until ten before we called it quits. I took Louis to his barracks, then went home. Tomorrow would be another long day.

Jina was already asleep when I got there, so I lay down beside her. I was dead to the world before my head hit the pillow.

When I woke up, I greeted my wife in the kitchen. A look of concern clouded her face as I explained what Louis and I would be doing all day. She didn't know who we were tailing, but she knew the risks. I assured her that everything would be all right, and she seemed to calm down visibly. Then she remembered Louis' meeting with Mihi's family the next night.

I told her not to worry. "I'll take it alone during that time if I can. The only way he'll miss it is if something breaks in the case right about then." She shrugged, still looking concerned, then turned back to her cooking. My breakfast waited on the table, so I plopped down in my chair. She was working on the evening meal that would probably have to be reheated by the time I made it home. With any luck I might be able to see my wife again before she went to sleep, but I doubted that very much.

Jina wanted to make sure something was waiting for me, no matter what time I returned. Then she could finish the rest of her work, such as laundry and shopping. She also cleaned the house at least twice during the day, like most Korean women. Even in the States, after working all day, she'd clean the house twice: once before heading off to work and again when she got home. She was something else.

I finished wolfing down my breakfast and got ready to get Louis. It would be close to seven thirty before we finally got to Compo's house, but we figured it was better to be early, rather than late. There was no telling what could go down before we got there. Louis was waiting at the door when I arrived at his barracks and hopped into the car as soon as it stopped. We were off the camp within minutes and heading out through the thin Saturday morning traffic. We arrived at our destination without complication and waited.

It was nearly noon before the MPI agent wandered through the front gate and climbed into his car, driving past us toward the main street. We let him turn before I got out of the car. Louis swung the car around and turned out after the agent, handling the wheel competently. I grabbed my bag and sat on the curb at the end of the block, taking out my radio to turn it on, and replacing it inside the bag.

I keyed the mike through the material and called for a radio check. My partner's voice returned through the opening in the bag a second later. "Roger, check. Looks like the destination is Camp Henry. Keep you posted."

I reached into the bag again, pulled out the latest issue of Alfred Hitchcock and leaned back against the utility box, facing straight toward the Compo house. I opened the magazine to the bent page and took up where I last left off.

Twenty minutes later my bag spoke again. "He bought a paper at the snack bar on Henry. Looks like he's headed home again. I'll let him swing in, then I'll circle around and pick you up at the other end."

"Roger," I responded, then continued reading. Compo's car pulled into the street and parked in front of his house. Louis drove by the intersection, not turning in. I stood and put my book back into the bag, then walked casually along the sidewalk that would take me past Compo's house to the other end of the alley.

Compo was already inside by the time I was even with his front door. I didn't look toward the building, but stopped directly across the street for a moment to watch some people playing soccer in the schoolyard. A minute later I was on my way again to meet Louis, who'd already parked in position. I climbed into the driver's seat after Louis pushed over to the other side. He'd get foot patrol next time.

Louis handed me a cup of coffee he'd brought back from the snack bar. I opened it and took a sip. It tasted pretty good, considering its source. The snack bars weren't known for making the best coffee in the world, that's for sure. It usually tasted a little bitter. But not today. It had to be the cup, so I complimented my partner on his choice of cups. He looked at me strangely and picked up the copy of Stars and Stripes that he'd bought while tailing Compo.

We alternated the reading and watching times until nightfall with no activity outside the house. They both exited as the streetlights came on, though, and headed their car toward the main road. We followed them through the Taegu streets and onto a country road leading northward out of the city. About twenty miles along this route was the town of Waegwan and Camp Carroll, home of the U.S. Army's Materiel Support Center for Korea. Between here and there were a winding mountain road and a couple of small hamlets. Then the road continued northward until it eventually reached Seoul.

It was the old military supply route between the capital and the southeastern port city of Pusan. Anyone willing to spend eighteen hours on that road to Seoul, however, should have had their head examined. The expressway was much faster. A five-mile stretch of construction skirted the mountain pass that would eventually cut about fifteen minutes from the drive and make the trip much safer.

We came off the mountain ridge and drove past the huge American petroleum terminal, into Waegwan, then made the right turn through Camp Carroll's little ville to the only gate that was open all night. Compo's car stopped short of the gate, however, and they stepped into the King Club. We turned around and pointed our rental car in the direction we'd come from, then locked it and went inside.

The King Club was known as a pretty good disco place. It was also known for having some of the prettiest hookers around, to include those in Taegu. The rumors proved correct. The club was filled nearly to capacity and music blared through the closed doors, clearly audible across the street. Modern American tunes filled every inch that wasn't occupied by Americans and hookers. About twenty couples filled the dance floor, the Compos among them. They looked as if they were really enjoying themselves.

Louis and I grabbed the only two available stools at the bar and ordered Cokes. We'd take turns casually watching them while trying to look like we were waiting for friends. This went on until two in the morning, with no unusual movement, save for a few of the dancers. Then they left. Louis slipped out the door first, buying some fried onion rings across the street, next to their car. I went out to our car about the same time they'd finished turning theirs around, heading toward Waegwan.

Louis and I took a little-known road on the other side of the tracks that would intersect with their road just south of the city. We liked to throw people off in case they thought they were being followed. They'd automatically think we weren't following them, or that they'd lost us. Our prey would pretty much be at ease by the time we linked up with them. We came out on the main road and waited at a service station just before the entrance to the expressway.

They passed us and took a left onto the highway, going through the tollbooth to pay their fare and collect their ticket. Louis reached into the glove box and handed me the "Official Business" sign displayed in Government rental cars. I placed it on the dash in front of me. We'd only need it to gain toll-free access to the expressway and for the exit in Taegu. We were allowed to zip right through and got the Compo car in our sights again.

They were about a half-kilometer in front of us, driving at the national speed of a hundred kilometers per hour, or about sixty miles an hour. We kept our distance, sometimes letting other vehicles play leap frog around us to disguise our presence even more, then followed them through the tollbooth on the western side of Taegu. They went straight home and inside the house. The lights were turned out within the hour, but we waited another thirty minutes before leaving, then went to catch some sleep ourselves. It had been a long day, to say the least, and we were both very tired.

It was four o'clock when I got home, and the eastern sky was already beginning to show light. I undressed and crawled under the sheets, after setting the alarm for eight. Jina was sound asleep and didn't even stir as I kissed her on the forehead. She must have waited up late for me or the kiss would have woken her. I laid my head on the pillow and drifted off to sleep.

My eyes had only been closed for a second when the phone rang. I reached for it to find a dial tone and the ringing continued. Was it time to get up already? I reached for the stop button on the alarm clock.

I went into the bathroom to shower and swallowed two Tylenols. The hot spray almost woke me up. Jina had brewed the coffee and left a note telling me she was at church. I poured a cup and placed the already cooked breakfast in the microwave, then dialed Louis' room. His groggy voice told me he'd slept right through his alarm, but that he'd be up and about in no time. I hung up and ate, realizing I was famished, but not really tasting anything. The coffee helped get me alert, and I was out of the house within the hour.

Louis was locking his door when I arrived, so I waited for him to join me in the hallway. What was the point in wasting energy I didn't have? We went out to the car and down to the 19th Hole. Louis was hungry and I needed another cup or three of coffee. We made it to Compo's house before ten and started the daylong vigil once again, shifting off to take naps this time.

The couple came out in mid-afternoon while Louis was napping. He awoke immediately as I started the car. We were heading for Camp Walker's back gate this time.

We drove through the gate, flashing our badges, just as Compo's car rounded the bend past his office, and staying within the posted twenty-five miles per hour speed limit. By the time we rounded the bend, we saw that Compo had taken a right turn and was traveling along the west side of the golf course. We followed at a discreet distance as they turned left at the first intersection, then left again into the commissary parking lot. I let Louis out on the street, then continued on. He'd keep an eye on them while I went back to the office to change rental cars. They'd taken a pretty good look at us in their mirror. Louis was standing outside the door of the commissary when I returned. We walked around to the side to talk.

"They've got some regular shopping in there, but they're also picking up two of everything on the black market list, it seems." Louis was pretty observant about things like that. He had the list nearly memorized. The Compos either lived the lush life on their double pay checks, or they were buying things for illegal resale. We radioed in to the duty agent that we might need a backup team soon, and told them to be standing by on a moment's notice.

Our suspects came out the door about five minutes later, the old Korean man who'd bagged their groceries was in tow with their spoils. Once their ten bags were loaded, they drove out of the parking lot, made a left, crossed the first intersection, then turned left again at the Burger King. Immediately after, they turned in at the liquor store, got out of the car and went inside. They returned about ten minutes later with two cases of Budweiser and a brown bag. The bag looked full, but with what, we had no idea. We'd have to check it later if we got the chance.

We tailed them to the PX and, while I followed them inside, Louis stayed behind to look in the bag through the car window, then joined me inside. "They've got one of those sixty-two dollar bottles of Chivas in there and some wine. Do you think they're really into drinking that exclusive stuff?" he asked, knowing full well it would net the seller at least double on the black market.

I let it drop. The only people who usually bought that stuff for their own consumption were officers or high-ranking civilians. None of the enlisted people could afford that kind of drink. This couple was earning two military paychecks, so it wasn't completely out of the question. I'd bought a bottle or two before to impress people.

I asked Louis to radio in for additional Korean National Police backup, giving them the usual briefing about wanting to search a Korean national on the city streets. He returned to my side within ten minutes and announced that the KNPs would be waiting for our call to provide necessary assistance. They were aware that this was in connection with the murder and the false ration cards, so they were more than eager to help. Mr. Park was a black eye for even the police force, and they wanted to help set that straight. They also knew that, if we broke the case with their assistance, it would look good for their promotions.

The Compos had several three-packs of TDK video cassettes, some baby clothes that later proved to be Osh Kosh (very high on the black marketing list), a steam iron, portable ironing board, and several other items that sold pretty easily on the market. None of the PX items had a singular value of more than fifty dollars but, coupled with the items they'd bought in the commissary and liquor store, the Compos stood to profit by a couple hundred bucks if they sold everything. We returned to the car to await their departure and discuss our plan of action. If it was coming down at all, the odds were stacked heavily that it would happen sometime today. When they came out and loaded the car we were ready.

Following them home was easy and, once they'd unloaded the car, all we had to do was wait. The agent came outside several times to look up and down the street during the next couple of hours, which forced us to move the car a few times and even exchange it once. We sure didn't get any napping time. But our vigilance paid off as dusk fell, when an older Korean lady entered their house. We called for our office reinforcements and the Korean police, and briefed them as soon as they arrived.

We had the Korean police follow the lady when she left. They understood and positioned themselves. The other CID team was to watch the Compos if we had to leave the scene. I was sure they were going to deal all the stuff tonight, if they were going to do it at all. And I was sure it was going down now. That meant the Korean lady would have to make several trips or have someone else help. It also meant a possible lapse between the time of the financial transaction and the movement of goods. That might complicate things a bit, but not much. I was counting on the Korean National Police to overcome that obstacle with their unique method of handling that type of situation.

A full moon rose in the east as the last light of the sun disappeared from the sky. The moon, combined with the streetlights, would make our job a little easier, but not real easy. The Korean lady had been inside about an hour and we were still waiting. Thank God it wasn't winter or even the monsoon season. Otherwise we'd all have pneumonia before the night was out. The thermometer on the car dashboard finally registered under ninety degrees as the sun set. Now it was hovering just under eighty, but the humidity was still with us.

Thunder rumbled from still unseen clouds off in the distance. I hoped this would be finished before that thunder made its way here, but I never really held much hope. My luck usually wasn't that good.

Three young men on bicycles soon arrived, turning up the road from the same direction the lady had come. We were at the far end of the block, just a group of people to them. From that distance, they couldn't tell whether or not we were police, so they weren't worried. We didn't take much notice of them, either, but when they brought the bikes to a stop outside the Compo's gate and rang for entry, they gained our undivided attention.

They were buzzed in and took the bikes with them. The Korean policeman who was with us ran to brief his buddies and was back inside of two minutes. They'd have to run to keep up with these guys. I'd hate to have been in their shoes, but they were all relatively young, except for the captain. I guessed him to be in his mid-fifties.

The gate opened twenty minutes later and the lady stepped out, followed closely by the three bikers. She now had a large cloth bag perched on her head, that she held in place with one hand while keeping her balance with the other. The backs of the three bikes were also loaded with cloth bags. I signaled to our Korean police friends that we could take them immediately. The snatch was made just as they rounded the corner at the far intersection. The second CID team stayed just out of sight near the gate. We instructed them to detain the Compos if they tried to leave, and went around the corner to get a glimpse of our catch of the day.

"It's all the stuff we saw them buy today, minus only a few things," Louis announced, as he held up the expensive liquor. The Korean policeman who doubled as our translator explained to his partners what we'd just said, and they beamed with pride, as if they'd masterminded the entire bust. I asked them to take those four down to the local station for the ritual questioning, letting them know we'd be collecting the Americans and bringing them along as well. They happily complied.

We returned to the rental car and radioed the duty agent to notify the boss that we were apprehending the Compos. We requested that he contact us by radio, and we'd be waiting. He was on the radio within minutes and we asked him to change to our secure channel so the military police and MPI couldn't listen in. The change was made, and we recited what we had for evidence. He seemed pleased and disappointed at the same time. Pleased that we'd made headway into the case, and disappointed that it was a fellow cop. We shared his unspoken sentiments. Every good cop does. He told us to pick up our suspects and meet him back at the office. We broke the connection and rang the gate bell.

Compo was all smiles as he personally opened the gate, rather than buzz us in. The smile evaporated when I informed him that we were there on business rather than pleasure. Louis read him his rights, and I placed the handcuffs on him as the other team made its way inside to collect his wife.

Compo began to object, asking us where the necessary Korean police representation was. He knew they had to be present when making an off-post apprehension. Our English-speaking pal appeared from behind me and announced his presence. Compo went slack, all protest draining from him. He did exactly as we ordered from then on. We asked our Korean police friend to remain outside while we sealed the house, making sure no one could disturb whatever evidence lay within.

"I would be pleased to assist in any way," he said, smiling from ear to ear. He knew he'd proven his worth that night. We loaded the Compos into the rental car and drove to the police substation where the woman and three young men had been taken. The previous group was arguing a losing battle as we entered, but fell silent when they saw the Compos herded in with handcuffs. They knew they'd lost their argument without a doubt.

The lady, thinking that the Compos had already betrayed her, started to plea bargain with the Korean cops, pointing to the agent and saying that he cooked up the entire deal. We knew she'd probably been in the business since before Compo was born, but all we needed was that ID on him. That was why we had brought them there. With that situation under control, I told the Koreans that our other team would inventory the goods and take them to post. We left just as they entered the station.

The colonel was waiting at the office when we arrived. He looked freshly showered and shaved, but then, all officers always did. He motioned for us to go into his office, which we did, taking seats on the two sofas that were provided for meetings.

I sat next to Compo while Louis stayed with Compo's wife. The colonel took his chair behind the desk. There was a period of silence before the colonel asked what we had on the couple.

Louis briefed him on the events leading up to the surveillance, which the colonel was already aware of. This was done to let the Compos know we'd been aware of them for longer than just that day. Leaving out the boring wait-and-follow sessions, he jumped right to the period when the couple made their purchases, and the subsequent visits by the Korean lady and her cyclists.

He finished by telling Colonel Walsh that the other team was taking inventory of the goods and collecting statements from the other four culprits. They were with the Korean police and would return shortly, he said. There was silence again as the colonel sorted out the information. Then he looked at Compo.

"You've been read your rights and I know you understand them," he started. "Do you have anything to say for yourself?" Silence. He let that silence fill the air before speaking again. "Get these two out of here."

We led the two suspects to separate rooms. The agent was locked in a holding room when we started on the specialist, leading her into my office and closing the door.

She was young, her ID card noting that she was only nineteen years old. Standing five feet six inches with dirty brown shoulder-length hair, she seemed somewhat plain Jane-ish. I couldn't really tell about the figure through her loose blouse and long house skirt, but she seemed neither overly chunky nor thin.

Her eyes were deep set and alert. They were a light blue, almost like ice. Her nose was delicately small and her chin strong. Her lips were full and set in a naturally pouting sensuality. The hands were well manicured and, with the cuffs off, lay flat on her thighs. She stared straight ahead, volunteering nothing as of yet. I didn't prod her, but instead typed up the beginning of the report from her ID card and Ration Control Plate. Louis paced back and forth quietly in front of the door as I typed.

I swung around in my chair to face her when I finished. She was still staring at the same spot on the wall. She hadn't moved an inch. I could see her blouse rise and fall softly with her breathing. That was the only outward sign of life. She looked calm and composed, but there was an unnatural whiteness to her facial color. She apparently still hadn't recovered from the shock of the arrest.

I watched for a second to see if I could find any reaction whatsoever. None. Louis sat down on the sofa.

"Tell me about it," I said. Silence.

"Look," Louis said. "We can either go hard on you two or we can make it easier. If we have to dig for all the answers, we might just be inclined to forget about any kind words that might lighten the sentence." Silence.

"He's right," I said. "The easier you make it for us, the easier we can make it for you." Silence. It was amazing. She hadn't blinked or moved in any way other than to breathe. We had to try another tack.

"The Korean police will make that woman talk," I said. "She's already blabbed that Ernie's the culprit. She was bargaining with them as we left, just to make her sentence lighter and to hang the blame on both of you." Her resolve faltered. First her eyes moved slightly and then she blinked, allowing a tear to roll down her face. Her hands clasped each other in her lap. She breathed harder for a while, sometimes allowing her ample breasts to make contact against the loose blouse. I thought we'd have to call for an ambulance. Then she took two deep breaths, with the blouse straining to contain her flesh, and spoke in a low whisper.

"He told me not to say anything. He said it would be all right. Ernie said that giving to an orphanage wasn't black marketing. He said that there were exceptions to the regulations for that. He knows all that stuff, 'cause he's MPI."

Louis and I just looked at each other, dumbfounded. Had we stumbled onto a case of legitimate orphanage donations? I signaled for Louis to go to the colonel's office with me for a second and we left, locking the door from the outside so she couldn't leave.

He invited us right in and we briefed him on the latest outcome. His eyebrows raised and he picked up the phone. It was time to notify the military police commander that we had one of his agents, and find out if there was any record of approval for orphanage donations. We left and went down the hall to the lockup where we had left Ernie.

I fed a sheet of paper into the typewriter and, without saying anything, started typing the top of the report from his ID card. I broke the silence when I stopped. "Is there anything you'd like to get off your chest before I start the tape recorder?" He replied with a simple "no."

I turned on the recorder and, as I started to talk, I looked at him. His mouth was already starting to work, so I held my words for a moment. Then he burst out with his explanation.

"You guys are in big trouble now," he nearly screamed. I asked how. "Because it's legal to give to an orphanage, that's how." I asked him to explain.

He said that he and his wife sponsored an orphanage and every week they shopped for things for the children. It was an

Amerasian orphanage — sons and daughters of American men and Korean women who were abandoned after their fathers returned to the States. Most of the men didn't even know there were children born from the relationship, but some did. Compo recited a U.S. Forces Korea regulation that provided an exception to the ration controls in cases like this. I knew the Reg well, and so did Louis. We also knew that each one had to be requested and approved.

"And do you have the proper written approval from your chain of command for these donations?" His face went blank and he echoed, "Approval?"

"Yes," Louis said. "In order to donate duty-free goods to orphanages, there must be a safeguarding approval from the chain to guard against abuse of the privilege. Otherwise you're still black marketing." That shook him up.

Either he hadn't read the Reg thoroughly or he'd overlooked that part when constructing his verbal highway out of this jam. We'd know soon enough when his commander arrived with his ration file. That would at least show us if he had permission. The Korean police would tell us if the Korean lady with his shopping in her possession was connected with an orphanage in the area. That wasn't likely, though, since I'd met her before in my official travels. We informed Compo that his commander was on the way over, and that we'd know for sure in a few minutes about his self-proclaimed innocence.

We left him to stew, and briefed the colonel on what he'd said so far. He said he'd call us in when the MP commander arrived, but it was better if they had some "commander time" before. He needed to be well informed when that happened. We returned to my office and Specialist Amanda Compo.

She was where we'd left her, bent over in the chair with her head in her hands, sobbing quietly. She looked up with red eyes and tear-stained cheeks when I walked around my desk to sit down.

"Are we going to jail?" she asked. I told her that I truthfully didn't know. If their story about orphanage donations panned out, they'd be free to go home in less than an hour, with no more than a slap on the wrist. If it didn't, their commanders might opt to take custody of them until morning.

I took the time to dial her company and spoke with the charge of quarters, who said he'd call the commander at home right away. The phone rang back in a few minutes and I talked with Captain Grant about his soldier. He said he'd be down right away and we hung up.

Louis and I decided to wait and see what the outcome would be before going further with the suspects. We retired to the lounge for a cup of coffee. That's when we both remembered the meeting Louis was supposed to have with Mihi's family hours ago. I dialed the home number. Jina answered on the first ring. She suspected why we were late and told me she had explained everything to Mihi.

"She was angry when she left, but she went to explain it to her family anyway." I apologized profusely, taking full responsibility. Like the loving and patient wife she was, Jina said she understood, but felt bad for Mihi. I asked her to tell Mihi that Louis would definitely be there any time they wanted the next day, because I was giving him the day off. She agreed to try and said she'd call back.

Louis thanked me several times, even though he knew it was only a gamble and that this case might have ruined his chances with Mihi. Korean patriarchs didn't think well of foreigners who stood them up. It could seriously hurt their chances as a couple, but I said I'd go there with Jina to explain if it would help. Somehow I thought that wouldn't be necessary though. Jina was good at that sort of thing.

The entrance of the MP commander, Colonel Thornton, signaled that it was time to get back to the case. I escorted him to the colonel's office, announced his arrival, and closed the door after he entered. They'd talk for a few minutes, then he'd want to see the suspects. I expected Amanda's company commander to arrive before they exited the office. Until then, we'd leave the suspects alone and separated. We returned to the lounge and our coffee. It would do them good to stew awhile.

About ten minutes later, the duty agent announced the arrival of Captain Grant. We went to the front office to greet him. He'd brought his soldier's ration control file.

"Captain," I said, hand outstretched, greeting him and introducing Louis and myself as the agents in charge of the case. "We have Specialist Compo and her husband in separate offices. Colonel Thornton from the MPs is here. That's her husband's commander," I added. He nodded.

"I brought the file you wanted," Grant said, handing the relatively thin folder to me. "Now, what can you tell me about the allegations?"

We filled him in, then brought him into my office to see his soldier.

Amanda Compo turned when the door opened and, seeing her commander, stood at attention in front of her chair. He told her to be seated and took a seat on the sofa. The door opened again and Colonel Walsh stuck his head inside. "I need Louis with us when we see her husband," he said, and Louis left to escort them.

Captain Grant opened the ration file on Amanda Compo. He looked at the single sheet of paper in the file, then handed the entire file to me. I opened it to find a copy of the initial application for her ration card and nothing else. I noted this for the report, then turned on the recorder and noted it on tape, too.

Handing the file back to the captain, I repeated what she'd told us thus far. She added nothing to this. The captain took his turn first.

"Where is the request and approval for the exception to policy?" he asked. She was silent for a second, then told him she thought her husband had it. She said that he'd told her of the policy and requested the exception. Suddenly, the ajumah was coming to the house every week to pick up things for the orphanage. I asked her if she'd ever seen the approval. She hadn't.

"Damn it," the captain said almost under his breath. "You've been in the Army long enough to know you should have your backup copy with you. That's standard procedure." He seemed fit to be tied, but at least he wasn't screaming in his rage. The door opened again and Louis asked me to step into the outer office with Captain Grant. We left to see what he needed. The boss and Colonel Thornton were already there when we arrived.

"He didn't have any approval to give anything to any orphanage," the colonel told me.

Colonel Thornton agreed. "There's nothing in his file to even suggest that he requested an exception. I have one of the best damned clerks in the Army, and that file copy would be here if there was one in existence. You guys can keep him here for the night while I decide what to do," he said, then bade farewell to our boss and stormed out into the night. Captain Grant knew he'd also lost an otherwise perfectly good soldier from his unit and looked to the floor, possibly for an answer that wasn't there.

I told him he could take custody of her and keep her in the barracks, but that we'd have to retain her ration card. He understood that, as well as the part I didn't have to say. It wouldn't have been ethical to keep her overnight in the only detention cell with her husband. They could plan a possible escape from their predicament. I told him the house was off limits until we could search it for anything that might be pertinent to the case. I drew up the custody slip and he signed it. Louis went to get her.

"I'll have her in the barracks. She'll be reporting to the charge of quarters every two hours. She'll remain there all day tomorrow if you need to speak with her again."

Amanda Compo was brought out and we let her leave with her commander. The colonel told us to make sure the special agent was secured for the night under the attention of the duty agent. "You can continue tomorrow. Right now I think we all need some rest."

"Right, sir. By the way, I'm giving Agent Linke the day off tomorrow while I work. I'll take Tuesday off, if possible, while he covers. We'll still be available on standby." He OKed it, knowing that we'd put in more hours over the weekend than most people put in during an entire week with overtime. The duty agent spoke up then.

"By the way, Jim, your wife called. The meeting's set for noon tomorrow." I thanked him and saw the colonel waiting for an update.

"It's not about the case sir. This one's a private deal for Louis."

He nodded and smiled, then shut out the lights in his office and went home. I saw the clock nearing midnight and realized how very long the weekend had been. We dropped our radios into the rechargers. I left Louis at the barracks before going home. It would be a short night for me, having to wake up at five for physical training. I groaned at the thought.

Light was just spreading across the eastern sky when I hammered the off button on my alarm clock. Jina was still sleeping, as she had been for a few hours before I got home. I saw that her alarm was set for half past six so she could have breakfast ready by the time I returned. I quietly made a cup of instant coffee in the microwave, then ducked out.

PT's hard enough when you're well rested. When you're dead tired from a working weekend, it's pure murder. But I survived, like always, even turning in the authorization for Louis to be absent from the day's ritual. We didn't need the first sergeant on our case about missing PT, that's for sure.

I went home to shower, with the mixed smells of breakfast waking me up even more than the grueling torture of PT. It was waiting on the table by the time I finished dressing, and I ate heartily. I realized I hadn't eaten anything since breakfast the day before.

"Rough weekend, huh?" Jina asked after I'd washed down the last morsels with coffee. Then she took up a half-joking tone.

"Mihi says that if Louis isn't there to meet her family by quarter to twelve, he can forget about her and go back to Kangnung."

I assured her that I'd given Louis the day off, and that I'd take a lunch break to take him there myself. I asked her to tell the family that the missed appointment was my fault. "Tell them we're on a case. Sometimes the crap hits the fan."

"I know that, honey. Mihi's just not used to it yet. It will take time. It took me years before I finally accepted it," she said.

I kissed her and headed out the door. I was going to have a full day, so I wanted to start early so I could finish up late at night, rather than early in the morning.

I called Captain Grant to let him know that I would release some of Specialist Compo's personal effects and clothes as soon as I could. "Could you have someone drive around there about ten or so? I'll give them what I can release and they can bring it back to her." He agreed to have his supply sergeant there to inventory and bring the articles to her. I told Miss Paek where I'd be, and grabbed my radio. Then I was off to the Compo house to see what I could find.

I heard the sedan pull up at precisely ten o'clock, and looked out the window to see Grant's supply sergeant ringing at the gate. I buzzed him in and let him sit on the sofa that I'd already cleared. A suitcase with some items she might need was sitting open on the coffee table, and he took two inventory sheets out of his pocket.

"Here," I said, handing him two that were already completed, except for his signature. "I saved you some writing. Make sure it's all there."

He thanked me and went over the list, checking it against what was in the case. He closed the bag, signed my receipt and left. The entire process took only a few minutes, and I was back into my work as soon as he closed the gate behind him. Luckily, this house had air conditioning, unlike Rostock's, and it hadn't been closed up for a month. That would make the day and the task of searching it from top to bottom a little more acceptable. I bent to it.

I stopped and locked up the house at about a quarter after eleven. It was time to round up Louis and take him to his appointment, then get something to eat. I was starved again. We arrived to find Mihi dressed very sharply, with her hair tied up. She was simply gorgeous and, when she laid eyes on Louis, her radiant smile added to the sensuous beauty already in evidence.

Jina, who was going to help explain the role of a CID agent and the late nights it would bring (one of which they'd already experienced), was dressed beautifully also, with her hair flowing down her back. They both wore heels. Wow! Louis' eyes echoed the thought.

"Your lunch is on the stove, honey." I kissed her on the cheek to keep from smearing her lipstick, and they all left, high heels clicking a staccato on the concrete alley floor. I listened until they couldn't be heard anymore, then turned my thoughts to the stove where I found my midday fare.

I served it up and sat down, turning on the TV to catch the CNN noon news. That's when AFKN aired it in Korea (it was actually the previous day's evening news). I watched about murders, peace talks and stocks, then sports as I devoured the meal. After that came the local weather forecast from an air force meteorologist in Seoul.

A cool front was moving through western China and would roll over Korea the next day, touching off some severe thunderstorms. A typhoon was wreaking havoc on the tiny island of Guam, but was expected to pass to the north, just east of Japan. The cold front left Korea unscathed. Weighing the thunderstorms as the lesser of the two evils, I concluded that we were pretty lucky this time, even if we got smacked with some bad weather.

I finished up the final morsels of my lunch, flicked off the TV, and put my dishes in the sink, then headed back to the Compo place to continue looking for the evidence I needed, but secretly hoping I wouldn't find in their home.

Within the next hour I concluded that there was nothing of particular interest in the bedroom, I cleared the kitchen as well, and headed for the den.

The room was lined with three collapsible closets against one wall. Another wall was covered with family photographs. The wall with the door I just entered through had a large desk set against it. The final wall was bare, save for a frosted glass window that opened to the outside. The desk was locked, so I started with the closets.

One was filled with the agent's battle dress uniforms and suits for work. They were all clean and neatly pressed, some still in plastic bags from the laundry. The second was filled with his wife's uniforms and a few dresses, blouses and skirts. There didn't seem to be anything unusual in either closet. I undid the zipper on the third. As the cloth door fell away to reveal the inside, I noticed a few winter coats and jackets that belonged to the couple. On the floor of the closet were several small cardboard boxes. I took them out and laid them on the top of the desk, side by side.

The first contained several ration control receipts. Only a few were for high-value items; the rest were for smaller dollar limits. I separated them into the two categories, singling out those that noted cigarettes, alcohol and rice, and organized them by months.

They used their monthly allowance of ten cartons of cigarettes on a regular basis. If they didn't buy ten, it was nine or eight. The alcohol ration was used up every month. According to the receipts, they'd bought at least one bottle of the expensive Chivas every other month. I toured the house. There wasn't even an ashtray, let alone ashes and butts. Nor were there any cigarettes, despite a receipt showing they'd bought four cartons within the past few days. I noted this and placed the receipts in a bag, then in my pocket.

During that same search, I noticed there was no beer or any other kind of alcohol in that house. I knew the final destination for the Budweiser and Chivas they'd bought the day before, but there was no sign of remainder of their purchases for the past week. I made note of this, too, and those receipts also became evidence.

I returned to the den to get the receipts for the high-value items, taking them around with me as I attempted to locate everything in the house. Those items were all there. I went to the second box, which contained some important family papers, to include their pay vouchers, insurance forms and the like. At the bottom of the pile, though, were bills of sale showing they'd purchased items for more than fifty dollars from other service members. I checked around the house for those items and found none. I made notes regarding that and placed those forms in my pocket to keep the others warm. I'd have to start using another pocket soon.

Returning to the den, I opened the third box. Inside lay some old military ranks insignia, the pin-on type, and a few other odds and ends. There were also two silver rings and a gold class ring from a Palmer High School, with the initials E. A. C. engraved inside. I suspected the class ring belonged to the MPI agent and returned it to the box. There was nothing else. I closed all three boxes and placed them back on the floor, zipping all three closets closed. They were cleared now.

I turned my attention to the desk and tried to think of where Compo might have hidden the key. Nothing was taped to the underside of the desk, nor to the sides, so I pulled it away from the wall and checked behind. Nothing. I remembered a key holder near the front door of the house and went there to look. It held copies of the front door and gate keys and a set of car keys. One lone key stared at me from the end hook. It was a small and silver one that would normally be associated with office furniture, so I palmed it and took it to the den to give it a try. Voila! The top drawer slid open.

Several notebooks were inside. Some were filled with investigative notes, another had a list of phone numbers and names. The book that caught my eye, though, was s small blue one. Inside was a nude photo of Miss Lee, our Kangnung stripper. That photo didn't do her justice. But the notes found in the book intrigued me.

The handwritten listing of names and numbers didn't seem to be Compo's writing. But the numbers weren't phone numbers. These looked like ration card numbers, with the telltale "20s" and "30s" at the front of each. Those same numbers appeared later in the book with different names after some of them.

I had a feeling that the first list matched the false names on the cards, while the second listing contained names of real people who had used the cards at one time or another. I would have bet anything that the book had belonged to Rostock, and Compo had "liberated" it from his house before the case was handed over to CID. I made notes about the books and stuffed them into my pocket. That drawer was empty now and I slid it closed, then reached for the second one.

That drawer was filled with coupons, rubber bands, pens, pencils and the like. Nothing much of interest here. I closed it and moved to the bottom and final drawer.

It was stuck and I had to find a screwdriver to pry it loose. I noted this for the damage report I'd have to file, then opened the drawer the rest of the way. Lying alone in a plastic Ziplock bag was an Army .45 caliber pistol, the type used by the military police and officers — not by special investigators. We all used the .38 revolver, though we'll change to the 9mm after Pentagon approval. I pulled out my handkerchief and used it to lift the bag out of the drawer, so as not to smudge any possible fingerprints. Then I placed it in a larger evidence bag. This wasn't going into my pocket.

The weapon was the type used to kill Rostock. It was also the same type found missing from an arms room. Could they be one and the same?

I radioed the duty agent and asked him to send over the team that was investigating the missing weapon. He returned my call a few minutes later to report that they were on their way. I continued with my search of the den, removing pictures from the wall and searching their backs. Then I went outside to the heater room to check around the furnace. I hadn't gotten too far before the gate bell rang, announcing the other team's arrival. I went around front to let them in.

"Something here I'd like you to see," I said as we went inside. I'd worked together with both agents on various cases in the past. The team leader, Bill Fuller, and I graduated from training together. His partner, Mike Quinn, was a relative "newbie," having graduated only about three years ago. Taegu was his second assignment since joining the Army, whereas Bill and I had bounced around quite a bit in the past few years. Nothing against Mike, mind you, because he's a very promising young agent. He and Bill will make an excellent team, just as Louis and I do.

"This yours?" Bill asked, indicating the double-bagged weapon. I signaled for him to go ahead and inspect it. As he turned it over to read the serial number, Mike lifted his notebook from his inside jacket pocket. He read along as Bill called out the numbers from the firearm's side, then called out that it was a match.

I asked them to also run it through ballistics to see if it might be the same weapon that killed the ration control clerk. They agreed and took off as I returned to the heater room.

The initial survey showed that along with the heater pump and fuel tank, there were two inexpensive footlockers, several cardboard boxes, two bikes, a half-finished bag of charcoal and some lighter fluid. I started with the cardboard boxes, which had "COMPO" stenciled on the sides. The first few were empty, except for some smaller boxes inside. I'd guessed they were packing boxes, used for the next military move. Most soldiers move at least six times during a twenty-year career. The two larger boxes on the bottom were heavier, so I opened them where they were.

The first was filled with wrapped Korean Celadon pottery, which was stuffed with crumpled newspapers. I estimated the value of the box's contents to be about three to four thousand dollars. But it' wasn't unusual for a soldier to collect items of this nature during an overseas tour. Celadon was a nice gift, with its artistic design, greenish color and outer glaze, looking as if it was cracked in thousands of places. The finish was smooth, and all the designs were hand painted. The underside usually carried the hand-painted Chinese character depicting the artist's name. A search through each piece netted only the crumpled filling paper stuffed inside, so I spent the next couple of hours restuffing and wrapping the pottery, and replaced it inside the box.

I checked my watch and found it was well after six o'clock, so I locked the heater room door and returned to lock up the house, as well. I made sure all the keys were removed from the house and locked the gate on my way out. By the time I'd written up my daily report and secured the evidence I'd gathered, it was nine o'clock and nearly pitch black outside. I headed for home and some rest. It had been a long day and my bones felt every minute of it. I secretly thanked God that there was no PT in the morning, even though I'd probably have to give up my planned vacation day to finish searching the Compo house.

Jina and Mihi were sitting on the sofa when I opened the door. They had both changed to cut-offs and halter-tops. Mihi was talking at least a mile a minute and Jina could hardly get a word in edgewise. They both seemed to be having a lot of fun. Jina jumped up to greet me, planting a big kiss on my lips. Mihi giggled.

"Louis made it," she said when she finally stopped giggling long enough to talk. "My family gave approval to marry him." Jina nodded, then started telling me the intricate details of the meeting while she and Mihi warmed dinner up. Mihi interjected some details along the way. They were a well-oiled talking machine, going non-stop for the next thirty minutes. I ate my meal as soon as it was served, wolfing down every morsel. They finished capping off the day's interview about the same time I finished sopping up the sauces. When they looked at me for approval or something, I issued the appropriate congratulations, then asked if Louis had already gone home. I couldn't make it sound as though I was excited for them, even though I was. I was simply bushed.

"Oh, yes," Jina said. "He was very tired." I knew he would be, so I left it at that and excused myself to hit the sack. Mihi had gone by the time I came out of the bathroom, and Jina was washing dishes. I put my tired arms around her waist from behind and kissed her on the cheek, holding her very tightly. She turned around in my arms and kissed me back, slipping her wet hands around the back of my neck.

We embraced for a few minutes. Then she returned to her task, while I reached for the phone to let Louis know I'd meet him at the office in the morning. I also congratulated him on passing his "test," and jokingly asked when the big day would be. He mentioned what the girls had already told me — the big party Friday night. I told him we had already promised Mihi we'd be there, then broke the connection. It was time to get some sleep.

I was up and running shortly after the sun came up, brewing coffee and toasting Eggo waffles for breakfast. I didn't want to wake Jina because the day before had been a pretty big day for her. I spread some peanut butter on the Eggos and flicked on the news while I ate. Nothing new. Even the sports and weather were drab. Much of the same old stuff. The same crimes were being committed, the same teams were losing and the same humid weather was smothering the peninsula. I would have been happier if that nasty weather would take away some of the humidity. I turned off the set, put my dishes in the sink and dressed. I was out of the house by a quarter after seven. I could be at the office half an hour early if traffic didn't hold me up. Time enough to get rid of some paperwork before we briefed the colonel and went back to the Compo house.

Louis was already in when I got there, and he had taken charge of the paperwork that had been left on our desks. By the looks of things, he'd been there nearly an hour already. I poured each of us a cup of coffee and split the remainder of the work with Louis so we could cut through it quicker. I sat down and punched my brain into working mode and we had all of the paperwork squared away before eight. We retired to the lounge so I could fill him in on the previous day without being interrupted. His eyes bugged out when I mentioned the .45.

"What do you think the chances are that it's the one we're looking for?" he asked.

"Don't know. Guess we'll have to wait until it comes back from ballistics." The colonel walked in as we talked and sat down. I briefed him and told him that the weapon brought in by the other team the day before needed to go to Hawaii.

"I'll send Bill and Mike over with it today," he said. "I don't want anything to happen to that firearm."

He asked if we were done at the house, and I told him that we'd probably be out of there by late morning or early afternoon.

"Good. They're being released today and I want to be able to get them back into their home. But I don't want you to overlook anything." He got up and left the lounge, heading for his office to get that weapon off to the ballistics lab in Hawaii. Louis and I planned the remainder of the search while we were in the car. Louis would give the house a once over while I finished up in the heater room.

Chapter Eight

The front gate was ajar when we got there. We drew our weapons and radioed in for Korean Police assistance. We were advised that it would be there in a few minutes. When they arrived we all went in low, Louis and I first since the Korean police are rarely armed.

Someone had been there, but they were gone now. The only visible evidence of the visit were the unlocked doors and a missing box from the heater room — the one I hadn't checked out yet. I asked the Korean policemen to check around the neighborhood for information and radioed in to the office. I'd just finished briefing the colonel when the local officers returned from their queries in the surrounding area.

"A green car was here about six o'clock this morning. They saw a black man take a large box from the house and put it in the car. He drove away. They say he looked like he was in a big hurry, but after he turned the corner, they don't know where he went."

I asked them for a better description of the suspect and the car, and they took off again. The description we had was radioed in for an all points bulletin, but there wasn't much hope in finding him with such thin information. Louis and I began our search of the remaining items throughout the house.

We finished about noon and found nothing else missing. I went over the house once again after Louis, just to double and triple check. All else was intact. We locked up and returned to the office, requesting that the Korean police keep one man outside at all times. The report on the missing box would take about an hour, and it had to be completed before the Compos were released.

I had Miss Paek call the Korean police substation every hour for updates on our early morning raider. They still had very little to give us by five in the afternoon. The same with the Military Police. Their registration clerk was going through all the files for the Taegu area, and he'd called his counterparts in Seoul, Pyongtaek, Pusan, Kwangju, Kunsan and Osan. They assured us they'd let us know.

Louis and I decided to head for the Hilltop Club for a beer before going home, so we finished our reports, and headed up the hill. I telephoned Jina to tell her where we were, and she said she'd gather Mihi and meet us there. We decided it would be a good opportunity to celebrate Louis' latest fortune.

In direct contrast to the daytime events, the evening went pretty well. The girls were happy because they didn't have to cook and clean. They also had a little time with their men during the early evening hours. Jina warned Mihi that this was a rare case when married to a CID agent, and that she should take advantage of them whenever they came along.

A Filipino band was playing that night, so we even got in some dancing. That helped us clear work from our minds for a bit so that we could tackle it with a clear start later. Mihi found a couple of quarters in her purse, put them into a video poker machine, and pulled out a royal flush, giving her a whopping profit on the evening. She cashed in and we went home to have a small quiet party before getting some sleep. What a great way to cap off a bad day!

There was a message from the Military Police when we got in the next morning. The car we were seeking belonged to a Major Dwight Moss from a unit in Seoul.

Seoul? Then why was he removing a box from the house of a suspect here? The message went on to say that Moss was on leave and they weren't able to contact him yet. They had a bulletin out over the entire peninsula, though, to bring him in for questioning. They also contacted units that operated gasoline stations along the expressway. GIs rarely paid the exorbitant Korean gasoline prices. It seemed like all the bases were covered there.

A second message simply stated that Miss Lee would be in Taegu today and would call. Another from the duty agent said that agents Fuller and Quinn had arrived in Hawaii, and were on their way directly to the ballistics lab. Good. That would answer another question for us.

With no more messages, Louis and I got down to sorting out the paperwork. The batch on my desk contained the report about the now discovered missing weapon. Bill was cool about putting in a good word for me whenever he could. Especially when I inadvertently cracked a case for him. I did the same when the tables were turned.

The colonel briefed us after his arrival from a staff meeting, and we informed him what we were up against. He told us to keep plugging away, then retracted it almost immediately.

"Today might be a good time for you to take off, Jim. You've been at it straight since you returned. Take a break and let Louis cover the office for you for the day. It won't help matters any if you get worn out and miss something critical." I agreed and started making arrangements to skip out for a while. I'd keep the radio in case Louis got something that deserved my immediate attention, even though he protested.

"You need the day off, Jim, not a day on call," he said, as he scarfed a pile of paperwork out of my hands. The reports the company had been asking for during the week would probably now get done.

Louis finally kicked me out the door, and I realized I had nowhere to go, except home. Maybe some quality time with the little lady, I thought, as I hopped into the car. It was too bad the colonel hadn't mentioned this yesterday so that I could have slept in and missed PT. Miss PT, maybe, but sleep in? Fat chance! I'd been in the Army too long. Unless I'd been out all night, I couldn't sleep much past sunrise.

Jina was up and cleaning when I arrived. It surprised her to see me that early in the day. Her face immediately adopted that concerned look.

"Relax, sweetheart. Just a day off," I explained, as I took off my shoes and jacket. She was so happy that she jumped up, hugging and kissing me until we were both out of breath. We didn't waste any time. Holding hands and kissing the entire way, we migrated as one into the bedroom. About noon we transferred our passion into the shower. We were squeaky clean when we finished. She put on an apron (and nothing else) and marched in to the kitchen to fix us something to eat. I plopped down on the sofa, exhausted, to take a nap.

Lunch was on the table when I awoke, and Jina was on my lap, ready for another inning. Lunch went cold. Our hearts were into something a little more important at the time.

The doorbell rang as she was cleaning up the dishes, probably announcing the arrival of either Louis or Mihi. I picked up the intercom, listened, and asked Mihi to wait for a moment as we dressed. A couple of minutes later, it became a girl-talk afternoon.

They were just getting settled into a conversation about Louis when the phone rang. I picked it up and it was Miss Lee. The minute I said her name, a hush fell over the living room.

"Yes," I said. "Everything's fine. No, we haven't solved the case, yet. Yes, Louis is getting married. I'll pass your congratulations on to him. Just a moment." I cupped my hand over the phone as I spoke. "She'd like to talk to you, Mihi," I said, and handed her the phone. She didn't want to take it at first, but I insisted, so she put it to her face.

"Yoboseyo...Neh...Kam saham nida...Yeh..." The conversation went on for a few more minutes, then Mihi cupped her hand over the phone and spoke to my wife excitedly for a moment. Jina looked at me, then answered her. Mihi turned to the phone again and spoke rapid-fire into the mouthpiece.

"She'll be coming here for dinner, if that's OK," Jina said to me. It was really more of a statement than a question, since Mihi was already giving her directions. I didn't mind, though. It would give the girls a chance to meet her face-to-face, and possibly clear up any hidden doubts they may have had about our honor on the road.

When Mihi hung up, I grabbed the phone and dialed, explaining that Louis shouldn't be left out of this little get-together. Both ladies giggled and continued with their conversation, ignoring my phone call. I made arrangements to pick him up in half an hour. That would be close enough to the end of the business day for him to brief me on any new developments, and leave for the day.

The evening wouldn't be business, but rather a purely social event that would test our mettle against the worst our women could come up with. I left to get some things at the shoppette for the party and to pick up Louis, letting Jina know we'd be back in about an hour and a half.

The MPs hadn't found Major Moss or his car, yet. The Korean police hadn't come up with anything new about the burglary at the Compo's house. The Compos promptly filed a complaint that a valuable box had been stolen from their house while it was "sealed off" by CID, but they said they couldn't describe the contents as anything but "family heirlooms." The boys were held over in Hawaii for another day or two because a typhoon had closed the airport.

Louis and Miss Paek ordered up listings of all calls made from the phones of the suspects so far to see if there any more leads could be followed up. They'd be ready for Miss Paek to pick up on her way home tonight. Korean customs called to tell us that Mr. Park had finally confessed to illegal dealings in the black market, but denied any implication in the murder.

Other than that, the day had been pretty quiet, and Louis finished all the reports that we'd been ignoring for the past week. There'd be a new batch the next day. Sometimes it seemed like the Army thrived on reports, I thought. I turned to Miss Paek as we were leaving.

"See if you can get a listing of calls made from Moss' phone in Seoul. The address is on yesterday's blotter report from the MPs. She said she'd handle it, as we knew she would, and we headed out the door for our date with destiny.

All three women were there when we unloaded the sodas and beer from the car. They already seemed like old friends. Miss Lee was dressed much more conservatively this time. Personally, I was happy that she was dressed — period. They helped us get the groceries into the house, and Miss Lee offered her congratulations to Louis, topped off with a handshake and a peck on the cheek. He looked relieved about the handshake and the peck, considering our final show in Kyungpo.

The ladies rushed off to the kitchen to prepare dinner, while Louis and I watched AFKN for a while. I didn't care what they said. That old adage about too many cooks in the kitchen spoiling the stew just didn't apply to Korean households.

The table was finally set with a myriad of Oriental delights that watered the mouth, topped off with wine for all. It looked more like a holiday meal than a get-together of women wanting to playfully string their men up. The talk in the kitchen during the preparations was as non-stop as a flight from Anchorage to Seoul, with all three talking at once on occasion. I wondered how they could hear the questions and answer them when their own mouths, and someone else's, to boot, were going. Uncanny, these Korean women.

But the constant gab ceased when we were seated at the feast. Jina was on my right, followed by Louis, Mihi and, on my left, Miss Lee. I could tell by the seating arrangement that Mihi hadn't wanted Miss Lee to sit too close to her beau. Jina probably didn't care to have her sitting next to me either, but it was better than having her sit between us, I supposed. And since my loving, trusting wife was seated directly on the other side, a quick jab with the chopsticks would quell any possible hanky panky.

After dinner, Louis and I found out that Miss Lee had already told our women what happened in Kyungpo. "She says you were both real gentlemen," Mihi said with a smile. I wasn't sure, but I thought she was trying to elicit a response from one of us, preferably Louis. It didn't work. Jina chimed in.

"How was her show?" The question — and her eyes — were aimed directly at me. I had to choose my words carefully. If I didn't praise Miss Lee enough, I stood the chance of insulting her. This could have brought a wrath on me that was often seen by many people in Korea. On the other hand, if I praised her too much, that wrath could have been fired at me from the home front, which was a lot less desirable. I also had to choose my words quickly, for delay would give the impression that I was hiding something, and I would surely pay for that as well.

"It was a very good show. It was quite artsy," I chickened out. Louis chuckled until his eyes met Mihi's steady glare. Then he cleared his throat and looked down onto his empty plate. There was a slight twinkle in Jina's eyes, which gave her away. She was toying with me and she wanted me to know it. I reached under the table and squeezed her hand playfully. She smiled and squeezed back.

"What about you, Louis?" I asked, not wanting to be the only one under the gun. "What did you think of her show?" All eyes focused on him. Jina was trying hard not to laugh as he squirmed in his seat. Miss Lee was waiting for her compliment, and Mihi was pretending to see red. I noticed a touch of a smile on her lips, though, that gave her away. The women were playing with both of us in a concerted effort. This was just a little game with them — unless we really messed it up. It could get very ugly, indeed, with just the utterance of one wrong word or one wrong action, however small. I hoped Louis was up to this.

He took a second to compose his thoughts, then answered very nonchalantly. "Like we discussed right after the show, Jim. It brought a flavor of old tradition to the modern strip show. Very tastefully done." Mihi blew up.

"I don't care about her show. What did you think of her body with no clothes on, dancing right in front of your face?" The remark caught Louis off guard until Jina and Miss Lee started laughing. Mihi chimed in, laughing the hardest and holding her stomach. I thought she'd laugh herself out of her chair and onto the floor. Louis and I started laughing, too, enjoying the joke. We all settled down to friendly conversation after that. When the talk nearly died down, Miss Lee turned to me, finally approaching the subject that caused the visit in the first place.

"A man came to visit me at the club Sunday night. He was a big black man. He asked if I knew that Timmie was dead. When I told him I knew, he asked if I knew who was investigating. I told him you were. I hope I didn't do anything wrong. I thought about it all day Monday, then decided I'd better tell you about it."

"What else did he say?" Louis asked, all ears.

"He said he would come here and talk with you. That's what got me worried. You two are pretty good guys for being CID, and I didn't want anything to happen to you because of me."

"Do you know his name?" I asked.

"He wouldn't tell me, but I saw his car when he drove away. He was in an old green car. I remembered because I wondered how that car got through the mountains. It looked too old to be driven more than a few kilometers at one time."

I looked at Louis and he looked back at me. The theft at Compo's house was no mere coincidence. That was Major Moss and he'd planned to remove something before we could see it. That was definitely part of the case, and I didn't like the smell of it. He'd apparently stayed Sunday night in the Kangnung area, then drove all the way to Taegu on Monday. He would've been able to see me at Compo's house that evening, so he had waited until early morning to do his deed and leave. He was probably back in Seoul, laying low for a few days until he could get the box and its contents stashed. I got up and called the colonel at home. He answered on the second ring.

"Stewart here, sir. I just got some news on this Major Moss. I think he planned the heist and everything. I'll bet he's in Seoul trying to get rid of it before we can get to him. That box has probably got something in it that could break this case wide open."

Walsh was all ears and promised to call Seoul right away and have the search for Moss stepped up. I thanked him and hung up. The house was silent for a minute, as we all thought of the implications that little tidbit of information had brought about. Mihi and Jina had developed a new sense of respect for this stripper. So had Louis and I.

We finished the evening with small talk. Mihi invited Miss Lee to spend the night at her house, and Jina told Louis he could sleep in our den. We drove Miss Lee to her motel room for her bags. They returned her the room rent money, too, something unusual in Taegu. We drove to Mihi's house and promised to meet for lunch at the 19th Hole. Jina would sign them onto the post and escort them in, which was standard practice. The only thing Louis and I had to do was break away from whatever we were working on at half past eleven and meet them. We went back home and Jina set up a Korean mattress for Louis. The house was sound asleep before eleven.

Dawn woke both Louis and me at the same time. I let him use the bathroom first, while I made the coffee. I ducked in for a quick rinse when he was finished. We were ready to go by seven and headed out the door for the dining facility. A healthy western omelet would perk us up enough to get through the morning.

We got to the office just minutes before the colonel walked in. He told us that the folks in Seoul had begun escalating their search for Major Moss, and that they'd enlisted the aid of the local Korean CID, the Korean National Police, and even the Seoul Secret Police. It was turning into a regular manhunt. The colonel poured himself some coffee, asking us if we had anything new. Louis spoke up immediately, catching both of us off guard.

"I need your permission to get married sir," he blurted out. The boss just smiled.

"I've been wondering when you were going to ask me. You've been running around here with your head in the clouds since Tuesday. Well, let's get started while we're in a lull. C'mon into my office."

They went in and closed the door for the mandatory commander's counseling session. Louis was about to embark on the longest and most difficult singular trek in his life. Unlike marriage in the States, and in addition to what I've already explained about my marriage paperwork routine, a soldier overseas, no matter what the age or rank, must get permission from the commander, and Eighth U.S. Army.

The initial batch of paperwork is at least an inch thick. The secondary batch is another inch and a half. The background checks are accompanied by repeated requests and approvals for marriage, letters of counseling (two from each level), fingerprint sheets, eight copies of a very recent passport photo, and verifications of all types of information. The entire process takes about six months in most cases.

It could be expedited to one month for soldiers who knew how to do it, who to see and what to say. Most young soldiers didn't, though. The process was designed to make them think about how badly they really wanted the marriage — or to see if they were just horny.

No matter how you slice it, an international marriage, as the Army liked to call it, is no piece of cake. There are cultural, language and custom differences to overcome, some which take more than a few years. Once the new bride arrives in the States, however, the real fun begins. Because there's so much depression and homesickness, it gets difficult to fight for a good marriage. A soldier has to stay on his toes to work his assignment, while keeping his wife from feeling isolated in a country she knows little about. Experts claim that a full 60 percent of international marriages ultimately end in failure. Someone marrying outside America deserves a hearty round of applause for success, and needs a great deal of support from everyone. It's a rough road, and a helping hand is definitely appreciated.

Right now, Louis was getting the fatherly advice our colonel liked to hand out before the paperwork even started. He knew the stats well, and he'd put the necessary scare into my partner. He'd give his approval in the long run, though, because he also knew there were no barriers for love. And if this work lull kept up, I'd take Louis downtown to one of the emigration offices and get his paperwork started.

Miss Paek came in about fifteen minutes later with the phone listings we'd requested on our Taegu-area suspects. I was just starting to go over Compo's calls when Louis came out of the colonel's office. He took some of the stack and sat down to review it. We came up with some similarities during the next two hours, but still didn't have much to go on. None of the people called each other, but most called Rostock. One number came up frequently and recently from Compo's phone. It was the Seoul number for Major Dwight Moss. But no calls were made there within the past four days. Something hit me then.

Moss had been to Kangnung to see Miss Lee. She claimed not to know him. How did he know who she was and where she'd be? How did he know about her connection in the case? I passed this by Louis, and he agreed that there were more questions we had to pose to her.

We also had a list of questions to ask the major if they could round him up. But Seoul was a big city with more than ten million people. If he decided to desert, he could hide there for years before anyone found him. We had to hope someone would report seeing him or that he'd report back to his unit once his leave was up.

It was nearing half past eleven, so we packed up the lists and got ready for our luncheon date, informing the colonel where we'd be. I made sure to mention that it had turned out to be a semi-working lunch; that more questions had surfaced for our Miss Lee. He told us to take all the time we needed, and that he'd radio us if he had anything.

By the time we arrived at the 19th Hole, the girls were walking across the recreation center parking lot. I guessed they'd been shopping in the ville, or they would have come through the back gate and taken the bus. Instead, they'd come through the front gate, close to where we'd apprehended Mr. Park and Mrs. Stenberg. They were laughing and carrying on as they approached. We waited for them outside the door.

We decided to wait until after lunch before we started questioning, so as not to spoil the jovial atmosphere. The waitress brought our soft drinks within minutes and took our orders. Small talk floated across the table from various directions as we waited, but my partner and I only thought about the questions we'd ask and what answers they'd bring.

Other diners started arriving, filling the club before noon. Our lunch was delivered just as the last chair was filled. We bent to the delightful task of consuming our orders. We quietly sipped our coffee as the empty plates were carried off. When the waitress left, Louis began the not-so-delightful task of quietly questioning Miss Lee.

"Last night you told us you didn't know the black man who visited you in Kangnung. But how did he know you and the fact that you were all the way over in Kangnung?"

"I don't know," she answered thoughtfully. "Maybe he knows me from Timmie, or something."

"But that would mean he had to know you'd left Taegu," I stated. "Rostock couldn't have told him, because you said he was already dead when you left."

"That's right. I really don't know how, unless he knew about me from before, and knew that I have relatives in Kangnung. It wasn't too hard for you and Louis to find me."

I glanced at Louis. If this was all true, this elusive major was shrewd and involved in this thing big time. For him to have gone to all the trouble of locating and visiting her, and then drive to Taegu, there must have been something in that box that would incriminate him as well as the Compos. Either that or the Compos were involved, and their portion of the proceeds was stashed in that box that I'd waited too long to search.

We showed Miss Lee photos of the Compos, the Dobbses and Mrs. Stenberg, asking if she knew any of the people. She knew Mrs. Stenberg and Mrs. Dobbs in passing, she said, but denied ever seeing the other people. I asked her to think again real hard to see if she remembered anything about seeing Major

Moss at any time with her boyfriend. She claimed she wasn't aware, but volunteered to let us know if anything came to mind.

We decided to drop it at that, and changed the subject to the typhoon in Hawaii, which seemed to dominate the AFKN news. We turned to watch the big screen TV at the end of the dining room. The other guests had their eyes riveted to the scenes of death and destruction flashing across the screen as well. The big storm had crossed the islands, leaving many dead and millions of dollars in damage in its wake. The announcer stated that the airport would be reopening shortly, and that stranded tourists would soon be able to leave the islands.

That was good news. Hopefully Bill and Mike would be among the first to leave, and would return with some valuable evidence. We turned our attention back to our table after the report was finished, engaging in small talk again to lighten the mood.

"We're going shopping for a while," Jina announced as we prepared to leave. They said they were going to the Taegu Department Store downtown, then through the gigantic outside markets in the area. I pulled out my wallet to pay the lunch tab and handed her fifty dollars. Louis took my lead and handed another fifty to Mihi. With a joking smile, Miss Lee held her hand out. Louis and I looked at each other, then each laid a twenty in her palm.

She was shocked to actually get the money and tried to refuse it, but Mihi and Jina told her to take it. She placed it in her blazer pocket, bowed her head to the top of the table, and said thank you in Korean. We gave them a ride to the gate, where they signed out and caught a taxi. Louis and I headed back to the office and, hopefully, some new leads. We were getting nowhere fast in this case, and we needed more information to work on soon.

Miss Paek announced that the phone list from Moss' house had come over the fax. We reviewed it, finding some interesting facts.

Rather than a central circle being drawn from only Rostock's phone, a second had appeared around Moss'. Many of the same people were called frequently, along with many calls to Rostock's house. Rostock, however, never called Moss. That's why we hadn't gotten a lead on him prior to the break-in. In diagram form, we could draw a circle representing Rostock on one end of the piece of paper, and another on the other end to represent Moss. Lines drawn to various dots representing the other players could be drawn from both circles. Most of the calls were one way, going from the two major players to the others. Likewise, calls from Moss to Rostock were also one way on nearly a weekly basis.

We figured that was probably how Moss came to know of Miss Lee's existence, though we still wondered how he knew her by sight. Or had he just asked about her in the Kangnung area? I doubted that, since we weren't talking about a GI ville. The Koreans would be protective about women in such a city such as that, especially when a strange foreigner asked. We still had to go on the assumption that they'd met at least once, whether she knew it or not — or whether she admitted it or not. It only seemed natural. Moss would not only know where Rostock lived, but possibly the others as well. He had surely known where Compo lived, because he'd proven that recently.

That left only a few questions as far as Moss was concerned. How did he know we were searching the Compo house, and how did he know what to take away? Both of the Compos were under wraps from the time we took them in until Moss was near, or already in, the Kangnung area. Unless Mrs. Compo knew where to call him in Kangnung, she couldn't have made the call to alert him. Agent Compo was in our detention cell all night, so it couldn't have been him. No one outside the office knew we were going to raid the Compo house. Hell, we weren't even sure of it ourselves until moments before it happened. The only possibility left to consider was that he had already made arrangements to have the box picked up, and the rest was just a coincidence of timing. I usually didn't buy coincidences, but that seemed to be the only solution now.

The final question about Moss was whether or not he killed Rostock. If so, how did Compo get the weapon? Each question led to more questions, rather than answers. Would it ever end?

The colonel summoned us into his office as we were butting our heads against this clue that wasn't a clue, but was. After we were inside with the door closed behind us, the colonel explained that Moss had been picked up.

"It was a lead picked up at Camp Humphreys," he announced. "A new man in billeting there noted something suspicious about someone who was staying in one of the rooms. He accidentally poked a hole in a large box with his broom while he was cleaning the room.

"Moss nearly went berserk, even though the cleaner apologized. When he looked down to inspect the damage he'd caused, he caught a glimpse of American and Korean money through the hole before Moss pushed him out of the room, screaming at him.

"Thinking this all was strange, the cleaning man reported the incident to Mr. Cho, the billeting honcho up there, also in an effort to save his new job. Mr. Cho thought it was strange for someone to carry money in a box, as well, and called the MPs. They apprehended Moss as he was trying to stuff the box into his car. Mr. Cho says you have your father-in-law to thank, Jim."

I was shocked. I'd nearly forgotten he worked there now, especially since I'd been so intent on the case. But now my father-in-law's little accident paid off for us. We left the colonel's office and prepared a request to assume custody of Moss. The approval, signed by Lieutenant Milhans himself, came back almost as fast as it was faxed to Camp Humphreys. We cleared the way for travel and made plans to drive there in the morning to pick up Moss and the elusive box, and bring them back to Taegu. Maybe this was the break we needed.

We considered questioning the Compos about the missing box and their affiliation with Moss, but decided against it until we talked with Moss first. Because of their complaint about the missing box, it would probably look as though we were trying to discredit their claim. We knew the box had been stolen, but Agent Compo was accusing us of stealing it. Even though we were in the right, it would have looked like we were wrong and were trying to hamper our own investigation to achieve some personal end.

It was close to three thirty, and we had nothing left to accomplish during the afternoon, so we went to get some rest before the trek to Humphreys and back. It would be a long day on the highway.

Jina and Miss Lee were wearing the same style of dress when they returned that evening. "We all bought the same thing," Jina exclaimed, twirling about the living room. Miss Lee followed her example, both of them laughing away. "Mihi bought one, too," she added, as she sat down.

Miss Lee went to use the bathroom, and I told Jina about her father and our trip to Camp Humphreys the following day to pick up Moss. She wanted to go along, until I explained that we were using a government sedan and we couldn't take her. She understood that civilians, to include family, couldn't ride in official vehicles. She pretended to be sad at first, then a smile spread across her face. "I'll take the train. I'll see you up there before you come back, then spend a couple of days with my family."

I agreed, but asked not to have Mihi play housekeeper while she was away. She wanted to know why, so I told her that, since Mihi was now engaged, I didn't think it was proper for us to be in the same house together — alone — no matter how innocent. She agreed, and set about contracting for another lady, who I secretly prayed wasn't as young and beautiful.

Miss Lee vacated the bathroom and the girls plotted for her to spend the night on Louis' customary mattress in the den. I figured that was OK, as long as it was their idea. I was going to be out of the house early, anyway, so the thought of a cramped bathroom schedule didn't even enter the plan. I excused myself to get some sleep.

The women stayed up all night talking. They were still at it when I awoke. They'd changed from their identical dresses to two of my long dress shirts, with no bras. I could tell by the twin peaks trying to push their way through the fabric covering each of the ladies. It was a sight to see so early in the morning.

I walked past them to pour a cup of coffee that Jina had already made. I was making my way to the bathroom, sipping my coffee, when Miss Lee rose to her feet. When her legs and back straightened, the shirt rose and revealed that she wasn't wearing panties either. Was I ever glad that I was going to the john, because I don't think I could have explained my condition to my wife right then. She'd dressed in a light blue blouse with knee-length shorts by the time I returned. I was happy to see that she was also wearing a bra. She'd taken over the kitchen duties while Jina was dressing. I'd be driving them both to Dong Taegu train station before going to pick up the sedan and my partner, which meant I'd have to leave an hour early. Jina would meet me at Humphreys, while Miss Lee would continue on to Seoul, then catch her train to the eastern coast in time for the Friday night crowd at the club.

We were on the road by half past six, and I was able to pick Louis up about an hour later, allowing us to miss the brunt of Taegu's rush hour traffic. We were already climbing onto the expressway about the same time the city streets were starting to jam up.

I drove to the Kumgang service area, where we took a twenty-minute coffee break. Louis drove the rest of the way to Humphreys. Traffic was pretty light, considering it was a Friday morning, and we made pretty good time, getting to the MP station located just inside the walk-through gate at a little after ten.

After the necessary release forms were drawn up, we told the MP commander we'd be back after lunch to pick up our traveling companion. He informed us that the box and the suspect would be ready when we were. We headed for the CID field office to check in, then to billeting to thank my father-in-law. He was the real hero.

Mr. Cho asked Dad to come to the office, then translated for us. Dad was still a little shaken up about the incident, and he probably thought we were there to arrest him. Mr. Cho helped settle that point, and we took Dad to the snack bar for lunch. We headed back to the MP station at about twelve thirty, when Jina was supposed to meet me at the gate. She was waiting when we parked the car in front of the station, and I walked over to meet her. She was pleased that I'd taken Dad to lunch to thank him for his help.

"I will be home by Wednesday," she said, as we kissed goodbye. She walked out the gate and I retraced my footsteps across the street where Louis was waiting patiently. We strode in together.

The inventoried release for the box was the most interesting one I'd ever read. A mixture of Korean and American money totaled better than twenty-three thousand dollars. Some was stuffed into porcelain vases and the like, while most was banded in stacks of a thousand dollars each. There was also a box of .45 caliber ammunition and a fully loaded clip. Children's toys filled the remainder of the box.

I could see why Moss wanted the box, but there didn't seem to be anything that would incriminate anyone except the person who had the box in their possession. And even that had to be proven, because the money could have been totally legitimate, though I seriously doubted that. I identified the box as the one I'd seen at the Compo residence because their name was written on the outside with a china marker, like the others in the heater room.

We loaded it into the trunk, then went back inside to collect Moss. He was expectedly surly and refused to talk during the drive southward, except to agree that he had to use the john when we told him we were stopping at Kumgang. Louis cuffed Moss' wrist to his own, and I followed under the curious stares of locals who watched us navigate the busy parking lot and building. Moss held his head down while we were outside, but lifted it inside to drink the coffee we'd bought for him. He wasn't hungry, so we loaded him back into the car within half an hour and headed south again. Heavy clouds were starting to come in, and we wanted to beat any bad weather home.

We almost made it. A light rain started spotting the windshield as we turned off the expressway at Seo Taegu. By the time we pulled in the back gate of Camp Walker, it was raining so hard that our wipers set at full blast couldn't keep the windshield clear. We were driving about five miles per hour and still thought we were going a little too fast for conditions. Just getting out of the car and running in through the office door proved to be a soaking endeavor. Miss Paek ran back and forth to the ladies' room to bring us dry towels. Then she poured us each coffee, Moss taking his with him to his cell. We'd talk with him tomorrow.

I threw on a poncho that was hanging on the coat rack just for times like this, and ran out to get the box from the car. I brought it in, partially under the protection the poncho offered, as Louis held the door.

The colonel was already looking with great interest over the inventory sheet by the time I returned with the evidence. Standard procedures dictated recounting the money three times by different people before locking it up. Louis, the colonel and I started the task, which lasted until after Miss Paek had left to catch her bus at four thirty. We locked the money in bank bags, separating the American dollars from the Korean Won. It took four bags, mainly because of the small denominations.

Louis started taking toys out of the box to put in a large plastic bag before locking them up. One, a pink stuffed bunny, caught his eye. Or his hand, I should say. Then he turned it over several times before calling our attention to it. Then he grabbed a pair of scissors from a desk, slit the back open, reached in, and retrieved a roll of fifty-dollar bills banded together tightly.

He reached in again, but found nothing, then reached for another stuffed animal he'd already thrown in the bag. He slit that animal open and pulled out a wad of twenties. Two other stuffed animals revealed more money, bringing the adjusted total to nearly forty thousand dollars. What a haul. We looked in the box to see if it contained any more stuffed animals, but found that we'd rescued them all. All that remained was the Celadon pottery wrapped in paper. Some of the pieces had already given up cash, but we examined them more closely. In the hole in the bottom of one piece, we found a small piece of paper. It appeared to be signed in blood, by Rostock, Moss and Compo, the MPI agent. It read:

"The three persons undersigned hereby agree to divide equally the profits of our endeavor. The penalty for holding out will be death."

"There's a helluva motive," the colonel said. We agreed and Louis typed up a new inventory sheet containing the sum total of our new findings. We'd have a lot of questions for Moss in the morning, but it was after six now, and we were all bushed. Time for a little relaxation.

Since I was alone for the next few days, I invited Louis to join me at the Taegu Leaders' Club on Camp Henry. Many noncommissioned officers spent time there after work, watching the go-go dancers. There was a chance we would stumble across some valuable rumors and hearsay to follow up our investigation. That often happened in the clubs, where liquor plied lips loose — and loose lips sink ships. Luckily, no one had been caught in the club talking about defense secrets. That would have been punishable through a very high court at an extremely high price.

The storm that hit earlier had been a quickie. Leftover raindrops fell off the trees and overhead wires. The clouds pushed away and a hint of the setting sun peeked around the tail end of the clouds to the west. Rather than cool the air, the storm had made it stickier. We got into my Royale and I cranked up the air conditioner as high as it would go. The car might not cool off between the office and Camp Henry, but it would lessen much of the humidity inside.

We walked through the front door of the club, passed by the cashier's cage and turned right, going along the banks of slot machines. I instinctively reached into my pocket and approached a vacant video poker machine like the one Mihi had beat at the Hilltop Club on Camp Walker. I found a few nickels and dimes and about ten quarters. I put all but three-quarters back into my pocket and chucked one in, pushing the deal button. Up came two aces, a four, a seven and a nine. I held the aces and pushed deal again. Up popped two jacks and a three.

I noticed that I now had three credits to play. Louis slapped me on the shoulder in congratulations, but I was already becoming bored. I played all three credits at once, hoping I'd lose and could leave. The machine dealt me two jacks and three tens. I held them all and pressed deal, keeping the full house. I then released my newly won credits in the form of twenty-one quarters. Not bad for a minute's work.

Stuffing my booty into my pocket, I announced to Louis that the beer was on me. We walked into the crowded lounge and found a table near the back. The others were filled with soldiers wanting to watch the go-go dancers. A waitress appeared, took our order for two cheeseburgers and two Miller Lite drafts, then disappeared in the crowd.

The few conversations in the lounge were basically confined to each table because of the volume of the tape player. It would be a futile attempt to gather rumors here, but it was time away from the office and an empty house. The empty house. I thought about Louis spending every night alone in the barracks. What the hell, I thought. I leaned over so he could hear me.

"Since Jina's going to be in Pyongtaek until Wednesday, why don't you come over to the house every night 'til then?"

"Sounds good," he yelled. "But Mihi and I are going out tonight and tomorrow night. I'll stop by on Sunday, though."

I nodded, not wanting to yell again, and we again turned our attention to the surroundings.

I ordered two more beers about ten minutes later when the cheeseburgers arrived. When the waitress returned with them, I asked her if she knew anything about Rostock. She shook her head, then leaned toward me and said that her friend did. "They used to date," she yelled above the din, while pointing to another waitress. "Miss Chong over there is just coming back to work this week. She loved him very much. She's been off since they found him."

I slid her a modest tip for her help, and asked her to see if Miss Chong could talk to us after work. She reported back a few minutes later that tonight would be bad, but she was off the next day and would meet us here at noon. We accepted and let her get back to work as we ate. The remainder of the evening inside the lounge was uneventful. We headed back to the slot machines, and I gave Louis half of my quarters, signaling for him to play on the other bank of machines, while I listened for information on this side.

We played the quarters one at a time to make them last as long as possible. All I heard for the next twenty-five minutes was that so-and-so's girlfriend was cheating on him, and how Mrs. so-and-so lost a bundle at the machines and wouldn't be back until her husband's next pay day.

Another so-and-so lost so much money at the slots that she started borrowing money so her husband wouldn't notice. She then lost most of that. The lady talking said she might have to sell some things to make it up. I turned away and pulled out my notebook to write this information down. It might prove to be valuable later.

I hadn't been concentrating on the machine, and lost my money within the next fifteen minutes or so with little new information. I went to see how Louis was doing. Not too bad. He was playing a one-armed bandit and the pile of quarters in the basin that looked to be about ten times what I'd given him. I reached in and grabbed a full third of them. I guessed he still had about twenty dollars in there when I returned to my poker machine. Someone had moved into my spot, so I went looking for another vacant machine, ending up at a one-armed bandit myself.

I'd lost about half of what I'd picked up from Louis when I saw him go by with a basket brimming with quarters. "Jackpot" was all he said, grinning and heading for the cashier's cage. I gave up and joined him. The lady dumped the contents of the basket into the counting machine and pushed the button to activate it. She shut the machine off a minute later and counted out eighty-five dollars in bills, and shoved that and two quarters back through the window slot. Louis gave me forty dollars and we left.

I'd never been very good at those things anyway. We compared notes on the way back to the barracks, then I went home.

When I arrived, I found the house clean and dinner waiting to be warmed up on the stove. The new lady apparently knew not to wait for me. I didn't even know what she looked like. I felt just a little hungry, but not overly so. I sampled a bit from each pan and determined that the lady was a good cook. I ate a little, then hit the sack. Although Saturday wouldn't be an early day, I knew I wouldn't be sleeping much past sunrise. I also had to remember to pick Louis up in time for our noon meeting with Miss Chong at the Leaders' Club.

The dawning sun beat a silent rhythm on my eyelids, and I could hear birds singing somewhere close by. A rooster crowed in the distance. Funny. No matter how deep within the city you were, someone nearby always owned a rooster. I got up and stumbled into the kitchen to start the coffee in an effort to wake up. I was watching cartoons (professional development TV) on AFKN and sipping my coffee when Louis called.

"Can you help us find a house or apartment?" he asked without even saying "hi" first. "We decided to move in together while the paperwork's cooking." He'd agreed to assume responsibility for Mihi's college education, since her family would only pay if she remained in their house. I suggested he come over for breakfast and we hung up. I slipped into a pair of running shorts and a T-shirt, expecting the arrival of my maid within the hour, as well. I didn't want to be unpresentable when she got here. Then I settled back into the professional development programs.

Louis and the ajumah arrived about the same time. She gave us the once-over before asking if it would be breakfast for two. She didn't admit to understanding English, but instead pointed at each of us, then made eating motions with a questioning look on her matronly face. I nodded yes and she immediately set about banging pots and pans and dishes around the kitchen in the preparation.

She was quite a contrast from Mihi. I guessed her to be about forty-five and weighing in at nearly one hundred and fifty pounds while standing no taller than about five feet four inches. Her hair was in a perm that allowed for minimum fuss in the mornings, and she wore a loose print blouse with short sleeves. A floor-length skirt with a spandex waistband hugged her more than ample lower frame. Her size could have formed two complete Korean women about half her age, giving them both generous figures. But she was efficient, despite her size. Breakfast was served in about twenty minutes, and she immediately set about cleaning the floors, walls, windows, cabinets, and anything else that didn't move out of her way. She toiled away without so much as a word.

Louis and I discussed consulting a real estate dealer, then discarded that idea. When dealing with Americans, they collected their commission from both ends of the rainbow, rather than from the landlord only, letting the language barrier work in their favor. I recommended that the girls work together as a team, using my car to get around if necessary. The phone rang.

She must have known we were talking about her, because Jina was calling to see if everything was OK. I answered that it was, and she asked to speak to the cleaning lady. The phone came back to me when she was finished giving instructions. I mentioned Louis' plea for help in finding suitable living arrangements and my possible solution. She liked the idea, but rejected using the car. "If they see GI license plates, the price goes up," she said simply, adding that traveling by taxi and on foot was better. It was settled. The women were the bosses in situations such as this, because, simply put, it was their home turf and they knew better than we did. Louis and I reverted to small talk until the ajumah left.

Louis must have been reading my mind because, as soon as the outer gate closed, he said, "Let's save Moss for this afternoon." I agreed wholeheartedly, hoping that the uncertainty about us not being there first thing in the morning would soften the surly suspect up enough to make questioning a little easier. We decided to visit one of the local emigration offices to get Louis' marriage paperwork rolling. I dressed and we were out the door within minutes. After Louis filled out the initial form and obtain a list of things he'd need, he set up an appointment for Mihi to visit the office and called her. She'd also have to fill out several forms and provide many documents to prove her identity. This was no simple task.

Chapter Nine

We headed for the Leaders' Club at about eleven thirty to meet Miss Chong. She was waiting in the lounge, which looked quite different when it was empty. There was also no music, which added to the stark difference. We identified ourselves and showed our badges as we joined her. A waitress folding napkins in a far corner took our order for coffee and headed off to the kitchen. We got right down to it.

"We believe you knew Staff Sergeant Rostock," Louis led in.

"Yes. He was my boyfriend about two years ago," she replied. It was a short story. This beautiful lady had been swept off her feet by our victim during the early stages of his assignment here. A little later, something else caught his eye and number one was out of the house to make room for number two.

It was plain to see what had attracted the sergeant to the waitress. Her petite frame and ready smile were infectious. In her waitress outfit, her strong, shapely legs were a beautiful sight. Imagination brought the rest of the body into the mind's eye. Nice contours, not too small, but not large by any stretch of the imagination. Today, in the light of day and wearing blue jeans, she looked even more beautiful. If I was single I probably would have been making moves on her myself. I wondered why any man involved with this gorgeous young thing would wander off. Then I remembered who he'd wandered off with. I decided that it would have been a close call in my book.

I guess the solution came much easier for Rostock. Miss Chong, being much more conservative, wouldn't have even considered being a go-go dancer, let alone a stripper. She lived with Rostock and gave freely of her body, but not like a whore. Theirs was a quiet type of love. Rostock had swayed toward the more glamorous and adventurous Miss Lee within days of meeting her, according to the story.

There were tears in her eyes. I could tell she still loved him, and that she missed him even when he was alive and living with someone else. I guess he hadn't known — or didn't care — that she'd given him her heart, as well as her body. Now he was gone and she'd never get him back. She burst into tears and I gave her my handkerchief to sop up the flow flooding down her cheeks.

We let her compose herself for a minute before we continued. Then we laid some photographs on the table. She wiped away the last remnants of tears to look at photos of the Stenbergs, Park, Moss, the Dobbses and the Compos.

"Did you ever see any of these people visit the house when you lived with him?" I asked. She said she hadn't because of her work at the club. She worked most evenings while he was at home. But she had seen him at the club one night with the black man, she said, pointing to Moss' photo. She said that meeting took place about a year and a half ago. Louis made note of that as I went on with several other questions.

She said that she hadn't noticed anything strange, really, because of her work, and she didn't know anyone who'd want to kill Rostock. She denied even having thoughts about disposing of him. Though she loved him dearly, she said, she accepted the fact that he lived with another woman. Miss Chong had only hoped and prayed that he would return to her arms and marry her when it was all over. The tears flowed again, and my handkerchief once more became gainfully employed. But this wasn't getting us any hard information, except that Rostock had known Moss for at least a year and a half, and Moss had come to Taegu to meet with him at least once.

We offered to buy her lunch, which she accepted, so we adjourned to the dining room. We learned during a seafood meal that Oki, as she was known by her friends and family, was the eldest daughter of a Taegu policeman. She was born twenty-three years ago and had a Korean boyfriend before finding a job at the on-post club. Her boyfriend didn't want any part of a woman who "flirted with Americans," and he left her for someone else, even though she served drinks and food, but never flirted with the customers. She said she didn't miss him, and realized after a while that she hadn't even loved him. The separation caused her to turn away from Korean men to seek an American boyfriend. That was when she met Rostock.

She liked him almost immediately. He didn't drink too much and he joked and laughed a lot. When he finally asked her out for a date, she said "yes" without even thinking twice.

"I'll always have a place in my heart for Tim. I'll never forget him. But I know he can never come back now. I must find someone else to care for me."

Even being the first-born, her family didn't have too much money, and there were no funds to send her to college. She became a waitress about a year after graduating from high school because it was the only job open to her. She told us that men got available jobs first, even if a Korean girl had a college degree. I was strongly aware of that. Though much was changing every day, as women gained new ground with the economic boom, Korea was still basically a male-oriented society. Someone with only a high school education usually led a life of being a waitress, dancer or prostitute, for the most part. Or she married a foreigner and left the country.

It was a sad tale, but was nonetheless all too common in the Land of the Morning Calm.

We finished lunch and offered to drive her home, thanking her for her time and cooperation. She directed us out the gate and into a section of town near the Bongduk Market. The street was lined with Ginkgoes, the familiar pistachio-bearing trees. She finally asked us to stop near a large gate that was painted green. She thanked us for the lift and climbed out of the car, disappearing inside the gate. I turned the car around and headed for Camp Walker. It was time to talk with Moss.

Because he'd been bold enough to break into Compo's house in the middle of an investigation and flee, and then become violent with a Korean cleaning man, we felt we should wear our weapons. Louis and I clipped the holsters to the backs of our belts, and walked in ready for any eventuality.

When we arrived at the detention cell, we found that Moss hadn't eaten any breakfast or lunch, though they had been brought for him. We moved the trays aside before unlocking the door. I covered as Louis cuffed and led him out of the cell, into my office. We followed this routine only when we feared the worst from a visitor. We definitely did with Moss.

He was big, standing about six feet two inches tall and weighing in the neighborhood of two hundred and twenty pounds. His close-cropped hair was turning gray the at temples and in the moustache. His arms were as big as trees. I guessed that he worked out regularly at the gym. Louis sat him down in the chair next to my desk, while I stood behind my chair. Louis took up his position by the door behind Moss, with his hand near his holster.

I read him his rights again and made sure he understood them, then asked why he hadn't eaten. He didn't answer and he didn't look up. He just stared at the floor a few feet in front of his chair. I went right to the subject at hand, informing him why he'd been brought to Taegu, and what he was being charged with.

"Breaking and entering and burglary are serious enough charges, major," I started. "Add those to conspiracy to commit murder, murder, conspiracy to commit a felony, unlawful disposition of duty-free goods, aggravated assault on a Korean National and a few others, and you're looking at a lot of time at Leavenworth. We could probably cut that time by half if you'd come clean with us."

Nothing. It was Louis' turn.

"We know about the pact between you, Rostock and Compo. Compo's almost ready to talk. He's so scared right now, he's almost ready to confess to everything himself." He was lying, of course. We hadn't even seen Compo since we recovered the box. But Moss didn't know that. He raised his head high enough to look me straight in the eye. Something in his eyes told me that he thought he was off the hook on the murder charge. But after a few moments, Louis continued. "But he won't. He doesn't want to hang by himself. He wants company. Besides," and he paused there for just a second. "He says you murdered Rostock."

That got to him. Moss' eyes widened and his jaw tightened. Sweat started beading on his forehead, despite the air conditioning on full force. "He's lying," he said quietly between clenched teeth. I slipped my hand down to turn on the tape recorder, and asked him to repeat what he had said.

"I said he's lying. The little sneak bastard is lying. I didn't kill Rostock. He did."

"Who did?" I asked.

"Compo. He killed him and now he's trying to pin it on me."

"Tell us something that might make us believe any of this," Louis said from behind him. It looked like the story was about to unfold — at least one version of it anyway.

"I met Rostock in Seoul when he was learning how to be a ration control clerk. We had a few beers at the club during the evenings he was there.

"One of those times he was pretty much under the weather. I guess he'd had about twelve beers. Out of the blue he started talking about having the prime job that could make him a bundle of money. All he needed was a fence outside the Taegu area to make it a reality.

"I thought he was joking, but I mumbled something to that fact that I could probably unload some of the stuff in Seoul, if that's what he was thinking. I was pretty much trashed. Hell, I'd had seven or eight doubles. I didn't know what I was saying. I guess I offered to bring him back to my place for the night so we could talk about it.

"We kept drinking after we got there, and his whole plan sounded ludicrous, but I went along with him, figuring he'd forget about it in the morning. He didn't."

Moss stopped to compose his thoughts and Louis, realizing that our prisoner was calmed for the moment, took a seat on the sofa next to the door. We were all ears when Moss started again.

"When I woke up, he was at the table writing something down. I went over to see what it was. It was notes from the previous evening. He said he had it all recorded and that if I didn't do what he wanted, he'd expose me to the command and ruin my career.

"He had quotes and everything. I told him to forget it. We'd been drunk and out of control. He wouldn't. He kept pushing, so I tried to grab the notes. He stuffed them into his pocket and ran out the door. I still figured he was joshing me, so I put it out of my mind.

"I didn't see him either of the next two nights at the club. I knew he was going back to Taegu at the end of the week, so I figured he'd forgotten about that crazy plan. I decided to forget all about it and passed it off as two drunks bullshitting on a lonely night.

"That changed a week later, when he called me from Taegu. He told me to drive there and meet him just outside the Camp Henry gate. I told him he was barking up the wrong tree and started to hang up on him. Then he said he'd gotten statements from witnesses saying that we were seen together and then left the club together.

"I'm not a homosexual, but you know the Army doesn't need proof. All that's needed to trash an officer's career is an accusation or even a rumor. I listened a little longer. This man was truly crazy, and I needed time to get away free and clear from him. I finally agreed to meet him in Taegu. Only then would he let me hang up.

"I headed south that Saturday. He took me to his house out in the ville, where we talked. He'd planned it all out. He would forge ration applications and get a few false cards, making the names up as he went along. Then he'd give people those cards and have them buy things to bring to him. That way, people could buy things that wouldn't show up on their own ration records. He planned to pay them a little more than they paid for the item, then take everything to Seoul. He'd give me the stuff and I'd fence it all, returning his costs and half of the profit by depositing it in his bank account at the Seoul branch. The other half was mine.

"I knew he was whacko, but I also knew he was serious about the deal. I knew it could ruin me, but I couldn't back out without having time to plan so it wouldn't ruin my career. I've got seventeen years in, damnit! You don't get any retirement for anything less than twenty on the nose." His voice broke and he started sobbing. We gave him a little time to compose himself. At least a version of the story about the cards and the black marketing was unfolding. Maybe the rest would come to light today, as well.

He was more confident when he started talking again, seeming to realize that getting it off his chest was the best remedy. I think he knew his Army career was finished anyway. There was no legal way we could even attempt to save him. The entire thing had just gone too far.

"I went back to Seoul that night, carrying several big bags of rice, about twenty cartons of cigarettes and five small stereos. I had a week to unload them or he'd bring the stories out into the open. I did as I was told."

Rostock made the trip to Seoul every other week to get new ration cards — most legitimate, but some false. He brought the items bought on post in Taegu. He stopped by Moss' house and unloaded the truck, then got the cards and headed back to Taegu the same day.

Moss returned home from work and started to call a few black market ajumahs to dispose of the goods and collect the money. The following day he made the deposit in Rostock's account. He hid his share of the money in his house so there'd be no "extra" money going into his account. He had planned to turn it all in when he finally got out from under Rostock's thumb. But Louis and I knew from experience that he had gotten in too deep since that first transaction, even if he hadn't realized it. It was only a matter of time before he was caught, unless he was one of the lucky few who went back to the States before we got him. Those people were very rare, however.

"About a year ago, I made another trip to Taegu, this time for a business conference. Rostock found out about it and called me to join him for dinner. I wanted to refuse, but I was afraid he'd spill his tales to the brass, so I went. His girlfriend was there, but she was asleep. I was worried that she'd wake up and hear us talking, but Rostock said he'd loaded her with a tranquilizer or something because she was sick. She was a looker too. I had to admire that in Rostock. He had excellent taste in women. I saw the other one in the Leaders' Club. She was a waitress there.

"Anyway, we talked and he loaded up my car with some of the new merchandise, mentioning that he could make a double load that week since I was in Taegu. When the conference finished the next afternoon, I drove back and put the stuff in my house. By that time the ajumahs and I had a pre-established day they would visit every two weeks. When Rostock brought up his load, I'd get rid of it all at one time.

"The next trip he made to Seoul, he left a letter with the stuff, telling me to call him after ten that night. I did, and he mentioned there was a problem. I started worrying about my career even more then. He told me there was an MPI agent watching him, and that he'd probably have to buy him off or knock him off. I didn't like the idea of killing, but I also didn't like the smell of an agent of any sort in our operation. He'd probably get what he could out of us, then haul us in anyway. Or kill us one night and try to say we were resisting arrest. But what could I do?

"He wanted us to meet at Camp Carroll that weekend to discuss what could be done. He told me to meet him at the King Club in the ville there. That Saturday morning, I drove down there and got a room about a block from the club so I'd be close enough to walk. I met him at the appointed time.

He wasn't alone, though. He introduced Compo, saying that he was the MPI agent that he'd "bought." Compo assured us everything would be fine as long as the scam went along as planned. He even mentioned how he could be the protection against unwanted investigations and surveillance."

While he gathered his thoughts, I took the opportunity to replace the cassette in the recorder with a fresh one. Who knew how long this next stretch would be?

Over the next two hours and three tapes, Moss recounted how they'd gone back to his hotel room and drew up the agreement we'd found, with Moss depositing the proceeds into an additional bank account. Base funds would still be provided by Rostock and would be repaid to him, while the profits would be divided equally. Moss still kept his share at his house, occasionally changing some for different denominations at a variety of places, in case it was marked. He stopped for a second when I asked him exactly where the money was hidden. When told us, Louis picked up the phone and called Seoul to confiscate and inventory the money. Moss went on, saying that Compo started figuring more prominently in the scheme.

"Pretty soon, Compo was making trips to Seoul with some things, and he suggested I make trips to Taegu every so often to increase our sales base. During one of his visits, he gave me one of the phony cards and actually ordered me to buy things. He wanted me to buy some things that were controlled items for enlisted people, but that officers could buy without authorization. I didn't want to, but I was stuck between a rock and a hard place. I had no choice..."

Among the items he'd listed as buying with the phony card in Seoul were a stereo, two electric blankets, some video equipment and a TV. The rest were the regular, nobody-cares, but still saleable items, such as rice, meats and sundries.

By now we were spinning our wheels in the midst of the black marketing scam, and were getting nowhere closer to solving the murder. We needed more on that, so I steered Moss in that direction.

"Compo said that when he was on one of his trips in Seoul about two months ago, Rostock went to his house to rape his wife or something. The next thing I knew, Compo was asking where he could get a gun without having it traced back to him. I had no idea and told him so. In America, you can buy a gun on any street corner, but in Korea, only the soldiers and the police have them. He was fit to be tied, and said he'd get even with Rostock.

"When I saw the news about Rostock on AFKN last month, I put in for leave and started snooping around for everything connecting us. It took me awhile, but I finally found his girlfriend. I'd been searching all over Taegu and finally caught wind of her in the Kangnung area. It took me two days to find her at that club in Kyungpo. That's when I found out you two were on the case, instead of Compo.

"At that time, though, I didn't know you had Compo. I'd already been on the road for about two weeks. I'd heard that Mr. Park had gotten busted, along with a bunch of other people they'd conned into buying things for them. I didn't even know Mr. Park was with customs until he got busted. I didn't get a chance to find anything at Rostock's house. You guys had already found everything by the time I arrived."

I interrupted him.

"But MPI had the case for the first weeks after Rostock's death. They didn't even know about the ration card scam then. Why didn't you go there one night and get all the cards then?"

"Compo was supposed to take care of it," he answered, with his look telling me that I'd missed a major part. He filled it in for me, though. "He was the team chief on the investigation. He told me they wouldn't find anything there to incriminate us because he'd taken it and buried it." Louis and I exchanged looks. That was an interesting twist.

I made a note to check on the identity of the other investigating officers who were on the case before we took over. "So what made you break into Compo's house after I left for the evening last week?"

"I was waiting for Compo to come home from work. He didn't show up, but you came out of the house, locking the gate behind you. That meant Compo had been caught. I didn't know what you'd gotten out of there, but I hoped you hadn't gotten the box that I knew was there. That was the one thing we'd agreed on, that Rostock or I would take control of that box if anything happened to Compo, or if he turned on us. He'd bragged about it once while we were drinking. I don't think he remembered doing that, or he would have changed the hiding place.

"With Rostock dead, the deed fell into my hands. After you left, a bunch of college punks started hanging around, so I figured to return in the morning before you got there. I knew I had to have at least an hour to get the box and be gone before you arrived. I got there just before the trash truck, so I was inside before all the ajumahs came out to the street.

"It took me awhile to find where he'd hidden it, but I figured that if he'd hidden the money in stuffed toys and didn't have children, the box would have to be where his wife wouldn't really notice it. She thought he was buying stuff for an orphanage, not keeping it to hide his ill-begotten loot. She didn't know anything about the scam as far as I know." He looked up at me. "I guess she does now, huh?" I nodded.

It was getting late, and I wanted to give Moss time to regain his thoughts. Maybe he would think of something else by morning. I asked him if he wanted a chaplain to provide him with a service, and he said yes. He said he was Catholic, so I dialed the on-call number and made the request. It was set to take place between masses and I informed the duty agent of the attending chaplain's name. His replacement in the morning would have to accompany the clergy, even though the priest wouldn't be allowed in the cell with Moss.

When I hung up, I asked Moss if something was wrong with the food, since he hadn't eaten all day. He said he guessed it was because of nerves, but that he was starved now. Rather than have him eat cold food, I told him I'd bring him something, and asked if he had any preferences. Fried chicken was his choice, so I called the 19th Hole and ordered two dinners to go. If he was starved, he would probably eat both of them. Louis and I escorted him back to his cell after a brief pause in the men's room. I told him the dinner would be there within half an hour, and we left.

Remembering his date with Mihi, I took Louis up the hill to his barracks, then stopped at the 19th Hole for Moss' dinners. I returned to the office just long enough to give the duty agent Moss' meals before heading home, myself. It was starting to get dark, and I found the smell of the chicken dinners reminding me of how hungry I was. No matter what my new cook had prepared, I felt confident that I'd devour all of it.

As soon as I got home, I called to remind the duty agent that the prisoner was to have no visitors, save for a lawyer and the priest I'd arranged. I also didn't want him making phone calls, except for one to the Staff Judge Advocate's on-call representative, if he hadn't already. As an afterthought, I asked him to remove the dinner dishes as soon as Moss was finished eating. I didn't want him committing suicide by eating chicken bones.

We'd have to talk to Compo again, but it could wait 'til morning. Even if he tried to run, a GI couldn't hide for long in Korea, and he couldn't leave the country without leave or travel orders and identification. His ID card was in our safe.

I sat down to eat whatever was on the stove. Last night's dinner remains had disappeared, and were replaced with a marinated steak dinner. I watched the AFKN Saturday night movie as I dined. With any luck, the case would be totally wrapped up by this time next week. Too bad these cases weren't as easy as the one I was watching on the tube.

Sunday morning announced itself with a drizzling rain. The clouds were low and visibility was just about nil. I called Louis' room to make sure he was up, and got no answer. I called the office to see if he was there, leaving word for him to call if he showed up. I shuffled over to the kitchen to make some coffee and the phone rang. It was Louis. He'd been indisposed when I called. I reminded him about our task of picking Compo up. Then we disconnected.

Since it was Sunday, ajumah probably wouldn't be coming in, and I threw on some sausages while I dressed, then cooked up eggs and toast. I dug out my Army London Fog from the closet after breakfast and headed out the door. It looked like it was going to be nasty all day, so I wanted to spend most of it in the office.

I picked up my partner at the barracks and we stopped at the 19th Hole for his breakfast and my third cup of coffee. I told Louis to find us a table while I called the office to get the backup team. The duty agent informed me that Bill and Mike had returned from Hawaii the previous evening and volunteered to help if needed. He'd have them there by ten o'clock.

Coffee had already been served by the time I got to the table, so I took off my raincoat and sat down to hug my cup until it was empty. Another one after that might be a good idea this morning. My mind was still clouded by cobwebs.

Louis looked a bit tired, but otherwise pretty cheerful. He and Mihi had gone dancing at the clubs last night. They hadn't missed any of the nearly twenty clubs in the ville, he claimed. I knew that had to have been a tiring episode. But his cheerful attitude seemed to make it all worthwhile. I hoped she wouldn't make an old man out of him before his retirement. We paid the check and vacated the dining room about a quarter to ten, after a few more cups of coffee got us motivated. Bill and Mike were waiting in the lounge when we arrived at the office.

"I hear you two guys had some fun in Hawaii," I joked, referring to the typhoon that visited during their stay. They laughed. "We kept looking for you on TV when they talked about the rescue operations. We weren't sure, though, which side of the operation you'd be on." That brought another laugh, and I thanked them both for volunteering to help so soon after their return.

"Hell," Bill said. "We'd rested enough in Hawaii. There wasn't anything to do there except look for TV cameras to jump in front of." We all laughed. I asked Bill for the briefing from ballistics.

"That was the gun that killed Rostock, all right," he answered. "I had it dusted for fingerprints, as well, since we had extra time on our hands. Seems a certain MPI agent had his grubbies all over it. They raised an especially good relief off the trigger." That settled it. It looked as if Moss had been telling the truth. I started believing that he really was getting it all off his chest the day before during the interview. That would sure make it easier on us. I picked up the phone and asked the duty agent to get the colonel on the line for me. We'd have to brief him on the new developments before we moved, in case something backfired. The duty agent called back a minute later to announce that the colonel was on his way in, wanting the briefing in person.

He arrived within twenty minutes, and Louis started the show by running down what happened with Moss the previous day. Then Bill explained about the ballistics and forensics reports. Finally, it was my turn.

"We're going after him, sir. Bill and Mike will back us up. Here's the plan." They all listened while I sketched the scenario and contingency plans. When I was finished, the colonel said he'd notify the MP commander, then accompany us. He wanted to be in on this one, if only to act as witness to the proceedings. We went back to the lounge to double-check our weapons and radios, while the duty agent called the Korean police for local support. It was set.

The neighborhood was quiet when we arrived. The drizzle had been enough to coat the windshield with only intermittent use of the wipers. Bill and Mike followed us in their sedan. The colonel rode in the back seat of ours. We were all on the secure channel that was reserved for CID only.

When we got out of the cars, Bill went to one side alley, and Mike went to the other to cut off any possible escape over the wall. I went straight for the gate, with the colonel backing me up on the left and Louis to my right. This would be a textbook apprehension. The KNPs were walking around the corner as I rang the chime.

The sound of someone putting on shoes joined the chiming of church bells somewhere in the distance. A few seconds later, Amanda Compo opened the gate. She looked as if she hadn't slept in a month and her eyes were red. I flashed my badge, even though she knew who we were, and told her why we were there.

"He's not here," she replied. When I asked where he'd gone, she shrugged her shoulders, opening the gate wide to let us in. She closed the gate behind us, then led the way into the house. Louis and the colonel fanned out to either side of the house, while I went inside to look around. Bill and Mike kept a vigilant watch at the back corners of the residence, while the Korean police stayed in the front courtyard.

I looked inside every room, checking even the collapsible closets before returning to the living room. She was brewing a fresh pot of coffee. I noticed that dishes were piled in the sink and trashcans were filled and overflowing. A layer of dust covered everything, in stark contrast to the condition of the house during our last visit there as a team.

She was dressed in a flimsy robe and her hair was in curlers. Every now and then, when she reached for something, the robe would fall open momentarily to reveal that she was naked underneath. She reached for the folds of the robe and held it closed, working one-handed until she had to reach or use both hands again. I suggested she put something on and, as she did so, I ushered Louis and the colonel in. We took positions around the room in case we needed to act fast.

They shook their heads, indicating that they hadn't found him outside, and I returned the gesture with a nod. The Korean policeman came into the house and took a seat on the sofa. He didn't seem to care what this was about, and he looked as if he wanted to continue his nap back at the substation.

When Amanda returned to the living room, the Mr. Coffee was bubbling away in the kitchen. She was wearing a long T-shirt with cut-off shorts underneath, exposing a pair of gorgeous legs that weren't evident under the dress she'd worn at the interview. She'd also taken the curlers out and combed her hair. She still looked as if she hadn't slept recently, though the red was disappearing from her eyes. Probably a stiff dose of Visine or something. She sat down at the dining room table and looked at us for signs of who might start the discussion. Louis read her the Miranda Act again, which she said she understood. I asked where her husband was.

"I don't know. He left yesterday morning, saying he was going to report to the charge of quarters as ordered. He had to check in every three hours. He left here at a quarter to six and I haven't seen him since."

The colonel pulled out his radio, changed the channel to the regular MP band, and waited for a pause in the traffic so he could speak. When he got the chance, he called the MP desk sergeant and asked to have the commander join us at the house. Then he flicked back to our secure channel and informed Bill and Mike that there would soon be a visitor. If Compo had a radio and was in the area, he'd know we were there, but those chances didn't seem too high, since radios were highly accounted for.

"Who does he hang out with?" asked Louis. She listed a few names, which he copied down, asking where each person lived and worked. Some were MPs, of course. There was a mix of those who lived in the barracks and those who had houses downtown. Louis called the information in to the duty agent, instructing him to send teams to those places to look for Compo. Then he replaced the radio in his belt holster.

I guessed that Compo wasn't even in Taegu by now — he'd probably have gone either to Seoul or Pusan to hide until he could leave the country. That would be pretty difficult, unless he could get his hands on a passport, but I wasn't about to take any chances after getting this close to sewing up the case.

I radioed additional instructions to the duty agent telling him to call Seoul, Pusan and even Inchon, and provide them with a detailed description and a wire photo for an all points bulletin. The agents in Seoul would check Moss' house again, since Compo could go there. Whoever caught him would hold him until we got there.

I slipped outside while Louis and the colonel questioned Amanda some more. I was looking for signs of something being buried and freshly disturbed. A few places had no vegetation or paving, but one spot in particular caught my eye. The stone pathway next to a soft section of earth had been recently cleaned.

I went into the heater room and located the shovel I'd seen there earlier. It sunk easily into the ground. I removed shovel full after shovel full of dirt, until I was about two feet down and the spade struck something solid. I eased dirt from around the box and lifted it out, using my handkerchief to keep from smudging any prints. I took the box into the house and laid it on the coffee table in front of the colonel.

It was a green index card file box with no lock, like those commonly seen in about 90 percent of government offices. The colonel took my hanky and opened the lid. Compo's wife leaned over to look with as much curiosity as we had when the lid came up. She evidently hadn't seen the contents of this box before. Maybe Moss was telling the truth about her not being involved in this caper.

The contents took everyone by surprise. As the colonel took them out for inspection, we counted two passports with Compo's photo, both bearing different names. There were also two passports each for Moss and Rostock, none of which had correct names on them. The same held true for six military identification cards, all matching their passport counterparts. There were also six sets of false leave papers, "approved," but left undated. Destinations on all the leave papers were locations in the States. At the bottom of the box, however, were the most interesting of the items.

Six wallets contained IDs for the fictitious characters named on the passports, and each wallet held five thousand dollars in American Express Travelers Checks. The wallets were stored in an unsealed manila envelope. The colonel whistled lightly through his teeth then handed the box and its contents over to Louis for inventory.

We looked at Mrs. Compo, who returned our stares. We wouldn't get any information from her, because she apparently didn't know anything about the box until this very moment.

Since there was no identification for her in the box, it was clear that her husband was going to leave her behind if the crap hit the fan. In fact, it looked as if he really left but didn't take the box. Or did he take another set of IDs from the box? Moss might have that answer.

We left about an hour later, having gained no real information about where Compo might be. The MP commander hadn't been able to tell us anything either. He was going to find out why he hadn't been notified the minute Compo didn't show up for one of his reporting periods. Something had fallen through the cracks, and he wanted answers. He was boiling mad. I knew someone was going to get burned for this, and I was glad I wasn't wearing those shoes.

Back at the office, I took the tape recorder into the detention cell area. I wouldn't have to bring Moss out for the few questions I had. I stood outside, talking through the bars, and pointed the recorder in his direction to record his answers.

"What did Compo remove from Rostock's house and bury?"

"He wouldn't tell me. He said it was his insurance policy if things went bad."

"That's all he said?"

"He said it would hang us if you guys got hold of it." His eyes were on the floor.

"Where did he bury it?"

"I don't know. I told you everything he told me. Honest." I believed him and shut off the recorder, turning to leave. I stopped and faced him again. He looked up.

"Why are you telling us everything now?"

"My career's finished. I'm going to hang anyway. I just want to get it all off my shoulders." I nodded and went into the outer office.

The duty agent reported that units were in place at all ports of exit from Korea. I really didn't think Compo would take a chance on military transport with CID waiting for him at the other end. He'd travel commercial and try to hide in the crowd.

The agent added that the units had called in their interpreters to question people in the ticket booths, just in case Compo had already bought a ticket out. I grabbed a cup of coffee and went into my office to sit down for a while. Louis was busy marking the evidence we found, and the colonel had retired to his office to check with the MP commander. I had a minute to myself to think.

I made a mental note to talk with the commanders and first sergeants for the Dobbs' and Stenbergs after the investigation was completed. Then I just let my mind wander for a bit. I must have been off in space somewhere, because Louis had come in and sat down on the sofa without me realizing it. He'd been there for a few minutes before he broke me from my reverie. "You OK, Jim?"

"Huh?" I snapped back and looked around to see who was talking. By the time my eyes focused on him, he was already relaxed, sipping on his coffee. "Oh, yeah. I was just daydreaming. Trying to clear my head for a few minutes."

"It must have worked," he said with a smile. "You didn't even move when I walked in and said your name."

"I'm sorry man. What have you got?"

"The Seoul office called to say that a man fitting Compo's description had bought a ticket on tonight's Korean Air flight to New York — with American Express Travelers Checks. It leaves at five fifteen. I called the boys in Pusan and let them go home. Seoul has all their people at Kimpo Airport to pick him up."

"No," I said. Louis stared at me as if I was crazy. "He'd smell us a mile away, Louis. Call them off, but have one stick around to make sure he gets on that flight. We'll call New York Area Command at Fort Hamilton to pick him up at JFK." I thought for a moment before I asked the final question in my mind. "Did they say what name he was traveling under?"

"You're going to love this," he said with a smile, as he opened up his notebook. "His passport, ID and leave papers say he's Sergeant James Stewart." That hit me like a hammer. Louis went out to relay the latest instructions to Seoul, and I sat there dumbfounded. What nerve, I thought.

I went into the colonel's office to brief him on the new developments, but Louis had beaten me to it.

"I hear you've already bought a ticket to the States," he said as I entered. He was grinning from ear to ear. I said the only thing I could.

"How do you want to handle it, sir?"

"Let's try to talk the guys at Hamilton into bringing him back as far as Seoul. You and Louis can pick him up there, and fly him back from the supply point at Yongsan. I'll get the boys in Seoul to take you to Kimpo and bring you back. You'll use my bird," he finished, meaning his helicopter.

"And if the Stateside boys can't do that?"

"Then you two get a free trip to New York on Uncle Sam to haul him all the way back where he belongs." I nodded. We agreed that, with the thirteen-hour time difference between Korea and New York, it would be at least four in the morning before the other James Stewart was picked up. Adding the travel to Fort Hamilton and the processing, and they wouldn't be able to call us much before seven thirty. I told the colonel I'd take care of the reservations and travel orders in the morning, just in case. Once the day's reports were completed, there wasn't much to do in the office, so I informed the colonel that Louis and I were calling it a day. He agreed, saying he wasn't going to stick around either.

I gave instructions to the duty agent before I left, making sure he called me at home as soon as it was confirmed that Compo had left Kimpo and CID at Fort Hamilton had picked him up at JFK airport. As I walked out the door, I remembered that I'd have to pull my stint as duty agent for a while, as I rested up before the next case. It was a rotating duty. I always hated that part of the job, because the duty agent was an errand boy for the other agents. But, it was part of the territory. I learned to accept it, no matter how distasteful it was. Besides, I could trade off with Louis every now and then for the graveyard shift, just to break up the monotony.

We decided to run by the Hilltop Club for a brew. We realized we hadn't eaten since breakfast, and figured that one of their famous mushroom burgers would tide us over until ajumah fixed dinner. Louis didn't have a date with Mihi, because she had to be up early for classes and we had to be up early for PT, whether we went to New York or not.

Not long after we got there, Bill and Mike joined us. They were hungry, too, and had seen us pull into the parking lot, so they followed. I offered to buy their burgers for all the help they'd been giving us. They both accepted without hesitation.

We left by five to get home for the impending phone call. Ajumah was cooking when we arrived. She tried to tell me something about the phone, but I didn't understand until she put one hand to her ear and pointed a finger in the air, made dialing motions with the other, and repeated my wife's name over and over. I finally got the hint and dug out my address book for the number. Her mother recognized my voice right away and yelled for Jina to get to the phone. I heard her sweet voice a moment later.

"Hi, honey. What's up?"

"I just wanted to see if everything was OK," she replied, adding that Mrs. Kim, our housekeeper (now I knew her name), said I hadn't been eating too many meals at home. I told her about the latest developments on the case, and said that I might have to fly to New York with Louis to retrieve Compo. She didn't sound too happy at first, but brightened up when I said it wasn't definite.

"Besides, if we go, we'll just spend one night in New York and return by Wednesday." That cheered her up only minutely. Then she remembered that she wasn't due back in Taegu until Wednesday, so everything was OK again. I told her I was expecting a call about the case and would have to hang up, "but I'll call as soon as I know."

I hadn't taken my hand off the receiver when the phone rang. The duty agent said Compo had gotten on the flight and it was taxiing down the runway, "even as we speak." I told him he should become an impressionist and fill in for Willard Scott on the weather report. He laughed and hung the phone up in my ear.

I briefed my partner on the call and immediately dialed the colonel's home phone number to fill him in.

"I'll call New York right away so we'll be able to get an answer on our request by morning. Talk to you then," he said, before disconnecting the call on his end.

Mihi came by as we were sitting down to dinner, so I had her ask Mrs. Kim to set another place for dinner. The older lady gave me a dirty look until Mihi explained that she wasn't my girlfriend, but Louis' fiancée. Then a bright smile beamed at us through dry lips and gnarled teeth, and the extra place was set in record time. Mihi told her she could leave and we'd clean up when we were done. Ajumah was very happy about that, and was out the door before anyone could have said "gesundheit."

When Louis told Mihi that we might be going to New York, she nearly pitched a fit. He could only calm her down by promising he'd call while we were there. She was still upset, but seemed a little more complacent. I smiled. It would take time before they got accustomed to each other, like it did between Jina and me. Once the dishes were cleaned, we walked down to a neighborhood video rental store to check out a movie. We lucked out with Mihi's favorite actor, Chuck Norris, and brought the movie back for our evening's entertainment. She left as soon as the movie was finished, and Louis and I hit the sack. Tomorrow would possibly be a very long day, indeed.

Chapter Ten

The phone rang just as I turned over to shut the alarm off. I hit the button, then picked up the receiver on the second ring.

"He's in custody with the New York boys," the duty agent said, without so much as a "howdy-do." Damn. That was early. They must have radioed Fort Hamilton as soon as they locked on to him. I thanked him and hung up, then rolled off the mattress. Twenty minutes later, I was sipping a fresh cup of coffee and packing an overnight bag for a trip I might have to take. I called Louis to give him the news.

I grabbed my PT clothes and got ready to leave. Regardless of what happened, the Army always needed physically fit men and women. I quit the house by five thirty, taking the bag with me and throwing it in the trunk. Louis was ready when I picked him up, and we headed for the PT field to join the rest of the unit as it formed up. Although the colonel didn't have to participate because of wounds he suffered in 'Nam, he was there this morning. He greeted us as we got out of the car.

"He's there," he announced. "They pulled him off the plane while it was still on the taxiway. They got a lot of cooperation from the New York Port Authority."

He continued before I could ask about the status of the trip. "They've agreed to bring him to Seoul for us if we pay. I sent them the fund cite." It didn't matter that the Army was the Army and we were spending Army funds for an Army mission. Each unit was allocated money for their particular mission. When the money ran out, units either begged for more or suffered for the remainder of the fiscal year. Rather than have their unit put up with that hassle, the Fort Hamilton agents would travel at our expense so that we'd have to ask for emergency funds. It was only a couple of weeks until the first of the fiscal year, and we had enough for the trip, so we could suffer for that short period of time.

"They'll even bring him to Yongsan for us," the colonel went on, "and deposit him at the CID station there, if we want. But I told them you'd meet them at the airport to take custody and bring them in to Yongsan. They'll stay the night there and return to New York the next day."

Near the formation, I could hear the first sergeant calling for his soldiers to fall in. The colonel ambled over and told him that Louis and I were needed right away. When he came back, he said, "You guys don't need this shit today, do you?" He really didn't expect an answer, so we thanked him and took off. It wasn't every day that you could get out of physical training with the boss' backing for no reason. I took Louis to his barracks, where he grabbed his suit. Then he went with me to the house to get ready for work and have breakfast. We suddenly seemed to have plenty of time this morning.

I waited until seven o'clock to telephone Jina with the good news. She was happy. Mihi stopped by just after that and was similarly overjoyed that we wouldn't be going. We were all in pretty high spirits, considering it was Monday morning and all.

Mihi decided to skip classes and cook us some breakfast. Mrs. Kim was getting accustomed to the fact that I usually didn't eat breakfast at home and stopped coming in early. By eight o'clock, we were on our way to work.

Compo wasn't due to arrive with his escort until five o'clock Tuesday afternoon, so we had time to sew up loose ends and prepare for his arrival. We recapped what we already had and tried to think up questions that hadn't already been asked. Among the things we needed were a confession to the murder. That would go a long way right now. Of course, we also wanted to know why, and we had to find out who was in the chain for buying the illegal goods for the conspiracy. We decided to start with Moss. He seemed to be coming pretty clean right now. Maybe he'd come a little cleaner once we told him that the "long arm of the law" had just caught his ex-partner in New York.

We had a pretty comprehensive listing of what was bought and sold by noon. It spanned more than twenty typed pages. I estimated the monetary total at more than a quarter of a million dollars over the period of two years, according to our informant. All the ill-gotten gains would have to be turned over to the Korean authorities to pay for the customs taxes, of course, so it was being tallied from all different sources.

The money Moss stashed in his house was being held at the Yongsan CID office in Seoul, where we would pick it up when we went to get Compo. Compo's profits were in our evidence room. The profits realized by the murder victim prior to his demise were frozen in a Stateside account, and were ready to be turned over to us. That would pay about 75 percent of the taxes owed. The Korean government wouldn't be overjoyed, but they'd be a little happier getting that much. They would also get a list of the people Moss dealt with in Seoul, so they could attempt to extract the remainder of the fees due from them. And there was also Mr. Park.

All in all, we thought they'd be pretty happy, not to mention that a major black marketing ring had been closed.

We finished up whatever reports we could by three in the afternoon, then ducked out early for the day. Things were going so well that I hoped we'd have the case wrapped up before the weekend. Compo would be back Tuesday evening, and we'd question him all day Wednesday. If he spit it all out, we could start typing up the reports and finish sewing up the loose ends by close of business Friday. That would be extremely nice in my book. But it hinged on Compo's cooperation. We'd make sure we pressured him a little in an effort to speed things up. Besides, he was a cop gone bad. We had no inclination to make this any easier on him or save his feelings. He would go down this time. There was no question about that.

Bill and Mike volunteered to finish up the paperwork on Moss and prepare him for his court-martial. It would be much easier for him since he cooperated, but his career was still gone, and he'd serve time at Leavenworth for his crimes. There would also be a hearing on Rostock's actions, and his death benefits would be revoked since he'd died dishonorably. It looked like

Compo, however, was going to get the worst. With the charges of conspiracy, illegal disposition, coercion, using rank and position to impede an official investigation while conducting that investigation, violating restriction, fleeing from an investigation and murder, not to mention a host of lesser charges, he'd spend the rest of his life behind bars. His trial by court-martial would turn out to be little more than a formality before sentencing, with all the evidence stacked against him. He'd be lucky to see daylight again without a picture frame created by the bars of his cell.

Louis and I were walking out of the office when the phone rang. I hung back a second to see if it was for me. Miss Paek spoke in Korean, then hung up. I turned to leave, and she called me back.

"Miss Lee says she is coming to Taegu tomorrow night and needs to speak with you." I nodded, then took my leave. We headed for the house to relax. The chopper flight to Seoul and back the next day would wear us out, so we wanted to rest. No chance, though. Mihi greeted us at the door when we arrived.

As the sun rose the next morning, I immediately started brewing the coffee and Louis cooked. He wasn't as good a cook as Jina, but he'd do for a bachelor. We ate and cleaned up the dishes, discussing how we'd handle the day ahead of us. It was governed, for the most part, by Compo's arrival in the Republic, but that wasn't until after lunch. It would be a long day, however, with us getting back from Seoul well after nine in the evening. By the time we got back to the office, got Compo settled and returned home, it would be nearly midnight. We decided to ask the colonel for a reprieve on Wednesday's PT, with a commitment to make it up in the gym over the weekend. He usually had no qualms about that type of arrangement.

We arranged the request for transfer of bank funds from the States to Korea, then sent the list of Moss' Korean accomplices to the Seoul Korean Customs Office. We made fast work of the various reports and other paperwork that had come across our desks, getting everything out of the way before we left. The colonel came out of his office and told us that CID in Seoul was tied up, but MPI would loan us an agent for our mission in Seoul. Before long, it was time to get on the chopper, and we hadn't eaten lunch yet. We stopped at the snack bar on the way and grabbed some sandwiches to stuff into our pockets for the trip.

The chopper flight was uneventful, except that Special Agent Wilkins was waiting just off the tarmac at Supply Point 51 when the chopper touched down. She'd be our wheels to the airport and back. She wore a frilly pink blouse nearly covered by a black blazer, and a short, pleated skirt that blew up with the help of the helicopter rotor wash that hit the ground. The sight was truly beautiful, though she tried not nearly enough to hold the skirt down. The thigh-high stockings and pink garter straps stretched along her leggy lower half had no problem staying in view most of the time. Even a flash of black lace panties peeked out on frequent occasions. The skirt became more manageable as the rotors slowed their turns, but the vision was etched in the minds of everyone who stopped what they were doing to watch. Even the chopper crew had been immobilized during the unscheduled show. I don't know what everyone else thought, but "simply spectacular" was the way I described it.

"You're early," she yelled above the diminishing whine of the Blackhawk's turbine. She handed me the briefcase filled with money found at Moss' house, along with an inventory and receipt form for it. "You must have had a tail wind on the way up or something." Just then, one of Mother Nature's breezes frolicked with her skirt again, catching her totally off guard and lifting it high enough for all to notice that her panties were translucent and that she was a true redhead. I filed that vision away next to the previous one. This time her cheeks flushed a little, though not much. I signed the receipt and returned it to her.

I pulled my eyes away long enough to check my watch. True enough. We'd made the trip in a little under an hour, which would give us plenty of time to stop at the snack bar up on the main post to really fill our stomachs. The sandwiches we'd wolfed down a thousand feet above the expressway hadn't quite done the trick. Wilkins pointed the sedan in the right direction and hit the gas.

The lunch crowd was already gone, so we had our pick of tables. Louis and I briefed Wilkins on the case. She wasn't really a part of it, but had been involved in various aspects, so we felt as if she was nearly a team member. When we came to the part about Compo's alias when he left country, she let out a deep, rich laugh, truly enjoying that piece of information. She shifted in her seat and her skirt rode up on her leggy, strong, but not overly muscular, thighs.

"Look," she said, changing the subject and bringing her voice down to a husky near-whisper. She didn't try to adjust her skirt. "I hope I didn't offend you with what I said on the phone." I assured her that, though I'd been caught off guard, I hadn't been offended. I used the opportunity to repeat that I was a happily married man. She acknowledged and continued on, even though she really didn't have to.

"It's just that we American women get lonely at times. All you guys seem to go after the young Korean women and single American gals get left behind in the dust." She tugged the bottom of her skirt down and repositioned it across the tops of her creamy thighs. I could see from the corner of my eye that Louis was disappointed with this movement. I told her that, if I had been single when we met, she wouldn't have had anything to worry about, and I meant it. That seemed to cheer her up a bit, and she looked at her watch. "We'd better get going. Traffic's going to be a bitch." With that, we rose and left.

Compo's plane was about ten minutes late, but the official escorts and handcuffs prompted airport officials to let his party through without the customs hassle. They emerged from the gate less than a minute after the plane's engines shut down. The throng of Koreans awaiting their loved ones let out a long chorus of "ahhhs" when they saw Compo pass by, cuffed at the wrists and head held low. We went to meet them in the receiving area.

I identified myself and introduced Louis and Wilkins to our visitors, then led them out of the terminal and into the sedan.

The trip from Kimpo to Yongsan was quiet and we dropped the escorts off at the MP station. Wilkins made a beeline for the chopper pad, and we were loaded, with the rotors tearing at the air, before seven o'clock. We'd get back early if we didn't hit any headwinds, thanks to Wilkins' driving expertise through the city's streets. I looked out the side window as the chopper started rising and saw her standing there, one hand shielding her eyes from the setting sun, the other waving to us. Her short skirt was also waving brazenly in the rotor wash, this time riding well above the panties, but without a worry from her. Compo was cuffed to the chopper's frame, and I poked Louis in the ribs so he'd look and see the spectacular view falling away below us. The artistry of the moment wasn't lost on him. He was all attention until we could no longer see her. Then he started breathing again.

The chopper touched down in Taegu a little after eight and we hustled Compo into the waiting sedan for the trip back to the office. He hadn't said one word since we met him at Kimpo. We were probably going to have trouble getting him to talk, but that's what we were trained for. Unfortunately, so was he. He knew that all the veiled threats were usually just a load of bull to get people to spill the beans. That's why Louis and I had spent time intricately devising a different interview technique especially for him. We'd also enlisted the aid of his battalion commander. Compo would talk tomorrow or we'd throw the book at him.

Once we secured him for the night, we filled out our reports, tactfully leaving out the most memorable experience of the day. I looked at my watch. It was half past ten and, if we hurried, we'd get to the Hilltop Club just in time for one beer before they closed up for the night.

We missed the Hilltop by sheer moments, but dinner was waiting on the stove when we got home, so we popped open a couple of beers and chowed down. The fare was gone within minutes, and we were leaned back in our chairs, patting our stomachs, when the phone rang. I picked it up to hear Miss Lee's voice at the other end before I could even say "hello." I tried to beg off a visit because of the long day, but she insisted that it was urgent and related to the case, so I gave in. For protection from rumors, Louis called and invited Mihi over. She and Miss Lee arrived at the same time.

Miss Lee started in as soon as they sat on the sofa.

"I did not tell you everything I know about Timmie's death," she said. She immediately had our devoted attention. She began again after a long pause.

"Timmie was not a nice man. He butterflied on me a lot," she said, using the Korean bar girl word for cheating. "One night I came home and he was in bed with one of the women you showed me in the pictures." She described which one, and we knew it was Specialist Amanda Compo. "I was looking for something to stop him with when the woman's husband came in with a gun. I wasn't thinking too clearly and grabbed the gun from him before he could shoot. Then I shot my Timmie in the head. I just had to tell. I couldn't keep this lie from my friends any longer."

She broke down into uncontrolled sobbing, requiring extensive female comforting from Mihi. When she was able to continue, the rest of her story came out.

"I guess I fainted or something. I don't know. When I woke up, the man and woman were gone and so was the gun. I thought I'd been dreaming for a second, but when I looked around, there was Timmie. And he was dead. I couldn't stand to see him lying there naked, so I washed him and put some pants on him. I was very scared, so I left right then and hid. I didn't want to go to jail." Her voice trailed away on the last sentence, making it almost inaudible.

Louis, Mihi and I looked at each other, totally astonished. Here was a part of the case plopped into our laps when we least expected it. Worse yet, a confession by someone we'd come to know as a friend and taking the blame for one of the people we'd come to hate — a dirty cop. Until now, we'd been sure that Compo had pulled the trigger, either to double cross Rostock or because Rostock had double-crossed him. But if what she said was true, why did Compo take the gun and hide it in his house?

Mihi, on cue from Louis, called the Korean Police, who arrived in record time and led Miss Lee away. Louis and I busied ourselves, making notes about what she'd said. We'd compare those notes in the morning and write up the report. Seeing that we were going to be busy, Mihi excused herself after the police left. This had definitely been a serious turn of events, and we'd been caught with our pants down. Not like Rostock, of course, and not as serious. Within an hour, we called it a night, still partially in shock.

Wednesday morning started with the usual breakfast and coffee. Louis would return to the barracks tonight to sleep, so he set about packing his gym bag. We arrived at the office a little after eight, and Miss Paek handed me the message that the bank funds had been transferred, as requested. We still had to verify receipt by the bank at Camp Henry when it opened. All the illegal profits we knew about were now in one place, and would be turned over to the Korean authorities when the case was finished. We handed Miss Paek the notes we'd taken after Miss Lee's arrest and asked her to type them up for us.

A few other notes were lying on my desk, but they weren't anything related to the case, so I let them be. We retired to the lounge for another cup of coffee, and to review our procedures with Compo prior to getting started. We realized it was going to be another long day. When we felt we were totally ready, we collected Compo from the detention cell and led him into my office, shutting the door. Louis stood guard.

"Welcome back," I said, inflicting the first wound on his failed escape attempt. "How's the weather in New York?" He didn't answer, as I knew he wouldn't. I read him his rights, then listed the charges against him, substituting the attempted murder charge with first degree murder to catch his undivided attention. He didn't move and didn't talk. He just stared straight ahead at the blank wall. I sat down slowly, shuffling some papers on my desk.

"You know," said Louis from behind him. "The sooner you get started, the sooner we can get you tucked away in Leavenworth and get back to someone else who's worthy of our attention." Nothing again.

Minutes floated by as I watched him. Except for shallow breathing, he didn't move an inch. Then I dropped the bomb.

"Your wife is being charged as an accomplice to first degree murder. She'll be locked away for at least twenty years, too." He reacted by looking me straight in the eye. It was a hard, murderous stare, but he still said nothing for a while. Then he broke down. The first sign was a tear rolling down his cheek.

"She didn't do anything," he said quietly. I stood and walked around to the side of the desk, sitting on the edge of it, inches away from him. Louis got ready by placing his hand on the butt of his weapon, but he didn't draw it from the holster.

"Go on," I said simply.

He started slowly. Then, as he wound his web of half-truths, the story came faster, and maybe truer, about Rostock trying to molest his wife on several occasions. When he found out, he stole the gun after accounting for it during a routine inventory, went to Rostock's house and killed him. Simple as that.

I returned to my chair and shuffled papers again. After a couple of minutes, I said, "There's a witness."

He raised his head again, and there was a look of shock across his face. He knew there was no use in lying now. The real story came out this time, and it closely matched Moss' and Miss Lee's. Except that Miss Lee hadn't fainted. He'd actually knocked her out with an uppercut punch to the jaw.

"I was afraid she'd shoot Amanda and me next. I knocked her out, dragged my wife out from under Rostock's body, grabbed the gun, and got my wife dressed. Then we left."

"Why didn't you report the killing to the Korean police?" Louis asked.

He hesitated for a moment, then figured we knew everything by now anyway.

"Because of the other stuff," he said simply, teasing to see how much we knew.

"You mean the big black marketing ring you two had with Major Moss in Seoul and Mr. Park in Korean Customs?"

"You found the box." It was more of a statement than a question, as his eyes met mine. The murderous look of a few minutes ago had been replaced by one acknowledging all had been lost. I nodded, and his eyes drifted back down to look at his knees.

"If anyone investigated it besides me, I couldn't be sure I'd get any incriminating evidence out of there before my partner or anyone else found it. I made myself very visible and very available at work the next day when it was reported. It was only logical that I'd be tasked with the investigation.

"I found the two boxes in the closet and took them out without my partner knowing. Once I got them home, I found the unlocked box was the one I needed. I had an idea what was in the other, but I couldn't get it open without smashing it. I thought that if it was found without the box of passports, nothing would lead to me, and I returned it a couple of weeks later. By then, I was sure everything else had been removed."

"Why did you keep the gun?" I asked.

"I was about to return it to the unit when you guys picked me up the first time. I was scheduled for another inventory there. But then I was suspended and didn't have the opportunity anymore. You guys really screwed me there."

"Was your wife involved in the black marketing scheme?" Louis prodded.

"No. Amanda didn't know anything at first. She thought we were giving to an orphanage. After you guys picked us up, I had to tell her the truth. She wouldn't leave me alone."

"Then you went to see the ajumah later about payment, right?"

"Yeah."

"Why didn't you just send all the stuff up to Seoul to sell?"

"I wanted a little of the action all to myself," he said, almost in a murmur.

Louis brought it back to the killing. "Why didn't your wife report you after Rostock's death?"

"Are you kidding? She was in his bed voluntarily. Besides, I told her that since his girlfriend grabbed the gun, she was the one who killed him and we didn't have anything to do with it. It was better all around if she just forgot that it ever happened." He was near tears now, as Louis picked up the phone and instructed the duty agent to have Amanda Compo brought in again. He must love her very much to protect her, I thought, especially after he caught her sleeping with another man. I let him get it out of his system before continuing.

"How did you manage to get the weapon?"

"I faked a spot inventory. When the armorer wasn't watching, I stuffed it in my belt under my jacket."

"And you were going to return it the same way?"

"Yeah. Only this time I was actually scheduled for the inventory. It was easy to get, and it would have been a snap to return.

"Why didn't you just get rid of the box with the cards in it? That way you could have avoided turning the case over to us and you'd have been safe."

"I wanted Moss and him to get caught at what they were doing. I was going to plant all the evidence leading to Moss and erase any that was leading to me." He looked up at me questioningly. I answered before it crossed his lips.

"The Korean Telephone Authority provided us with listings of all the phone calls he'd made for a while before he was killed. Your number was on there quite regularly — about every other day." A look of shock crossed Compo's face for a moment, then disappeared. He nodded his understanding before hanging his head again. That little movement told me that he didn't know how frequent the calls had been. I guessed that Rostock and Amanda had been in contact for quite some time.

The interview went on throughout the morning, with breaks only to refill coffee cups and make trips to the bathroom. We obtained a partial list of people they'd coerced into helping, but Rostock knew the others, he said. Compo's wife hadn't known where he'd gone when he disappeared to the States, and he'd conned his way out of checking in with the unit's charge of quarters by producing a forged letter from the commander, saying that it was no longer necessary.

We broke for lunch, knowing that we'd received just about all the information he was going to give us. We briefed the colonel before leaving, and told him we planned to speak with Amanda Compo that afternoon. It looked as if we would have to charge her with adultery (which was standard Army policy), obstruction of justice, and being an accessory to the conspiracy and the killing after the fact. She'd be relatively lucky, since it was a GI who'd been the victim. If it had been a Korean, she would have spent about thirty years in the women's prison at Suwon. As it stood, she'd probably be out of Leavenworth in five years, dishonorably discharged from the Army and barred from ever returning to Korea again.

We tried to forget the case for the next forty-five minutes as we ate, but it kept at us. Several lives had been changed drastically by greed and lust. Those lives would never — could never — be repaired.

Bob Warner

Epilogue

As expected, the case was wrapped up neatly by Friday, reports and all. Amanda Compo confessed to sleeping with Rostock for nearly three months, though she claimed it was only to keep Rostock from causing her husband problems. She had no idea what problems, but Rostock had said it would ruin her husband's career. It didn't help in the end, after all.

Compo would stand trial for a host of charges that would put him behind bars for scores of years before being eligible for parole. Even if he beat several of the charges, he'd be convicted of the larger ones and would be dishonorably discharged after serving his prison sentence.

Moss would get the same treatment, with slightly different charges added to the list, along with breaking and entering, and disturbing a crime scene. All three would generally have no life for several years, and very little after that, with the marks they'd have on their records.

The Monday after we completed the main investigation, we started calling in people who had been coerced into purchasing goods for the ringmasters. Some who began enjoying the profits were charged, while others who were coerced the entire time were let off with warnings and administrative action by their commanders. The Dobbses and Stenbergs were among the latter, receiving nearly full pardons for their transgressions.

Miss Lee, who actually pulled the trigger, was charged by Korean authorities, based partly on testimony provided by Louis and me. She stood trial and was sentenced to twenty years at the women's correctional facility in Suwon. It was judged to be a crime of passion, and the sentence might have been reduced even lower, had she come forward earlier. She definitely would have gotten the maximum penalty of life if she hadn't come forward at all.

The money and the Celadon pottery found at the Compo house was turned over to the Korean government to recompense on the taxes due. The Koreans also rounded up another ten civilians in Seoul and Taegu who were involved in the activities. Between those people and their own Mr. Park, the government regained 100 percent of the money owed.

Mr. Park was never seen nor heard from again. The local office denied ever knowing him. Rumors have it that his family is receiving a monthly stipend until his return, however.

The young soldier who accepted the forged letter from Compo, and who ultimately allowed him the space to leave Korea, was reprimanded and given two weeks of extra duty for being so gullible and not verifying the authenticity of the letter.

Louis and I were rewarded by becoming the duty agent for the next five days. During the day, however, Louis was able to process his marriage paperwork and hand carry it around to the offices that had a say in his future of wedded bliss. He and Mihi were married in a civil ceremony in Seoul two months to the day after the case was closed. Then they had a chapel ceremony on Camp Walker, practically right across the street from his barracks.

We'll work more cases in Taegu until our tours are up, and then we've requested to be reassigned together to wherever the Army feels we're needed next.

About the Author

Raised in New England, Bob Warner was just an ordinary kid until his mother died. His loss brought his school grades in sharp decline from As to Fs and his demeanor from "nice neighborhood boy" to class clown and devil.

In a way, it's surprising he ever became a writer, since his grades were so bad he had to take some classes over three times to get a passing grade. English was one of those classes.

"My third sophomore English teacher, Mrs. Barbara Murphy, provided the catalyst, I guess," said Warner. "Even though my grades failed, I had fun with English composition classes and acting in some of the classic plays in class."

In response to his participation in various skits and his solo composition works, his teacher wrote in his yearbook, "With English accent you are great; as judge you keep the records straight. You write with logic and with art — if only it weren't in fits and starts."

"I think that's what propelled me toward thinking about being a writer," said Warner. "That and the fact that I was one high school credit short in Algebra to be a topographical surveyor."

He spent twenty years in the Army, starting as a journalist and working his way up to supervisor and magazine editor-in-chief, then retired. More than a third of his military career was spent in various assignments in Korea, where he witnessed some of the settings mentioned here.

9 780759 632608